# THE VILLAGE BEYOND

# THE
# VILLAGE
# BEYOND

By Livingston Biddle, Jr.

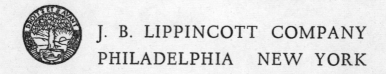

J. B. LIPPINCOTT COMPANY
PHILADELPHIA   NEW YORK

For my children

# THE VILLAGE BEYOND

# Part ONE

MICHAEL Allen sat at his bedroom desk, finishing the assortment of February bills, his large shoulders hunched over the writing surface, his brow knitted, his hands moving slowly, with an appearance of labor. They weren't exceptional bills; even with the Christmas expenses, some of which had been carried forward, they fitted into the family budget which Ruth had meticulously planned. Yet he never undertook the monthly task of making payments without a sense of misgiving, often approaching dread, and he was always relieved when the totals in the checkbook showed that the Allens were still solvent, that the savings account was still intact.

The savings amounted to approximately three thousand dollars—no great sum for a man who had worked for the same insurance firm for nearly eighteen years to have set aside; but the account was safe and clear and not connected with the mortgage or with taxes or with the money provided for the education of the two children, already in their early teens. It was money for the future, or for emergencies. Ruth used those phrases; but sometimes he saw it spent in an entirely different fashion.

Michael raised his shoulders and listened to the sleet sifting against the windowpanes. In the warmth of the room the sound was almost pleasant, suggesting winter in a small, snug house on the outskirts of Philadelphia. There was nothing to remind him sharply of Italy, no sudden association of sound and image; yet the idea of a return had been growing steadily and secretly in his mind. Perhaps the idea had been born two or even three years before, perhaps before that—possibly at a time when the savings account had stopped increasing and he had seen that his life and his career were becoming static, that a feeling of promise was slipping from him, that advancement was no longer to be expected. Perhaps the idea had come to him one day as he rode the Paoli Local commuters' train from Wynnewood into town, in some such prosaic manner; but it was difficult to ascribe to it any actual time or place, and for a while it had remained dormant because at first it had seemed impossible to realize: an impractical idea, one which Ruth might easily rebuff. For a while it had also seemed unnecessary and a luxury he could afford to postpone.

Now, however, the idea appeared abruptly immense, as if it had stretched out arms to welcome him; and he could see once more the village, the one special Italian village as it had been in wartime, ten years earlier, when he had been there as an American soldier. It was like a refuge his mind could withdraw into—a miraculous place, unlike any other; and sometimes when he was confused or worried or tense inside it appeared as a talisman capable of warding off discouragement, or the slyly intrusive whisperings of failure.

Perhaps it was naive to think that any place was endowed with magic, that magic had been there to begin with, or more particularly that it could be perceived again. But if this, or part of it were true, why did the village, its immediate surroundings beckon to him so? Why did he long so to return—this time with his wife? Was the idea too fanciful?

Michael reached for the loose pile of envelopes and started to address them. He could hear the sleet more distinctly. Maybe it would abate later on . . . January had been comparatively mild. Only over the holidays had there been snow on the ground— snow falling when he had driven home with Ruth from the annual New Year's Eve dance at the country club. He was thinking obliquely of how the New Year had begun in customary, traditional style. At least elements of the traditional were involved.

He and Ruth had stayed until the end of the party. As usual

they had joined up with the Ormonds and the Johnsons, the six of them seated at a table next to the dance floor with the huge tree gaudily lit in one corner. The party was always a major event; but for some reason this year, Michael thought, the voices had seemed overly raucous, as if pleasure could be summoned by shouting alone. He had found himself privately critical of the noise, of the paper hats, of the hat which Bettina Johnson had placed laughingly on his head. Yet these were people he had known for ages, behaving as they always did on New Year's Eve —people, like himself, in their late thirties, eager to usher out the old and receive the new . . . or seemingly so. But then the Johnsons had just bought a new house close to the club grounds and Bill Ormond had been promoted to an executive post at the Philadelphia City Bank, and there was cause for celebration.

Ruth had entered into the spirit of festivity. She had worn the brocaded blouse he had given her for Christmas and a dark skirt. Tall and slender and blond she had moved gracefully among the other dancers, her blue eyes and her smile quickly animated; and it would have been difficult to tell that the skirt had been bought at a sale during August, and presumptuous to say that she had not enjoyed herself tremendously. She had been drowsy in the car beside him as they drove home—past the Johnsons' new house, Dick in the car ahead skidding into the entrance, tooting the horn; Bettina waving, calling out goodnight.

He did not resent Dick's success or the success of others, Michael had told himself, but he had not spoken to Ruth until they had reached the short white strip of their own driveway.

Then he had said, "You okay, honey?"

Her head had come forward. "Why, we're home already."

"Safe and sound. I'll let you off here. I'll put the car away."

"Didn't you enjoy it?" she had asked. "You didn't, did you? Something depressed you. What was it?"

"Nothing depressed me, Ruth. . . . Nothing really."

"Anyway I had a good time," she had said, stifling a yawn with her glove. Her voice had seemed louder. "It's nice to dress up once and a while, and be out. We don't have too many chances."

"No, not too many. . . . Only sometimes I wish—"

"You wish what, darling?"

"That we could vary things a little. Stay at home maybe, have a bottle of champagne by ourselves. See the New Year in together."

"We'd probably both be asleep by midnight—"

He had smiled slightly. "Well—it would be a change."

"I must say it sounds rather appealing to me right now—my eyes are almost shut." She was getting out of the car. "I'll leave the key in the lock, Mike. Don't forget to bring it with you."

"No, I won't forget." He had watched her enter the house. Then he had kicked at the snow in front of the garage door and tugged at the handle, the door rising grudgingly—with a sudden loud clutter in the cold. . . .

They weren't as close to each other as they once had been, Michael reflected—not as close as in the beginning, or when the children were younger, when he had returned full of confidence to the firm of Dilks and Stanley after the war. And sometimes it occurred to him that they were going downhill together, not as a family particularly, but as husband and wife, quarreling more than before, or more than he could recall: small, unimportant quarrels that left small, unimportant scars that didn't quite heal.

That was the pattern they had drifted into without pausing to take cognizance. Maybe it was normal. Very few achieved great success. Yet his own impression of failure was somewhere at the root of the matter, he knew. It was hard to define exactly. It was even harder to admit, or to attempt to discuss. Ruth accepted it without talking in terms of success or failure. Ruth was eminently practical. Only at times were criticism or a sense of recognition implied. "No, Mikey," or "No, Priscilla," she would say to the children, "you know perfectly well we can't buy you things like that." She would make the refusal without rancor, but firmly so that it need not be repeated; and of course he could not intervene because requests of this nature, which were denied, *were* beyond their means. Not that the children often teased for what they could not have, or showed resentment afterward. They had about as much as the average among their friends. Yet it hurt him to be present when anything was denied—to feel implicit in Ruth's voice a tone of resignation, possibly unintentional but nonetheless emphatic to his own ears: you can't have this or that,

because you have only an average father. Look at him—see, he is
only average. . . .

He was exaggerating though, wasn't he? He was very fond
of Ruth. In a sense he depended on her. She was such a busy
person around the house; she kept it looking so spotless. Even in
this respect, however, there were times recently when he felt she
was unnaturally busy—not *unnaturally* busy, that wasn't quite
the right word—but as if goaded toward some new endeavor: this
*has* to be done, it can't wait another day. The new curtains in the
living room, for example. Ruth had spent hours sewing them,
hours searching for the right remnant of chintz at a bargain price.
The result was fine, the product of her skill; but the old curtains
would have lasted another season or two, Michael had thought,
and in an odd way the new ones rebuked him. They suggested,
if you made more money your wife could hire a seamstress, or a
decorator—she wouldn't have to work as hard. She was not conscious of the rebuke, however, or of the occasional hurt—certainly not fully conscious of them. She wasn't a complaining
wife; but she liked to excel, Michael thought. She enjoyed having
that ability herself.

He stood up and went over to the window and leaned down,
his arms pushing against the sill. The patch of lawn had turned
white below him. He could see the lights in the houses nearly
identical to his own, stone-and-clapboard houses spaced against
the inward curve of the road; and beyond these, the dimmer
lights of the larger and older and more lavish dwellings which
receded against a wooded slope.

Then, as he stood there, the idea and the memory it evoked
were in his mind again.

What would Ruth think of Italy? What would she see? Was
it too late to go back—too late to try to rediscover what had
never since been attained? Was it possible to salvage a marriage
by taking your wife back toward one place which meant more
than others? . . . But he was exaggerating again. The word salvage inferred an approaching crisis. He and Ruth were not in
that much danger. Or were they in danger without realizing it?
Did they antagonize each other more than superficially? Did the
small quarrels leave a residue which gradually became destruc-

tive? A nebulous destruction—unopposed. Or did Ruth oppose it—with new curtains for the living room? Did he oppose it with his longing for a return to Italy, for something vital which they both might share? Momentarily the thought intruded: I wonder how well I understand Ruth after all these years; I wonder how well she understands me.

In his confusion Michael half smiled. It's strange, he reflected, I believed I knew all about life once—only it wasn't anywhere near here. It was on a hillside, not a very remarkable-looking hillside, just one with a farm on top and a valley below and an Italian village on the opposite crest. The place had nothing to do with bills or New Year's Eve dances, or with stirrings of uncertainty, of discontent; and there wasn't any snow . . . It had been raining, he thought; when he had reached the village, there had been a light drizzle of rain. . . .

IT had been an extraordinary time in Michael's life, one as if set apart, though it had lasted for only part of a day.

He had become an ordnance officer during World War II. He had enlisted shortly after the attack on Pearl Harbor, not with any great feeling of patriotic fervor, but because it had seemed that eventually he must be in the war and that it was better to join than to wait. Ruth had agreed. They had been married almost five years then. Priscilla was two and a half and Mikey was still an infant; but Ruth had planned to live with the children in her family's house, an aging, roomy structure on a quiet street just beyond the city limits and not far from the tiny apartment which had been the young Allens' first home.

They had talked about the enlistment logically; he would go to school and get a commission, perhaps later on he might be stationed nearby. The separation, when it had come, however, had not seemed logical at all. He had been sent more than a thousand miles from Ruth, and when she had first visited him he had thought, "I deserted her in a fashion, I should have stayed with her and the children as long as I possibly could." But he had been commissioned and through the months that followed there were, of course, other men—close to thirty and with families left behind—in the Army. He had become adjusted to it and to his command, and he knew that Ruth was reasonably happy at home, possibly more relaxed than she had been in the crowded apartment. Yet they had seemed brave to each other and very much in love during the last leave before he was sent overseas.

He had not chosen to be an ordnance officer. That was the Army's choice. It had not seemed worth while to object. The job did not appear any more or less important than many others. He did not picture himself returning home covered with glory.

He merely pictured himself returning to Ruth and the children and buying the house they had wished for in the suburbs. He had risen to the rank of captain, and he was kept busy. In his spare time he even studied some Italian. Naples was a beautiful city, set above the curve of its Mediterranean bay; and it was a huge sprawling base and a center of excitement. Michael had never seen anything like it. Troops from all over the world passed through the Naples area, and came there on leave from the fighting. He felt himself lucky to be stationed within a few miles of the main street, the Via Roma. It wasn't a dangerous place. The danger was to the north.

Michael did not seek out the danger, but he did not shun it either. He went close to the front several times on inspection assignments which he might have delegated to another, and once the small convoy he had been in charge of had been strafed by a lone German plane, skimming in just above tree level, and there had been a shattering of glass and a brief ugly holocaust beside the road. He had not become rattled. He had knelt beside the three wounded men, had seen that the fire in the two burning trucks was put out. Kneeling there he had felt old and sad and yet in control of himself. But that had been an accident caused by the enemy and impossible to avoid. It had been very unlike the time on the hillside. Then there had been only Michael, no one else to help him.

He had gone forward to inspect part of a shipment of new guns which were not acting as they should. It was an early spring morning and a relief to get away from his office for the day's excursion. He had considered it in those terms. Normally the roads, beyond the range of German artillery, were safe enough to travel. Most of the counterbattery work took place after dark. It had been months since the attack on the convoy and now the line was stalled and probably would not move again until the fields and marshes below Cassino dried out sufficiently for the tanks. He would be to the right of Cassino, however, where the map told him the land would be hilly, almost mountainous. There would be plenty of shelter.

But the headquarters of the American artillery company he was searching for had been changed and moved ahead into the village to support a corner of the British-held front; and when he arrived the sky was overcast and the air colder, and rain was falling. The guns had been brought into a valley late the previous evening. They were firing sporadically. The ejection mechanism was faulty, a young lieutenant told him while they drove a short distance in a jeep and then stopped. The crews were having trouble with the empty casings on all except two.

Michael went on foot with the lieutenant, turning up the collar of his coat against the rain, smelling the soft earth, the dripping trees, hearing the gun ahead of him fire, although he could not see it because of the narrow path and the thicket of woods. Then he was quite close to it and could see the pocket where it was hidden and the men in ponchos working over the breech and the camouflage net and the long wet barrel.

He was leaning down, nodding, listening to the crew's complaints when the German shell hit. His head jerked sideways toward the slope of the hill.

The shell had hit below the crest. There was a black swirl of smoke and next to it, bent over and running, the figure of a man. Michael could see him distinctly, as if he had been suddenly and miraculously silhouetted there. Then the second shell hit and the man went down. He was about halfway up the slope. His clothing was gray, Michael saw. It was not a uniform.

The artillery crew had ducked behind the parapet banked in front of the gun. Michael heard the lieutenant say, "He's an Eyetie, Captain—some crazy wop. . . . Take cover!" The voice seemed loud and thin. The lieutenant was on his belly, his head partly raised. Michael was crouching, his knees jackknifed. He was staring at the man, waiting for him to move, but he was stretched out—not as you would expect a dead man to lie, however, although you couldn't really tell from a distance. He was only hurt, Michael thought. More shells were dropping, pockmarking the hill. Two or three whined over the gun and tore into the opposite slope. "Get down!" the lieutenant called. "Get down! . . ."

Michael was running, his eyes fastened on the gray figure. He had not noticed the low stone wall, how the hillside was terraced in long, sweeping semicircles. The wall was about three feet high, the top level with the soil above. It seemed much higher. He was pushing himself over the stones, watching another shell burst and another one near the hill's summit. He had the impression of incredible noise, of the black viciousness of the shells erupting heavily, as if with sudden personal intent. He was under the tangled branches of an olive tree. He hesitated, watching the drifting smoke. Fear grabbed at him. He could see clearly one of the shells entering his chest, piercing his throat below the thin protection of his helmet. Then he was running again, stooping, his boots digging into the hill, slipping in the mud.

He had reached the man. It seemed an enormous accomplishment. He was astonished to see that the eyes were open, that the face was old, a thick white stubble across the cheeks and chin. The lips were bluish, the face very pale and retracted turtle-wise into the hunch of the shoulders. The man moved. He was clutching Michael's hand.

"Are you hurt?" Michael was asking. "*È ferito?—*"

He did not finish. He was lying prone, the explosion ringing in his ears. His eardrums felt crushed. His nostrils and mouth seemed filled with smoke; for an instant he could not breathe.

"*È ferito?*" Michael repeated, as if he were shouting into a vacuum. The man did not answer. His eyes were stunned, opaque; but there was no trace of blood, no sign of a wound.

"All right," Michael shouted, "Come on!" He was bending over the old man, tugging at him. He had the notion that he could not carry him, that he would weigh a ton. He had partly lifted him, and then the old man was on his feet. Michael had his arm around the slender waist. They were sliding in the mud, moving rather absurdly, like a pair of drunks. They were at the wall. They were crouching at its base. The old man's teeth were set. He was shaking unbearably. Michael had a better grip on him. The smoke was in his nostrils still, but the noise seemed to have lessened. They were sliding again in the mud.

Michael could hear the sound of a cheer. He could see the gun suddenly a few yards away. The cheer grew louder and faded and became individual voices—the voice of the lieutenant: "My God, Captain, you oughta get a medal. . . . My God, here! Put the old bastard down." The crew had clustered around the three

of them. They were all sitting, kneeling behind the parapet. The
sound of firing had ceased.

The old man continued to shake. He was rubbing his hands and
legs; but there was apparently nothing wrong with him except
his terror. Michael could feel himself trembling. He was lighting
a cigarette for the old man. He noticed that his trench coat was
spattered with mud, possibly from the nearest explosion, but it
seemed that he was perfectly safe now, that nothing could touch
him. In his whole life he had never felt as exultant, as triumphant,
as happy. . . .

Even then he wondered why he had taken the risk. He had
never been quite able to find the reasons. Perhaps if he had been
like the others, battle-wise and fully aware of all the possibilities
involved, he would not have attempted to rescue anyone, or he
would have waited for an order and if none had come he would
have stayed within the relative safety of the earthworks around
the gun. Or perhaps if it had been a question of a fellow soldier,
the lieutenant would have behaved differently, and would have
gone himself or would have directed someone else to go. And
after all Michael had not actually saved the old man; he might
have been forcing him into greater peril. Suppose a shell had
dropped on them while they were making their escape, and suppose no more had landed further up the hill. But of course you
couldn't tell how it would be once you had committed yourself.
He had merely tried to save someone; and certainly the lieutenant
was right in not wanting to risk his neck or the lives of his men
for an unknown civilian. You could say that Michael alone was
in a position to act as he had. That had occurred to him later on.
At the time, however, he had only known that he had done something exceptional—a deed which, had he imagined it, he would
not have believed himself capable of performing.

They were laughing. "I felt as if I were on skates," Michael
said. "Roller skates going backward, or maybe they were skis."
The cigarette bobbed up and down between the old man's lips.
He was grinning, his eyes half closed, squinting at Michael. Then
the corporal who was nearest the parapet said, "Jesus Christ!
There's a whole bunch of them. Look! Here they come!"

Michael raised his head. It seemed he had not seen the farmhouse before, the tile roof outlined against the gray sky beyond the hill's summit. What appeared to be a family had emerged: a man, two women, and more remarkably, two small children. The man had a crate on his back. The women carried bundles on their heads. One of the children was carrying a white rooster. They were coming single file. Except for the way that the children did not deviate one step from the line of march, they made the hillside seem harmless, almost peaceful. To Michael they were at first like apparitions.

They came directly toward the gun. It wasn't until they were close that he saw that one of the women was young—a tall girl, perhaps not more than twenty, with a black sweater and skirt and dark hair. The old Italian had risen. He was talking suddenly, his voice climbing to a falsetto. Then he was weeping and the older woman had rushed toward him. Her face was pressed sideways to his. Michael heard her saying over and over again in Italian, "Father, my father!" The other man had lowered his burden. He advanced and was shaking Michael's hand. He had a stern grizzled face and a grip like steel. He was speaking rapidly. Michael could understand many of the words: they had seen him from the farm, they had been arguing with the old man about leaving because of the guns brought into the valley. The old man had wanted to leave; he had left too soon.

"Too soon?" the woman interrupted. "Not soon enough!"

"All right, not soon enough. But aren't we all safe now?"

"Thanks to the American we are. Not thanks to you."

"All right—not thanks to me."

"You say he isn't hurt, let him lie on the ground—let him rest while the Germans kill him."

"I don't say let him rest," the man objected temperately. "I only say he isn't hurt—that it's dangerous to move and better to wait until the bombardment is over."

"I suppose that's what the American thinks. That's why he runs up the hill."

"The American thinks in a different fashion . . . But is he hurt then? Show me where he's hurt. He isn't even scratched."

"You with your second sight. Now that it's over you have second sight."

The man looked at Michael. "I'm sorry," he said. "My wife is excited. You must excuse her . . . And I don't say you aren't brave, Captain. I don't say that at all."

"The brave gives thanks to the brave," the woman said.

The man shrugged. "We'll let it pass, Captain—you understand?"

"A little," Michael answered, smiling. "*Pochino.*"

"Good," the man said. "We won't waste the war in an argument." He inclined his head with dignity and with a touch of embarrassment. "We won't trouble you any longer. We're going to my brother's house." He pointed toward the village. "We will be safer there." He shook Michael's hand again and had turned and was hefting the crate to his shoulders.

The woman stepped toward Michael and put out her hand, her expression changing from scorn to sudden tenderness. "I do not speak English," she said, "but you understand, Captain—you understand, this is my father—"

"*Sì,* signora. . . . *Sì, capisco.*"

The old man was nodding, fumbling for speech, but the words were inaudible; and they were leaving, following the man with the crate. Michael saw him glance once toward the farm. It must be his, Michael thought; it must be hard to go away from it. Then he was watching the old man with his daughter and the girl and the children raggedly dressed. The girl was behind the others. She had raised her bundle, her arm angling upward to steady it, globules of moisture clinging to her sweater and skirt like dew on a spider web. Michael realized he had not heard her speak. She walked gracefully and somehow proudly, bending a trifle to shoo the children forward; but he was looking past her at the bobbing beak and eyes of the rooster. It seemed strangely pastoral to see a white rooster carried by a child through the woods.

MICHAEL was saying to the major at headquarters that the guns would be withdrawn for repair and that replacements would arrive soon, and the major said there was no special rush, they could get along well enough for the time being. The major was stocky and affable with a crew-cut and overhanging brows and a complexion through which red veins were criss-crossed. Next to him the lieutenant appeared younger than he had. The lieutenant could not wait to tell the story of the old man. He told it breathlessly, the major leaning back and chuckling and looking sideways at Michael. He said half jokingly, "We don't often get heroes sent up to us from Naples, Captain. Maybe we ought to break out what's left of the whisky."

It was good to relax. Michael had not known how tense he was until he had taken a chair and slid the heels of his boots out across the tile floor. His mind was filled with a sense of elation. He wondered where the old man was. He wished he could see him, but perhaps it was better the way it was. Tonight, Michael thought, I'll be back in Naples and the old man will be with his family.

The major poured another round of drinks. The lieutenant had returned to his post. There were just the two men sitting in the low-ceilinged room on the outskirts of the village. The occasional gunfire sounded muffled and distant. Once or twice a German shell dropped far away; but the major said he had had no casualties in over a week.

He reached for his glass. "It's funny," he was saying, "I've been wonderin' about you, Mike—and about me. I was in North Africa before I came here—and I was just sort of wonderin' if I'd have taken a chance for some Ay-rab sonofabitch who'd lost his camel in a mine field maybe. Would I crawl out to him, or would I tell him to go to hell?"

"Probably you'd crawl out and steal the camel," Michael said.

The major grinned. "You didn't get that old Dago's watch, did you—or his gold tooth?"

"I don't think he had any."

"Well, anyway, Mike—cheers!"

"Cheers!" Michael answered him, raising his glass.

"No, seriously—" the major said and stopped. A sergeant had appeared.

"Sir, there's a girl here, wants to see the captain."

"A girl?" the major asked.

"Yes, sir. An Italian."

"You know any Italian ladies, Mike?"

"Only slightly," Michael said.

"Okay, tell her to come in then, Al."

The girl entered the room. The two officers blinked at her and stood up. "I have a gift for the captain," she said in English.

The major advanced a step. "Okay, Al," he said. "Close the door." He faced the girl. "Now what was it again, honey?"

"I have a gift—a present. You recko-nize me, Captain?"

"Of course," Michael answered. "*Certamente.* How is the old man?"

"Oh, he is well. He is sleeping . . . You are surprised to see me?"

"I'm very surprised. Surprised to see you, surprised to hear you speak English."

"I learn it from my cousin," she said. "He was in the United States one time. I have taken many lessons from him—"

"And not from any of my soldiers around here, by any chance?" the major asked, peering at her.

"From my cousin, I said. The lessons are from him." She looked back at Michael. "Here—here is the present."

"It feels like a bottle," Michael said.

"*Sì!* A bottle of wine."

"Why didn't you speak earlier?" Michael asked.

"You think it is necessary?"

"Well, no—not necessary." He was smiling, holding the bottle wrapped in coarse brown paper.

"I do not speak before because there is much commotion and

because—" she glanced at the major—"my father thinks I should not speak with the soldiers. . . . That was my father, Captain, the one with the big box on his back." She had on the same black skirt and sweater pushed up a little above her wrists. She held her chin high, the dark hair spilling uncombed across her temples to the nape of her neck. Her nostrils were slightly flared. The large eyes were wide and bold. A faint amusement was in them and at the corner of her lips. "Who is this?" she asked.

"This is Major Hallahan," Michael said.

"He is an old friend?"

"A recent one," the major said. "One from today. And may I ask who you are?"

The girl smiled. "My name is Angelina Nardi. It is my grandfather the captain has saved."

"You didn't tell me there were angels connected with this business, Mike. That's what it means, doesn't it—Angelina?"

"Only a small one, Major."

"I wouldn't say a small one—by no means a small one. But come on and join up with the commonfolk." She looked at him quizzically. "I mean come on and sit down over here."

"For a minute, Major—then I must go."

"You must go—why? The captain would consider it very rude if you just said hello, here's a bottle of wine, and goodbye."

"He can walk back with me—to my uncle's house, if he likes."

"Why should he walk back to your uncle's house? It's probably miles. Very bad for the captain's feet."

She laughed. "All right, Major. I will sit down."

Michael was drawing out a chair, taking one himself, pulling the paper from the wine bottle.

"It is not very much, Captain. It is all we find."

"I think we should open it now, Angelina."

"Yes—if you wish."

"Of course he should open it now," the major said behind them, rummaging in the cupboard for another glass. "The whisky's nearly gone."

"You like the whisky best, Captain—or the wine?"

"Usually, *generalmente* the whisky," Michael said. "But in this case I like the wine."

She bowed her head a trifle, the gesture seeming suddenly personal and for a moment oddly sophisticated.

Michael was filling the glasses. "You have lived here a long time, Angelina? You were born here?"

"Yes, where you see the house today, the one I have come from with my parents and my two brothers. I was born there, but I do not live there always. When I am young my mother is sick and has no more children for a while and I go to live with another uncle in Napoli, and I work in a place to make clothing. I work all day, like this, with a needle and thread."

"And then?"

"And then the war has come—and I am sixteen years old, and my uncle is dead from the year before and my father writes to me and says to come back because it is better—and I do not want to come back, no not any, because Napoli is a big city and beautiful, you know?—and the war is not there yet. And once I go to Roma with my cousin and Roma is even bigger and more beautiful. But my father says that my mother would like me to help her for a while. . . . So I come back." She shrugged. "Maybe some day I will go away again."

"You don't marry any of the fellows in the village?" Hallahan asked.

She crinkled her nose. "No, Major. My father, my mother, my grandfather, they all say to me—marry Vincente, marry Rinaldo; but Vincente has a face like a fat pig and Rinaldo looks like an old horse who is very sick, and they will never go away from here. So I tell them no, no marriage."

"And the captain," Hallahan said. "What has he got a face like?"

She glanced at Michael, her eyes partly narrowed. "The captain," she said, "has a face like an American."

Michael laughed. "A young lady with spirit and tact." He lifted his glass. "How do you say it in Italian, Angelina—*buona fortuna?*"

"Sì. *Salute—buona fortuna.*" The three glasses clinked together and were put down. . .

The wine was a pale amber. Angelina said her father had made it from the grapes he had grown. It tasted musty and dry and yet raw, but they did not joke about it. They sat talking of Naples and of Rome until the men had finished the bottle and An-

gelina her glass. Then she said, "Now, Captain, it is time for you
to take me home."

"There's a couple of drops of whisky left," Hallahan said.
"Enough for you, Angelina—"

"No—no whisky, Major."

"Not even a drop?"

"No—thank you." She was standing. Michael had risen beside her.

"Okay, can't sell the whisky," Hallahan said. He got heavily
to his feet. "Okay, Mike, I guess you'll have to take care of her."
He winked. "Take good care."

"I'll do that," Michael answered, although he felt faintly embarrassed and for the first time during the day unsure of himself. But to be alone with the girl would please him, he knew.
He had been thinking of it while they talked.

"Goodbye, Major."

"*A rivederci*, angel face. Maybe you'll let me walk up to your
uncle's house another day."

"Yes—perhaps. Another day."

"This uncle is alive, is he?"

"Yes," she said, smiling. "He is very alive."

They went into the street, the sergeant watching them as they
crossed through the outer room. Evening had come, Michael
saw; and the rain had stopped. Men and women in drab, dark
clothes passed them—a man driving a small donkey loaded down
with sticks. The passers-by moved swiftly as if they wanted to
be indoors. Except for a woman who glanced sharply at Angelina
and at the silver bars on Michael's coat, they paid the soldier and
the girl little heed. The street was tucked under the hill, the village rising steeply above it, so that it seemed almost as if there
were but a single gray façade. A flickering of brightness was in
the sky to the north, but it did not enter the narrow climbing
lane into which she brought him.

"You have many thoughts, Captain."

"Yes, many—"

"They are about me?"

"In a way they are, Angelina."

"What means—in a way?"

He smiled. "It means they are about you."

She linked her arm through his. "This is how an American soldier walks with a girl—no?"

"Yes," he said, looking at the eyes that were half humorous and suddenly wistful. "Quite often."

"You are surprised that I come by myself with the wine?"

"I hadn't thought of it like that."

"Many Italian girls would not go by themselves. They would go with a father, a mother—a relative . . . But the wine is my idea. I think of it first. I say it to my father, and he say all right, it is a good idea, that he will go with me—but I tell him no, I will take it. It is a pleasure for me to take it, and he looks at me and says nothing—maybe because he knows I will not stay in the village always."

"So he doesn't have to care what other people think."

"*Sì—esattamente!* My father knows he does not have to care —but anyway it does him no good to care, because I do it just the same. He knows that too."

She gave her head an emphatic nod and Michael laughed. "How did you happen to find me, Angelina?"

"Oh—that is by luck. I think maybe I don't find you, but the first place I look there you are. I say to the man, the sergeant —where is the captain who has saved an old man?—and he knows right away, like that. It is so quick!"

"And more lucky than you think," Michael said. "Because if you'd come later, or tomorrow, I would have been gone."

"Gone? You go away?"

"I'm not with the major, Angelina. I'm only here for today. I'm stationed near Naples."

"Oh," she said. He could feel the pressure of her breast against his arm, the pressure of her hand. "I do not think I like you to go away."

"You shouldn't say that—"

"Why not? . . . Because it is foolish?" she asked, frowning. "All right, it is foolish. But wait! I have another idea. A wonderful idea! You will take me to Naples with you. I will hide in your car—very quietly. You will put me in your house, and I will cook for you. I am a very good cook. You don't believe it?"

"I believe it."

"But you smile, so you will not do it—will you?"

"I don't live in a house, Angelina. I live in a thing called a Nissen hut with a lot of other men. There wouldn't be any place for you—"

"Never mind," she said. "You don't do it. I am only making a joke. . . . You are married, Captain? Or Mike—I will call you Mike, like the major."

"Yes, Angelina, I'm married."

"And with children?"

"With two children. A boy and a girl."

"And you love them very much, even though you don't see them."

"Yes—"

"Some day I will get married," she said. "I will go to Napoli and stand on the Via Roma—and a big car will come, a big black car with white wheels—and the man will say to his driver, 'Stop! Wait! I see a girl over there, I want to marry her.' And he will be a very old man who will die soon. He will give me five million lire and a ring made of diamonds—and a dress made of gold." She smiled. "No, he will not be old. He will have a horse that is dying instead of a car—and his name will be Vincente Tomaso, and my father will be very proud. He will say—*finalmente*, Angelina, you have some sense!"

"No. I don't think you'll marry Vincente Tomaso."

"Why?"

"You're too full of life—"

"Too full of life—and too full of dreams. You think that is bad?"

"No—only sometimes the dreams can make you unhappy."

"You talk like my father," she said. "And my mother. They say this, too. They are very sad for me sometimes. They make a long face, like so—oh, very sad. But I am not sad. I like my dreams."

"That's because you believe in them."

"No—not always. The ones I like the most are the ones I do not see will happen—the ones, how do you say?—the ones *impossibile*."

"But not quite *impossibile*."

She smiled at him. "Okay—not quite."

They had reached a point where the lane, mounting the shoulder of the hill, dropped slightly and the stone walls, flanking the cobblestones, rose to frame a small vista of the countryside in front of them. Angelina stopped and was pointing.

"You see, Mike? There it is, the house where I was this morning. No, not there—more like this." She pushed his chin gently with her fingers.

"That little speck of white—"

"*Sì!* That is it. But wait, we can see it better from here. I will show you." She led him through an opening in the wall and through the doorway of a building unlike those they had passed —a partly broken building, apparently empty. They emerged to a terrace with pieces of broken stone across the floor.

The village rose almost perpendicularly to their left—like a fortress, Michael thought, rather eerie in the dusk. He was looking at the flickerings of gunfire playing across the range of mountains to the north, and at the white speck of the farm. The summit of a lower hill intervened between it and the pocket from which he had started. He was squinting. The white shape seemed so tiny. He could not visualize it as it had been closer. Then he was looking at the girl. He noticed the breeze rustling her hair and how serious the expression in the dark eyes had grown. They were nearly black: unusual eyes, the eyes of a child, the eyes of a woman, innocent and not innocent at all.

"Why do you do this today?" she asked. "I have wondered."

"I don't really know why, Angelina."

"Do you know it is Italian? Do you think to yourself there is an Italian?"

"I guess I knew it was an Italian. I don't remember thinking very much of anything. The nationality doesn't make much difference, do you think?"

"To me it makes a difference. Not because it is my grandfather, or like that, but because it is Italian. You understand?"

"Yes, but it isn't that important. It isn't that much of a thing —really."

"I do not think you will forget it, Mike."

"No," he said. "I won't forget about it, Angelina."

"So it is important then. Always you remember what is important." She walked a few steps from him and turned. "You are shy, are you not, Mike?"

"Am I?"

"Another would say, look at me. I do a great thing. I am brave—and beat his chest and wear his hat on one side. But I know you are not like this—not from when I see you first, when you are running up the hill, or with the soldiers, because then I am still full of the noise and the smoke and everything. But later I see you and I know you are kind."

"I don't remember looking especially kind," he said, smiling at her.

"Maybe you do not, but I see it—in your face. I do not see it in the major's face the same. Oh, he is nice and we laugh and talk, and I do not understand all, but he is like the other *soldati* who want this and this and this and tell it to you in the way they look."

"Maybe they can't help themselves."

"You tease me—but no, it is whether you give something or take something. It is very nice to give something." Her eyes brightened. "Like a cigarette. You have a cigarette, Mike?"

"A whole pack of them. Here—you can give one to me."

They sat on the edge of the terrace wall. Michael realized he had a peculiar impression of time. The morning, the early afternoon on the hill, the conversation with the major, the bottle of whisky, the bottle of wine seemed distant from him. Yet he remembered vividly how the shadows fell across the lane he had climbed, vines clinging beside it, the smell of dampness from the moss and stone. He remembered the clip-clop of the donkeys' hoofs, the face and cloak of the man who drove it; and he was acutely aware of Angelina, of her nearness, as if it had become detached from other things, and as if in a few minutes it would disappear. He watched her smoking the cigarette, holding it cupped so that the glow would not be visible, her long legs outstretched, bare below the skirt and ending in a pair of worn leather sandals.

The light from the mountain range played across her profile and died down. She wanted to go to Naples with him. She would go without question; but of course it couldn't be.

"It's not that I wouldn't like you to come with me," he said.

She glanced sideways. "We do not talk of it any more, Mike.

I don't think of it. I think of a long time ago, when I was a little girl. This house belong to a man who is not very rich, but more rich than my father. I look at the house many times and one day I come here, but not through the door. From this way, up over the wall. I climb it by myself, and sit there in the corner, like a small cat in the sun. It is very nice this—the *terrazza*. It has a little fountain—and a tree next to the fountain. A fig tree, I think you say—and after a while I get up and go to the tree and pick one of the fruit. Oh, it is very good and soft and sweet, and then a woman see me from where that window is, and she shout at me and say what I do to steal the fruit—and because she cannot catch me, I just stand by the fountain and make a face at her, and she shout at me very loud, but I do not care. I finish eating. I make a bow to her, as if she is a great lady, and stick out my tongue! Oh, she is furious, that woman—and I jump to the wall and down the other side. I laugh to myself for maybe an hour. It is very funny." She tossed the cigarette away and frowned. "I don't know why it would make me sad to think of it now—maybe because the tree is gone." Her eyes turned toward him again. "You think I talk too much, Mike?"

"I like to hear you talk. I like it very much."

"It is good English—no?"

"No, it's terrible," he said jokingly.

She grimaced. "But anyway you like it."

"Anyway I like it, and it's good English—and even if it were terrible English I would like that, too."

"Honest-ly?"

"Of course honestly."

"Am I very different to an American girl—or not?"

"Not very different, Angelina, but a little."

"How different, Mike?"

"Maybe you're a little more quick to express your feelings. You don't try to hide them, and one changes for another, and yet they're the same in a way—because they're intense feelings, I think."

"The American girl—she try to hide how she feels?"

"Sometimes."

"I never!" Angelina said. "I would not know how. But I am only one Italian girl."

"And I'm only one American and not a philosopher. How about your cousin, though, the one who was in the United States—what does he say about American girls?"

Angelina shook her head. "Oh he, my cousin! He says they have beautiful dresses, even the poor ones have three or four— and silk stockings, and lace to wear under the dress every day. Imagine! But he would never say they hide how they feel from him, because he thinks he knows all about the women from all over the world—"

She stood up. "*Che cosa?*" she was saying. "*Che cosa*, Gino?"

Michael saw that a child had come through the doorway opposite them. He wore a faded green jacket and baggy cloth trousers. He was clutching a cap. He walked stolidly toward them and halted and Michael remembered him with the rooster against his chest. He spoke hurriedly to his sister, his eyes moving away from the American. Angelina was answering, her voice angry and then tinged with humor. "He look for me," she said. "My father say for him to look, and someone say they think we go into the house. He is like a little dog after a bone. *Non è vero, Gino, come un' cane?*" She laughed and turned him round and gave him a gentle slap; and he ran across the terrace and stood grinning at them from the doorway and called out something, and Angelina picked up a pebble and shied it after him as he ducked inside.

"I am sorry," she said. "Now it is spoiled."

"It is spoiled, Angelina?"

"The surprise. I was going to make another surprise for you. My father say for me to bring you back, if you will go—in a little while, he say, so they can prepare. But he get worried, my father. He thinks I stay away too long—and maybe I do, but I do not play a trick on you, Mike. I only want to talk with you and not with the major; and I think you will come with me— even if I do not say about my father."

"You are full of surprises—"

"And the wine, that is my idea. I tell you the truth, and also when I say that my father wants to come with me and I will not let him. That is the truth. You believe it?"

"Certainly I believe it."

"The wine—it does not make you drunk. I do not like that to happen."

"No, I'm sober as a judge," Michael said.

"A judge?"

"A judge is a very upright fellow. He doesn't drink at all."

"Then you are not a judge," she said. "But I don't think you are drunk either. Come we will find my father. He will be, as always, in a rage."

They were descending by a different lane, steeper than the other and with steps built at intervals into the stone surface. Here and there people called out to Angelina from the doorways they passed. She walked more self-consciously now and did not hold his arm. It was not far. Michael heard the little boy shout and saw him dart through an entrance and then the father came out. He scowled at Angelina, but he was smiling at Michael and had taken his hand.

"*Ecco!*" Angelina said with a note of defiance. "*Ecco il capitano!*"

She went ahead of them into a room, low and oblong and crowded with more than a dozen men and women and children. Michael could see them in the lamplight, the shadows jagged on the walls as the men came to greet him. This was the uncle who owned the house, this man with the high bald forehead, the pointed nose, the thin corded neck. This was his son, a boy of fifteen or sixteen with thick black hair and bright flashing teeth, a slight reticence or envy in his smile. And this was another brother, more tall and rotund, with a moustache and with a gold chain across his waistcoat, worn a bit obtrusively as if he must have put it on for the occasion. Angelina was making the introductions—and here, at a table in the room's center, sitting beside a china bowl filled with hyacinths, was the old man. The women stood in a semicircle behind him, all smiling, all large-bosomed, all ruddy-complected and all dressed in black. The old man wore a gray shawl over his shoulders. He arose, his neck craning out as Michael advanced.

"*Capitano! Grazie mille—mille grazie—*"

"*Sta bene?*" Michael asked, gripping the bony fingers knotted with blue veins.

"*Sì, molto bene, capitano. Molto bene.*" He turned slightly toward the women and Michael was shaking hands with them, with
Angelina's mother. She leaned forward and embraced him, and
the old man was gesturing toward the chair next to his. "*Ecco,
capitano, una sedia. . . . Un' bicchiere di vino, capitano?*"

"*Sì, per favore. Grazie tanto.*"

The uncle with his bald forehead was pouring out the wine,
making a ceremony of it, holding the bottle delicately.

"*Per Lei,*" Michael said, "*per tutta la famiglia. Voglio che è
possibile per me di parlare bene italiano, ma il mio vocabu-
lario—*" He hesitated, turning to Angelina. "I wish you would
say how pleased I am to be here and how glad I am that your
grandfather is better."

Angelina struck a pose and threw up her arm. "*Silenzio!*" she
exclaimed. Michael heard the phrases tumble from her. Everyone was laughing.

"Anything else you wish me to say?"

"No, Angelina—*è abbastanza.*"

"He speaks so well," she told the others, "he should be a poli-
tician."

"*Non ha mangato, capitano?*" the old man asked.

"*No—ma non è necessario di—*"

"*Ah, sì! Un' piatto di pasta. È preparato. È pronto.*"

One of the women was bringing forward the tureen of pasta.
She ladled it out, serving Michael first. He noticed the white cloth
on the table, the way it seemed freshly ironed. He thought how
skillfully Angelina had maneuvered him away from the major's
headquarters. The pasta was steaming hot, bits of meat mixed
with the red tomato sauce. It would be a banquet dish for them
because of the meat.

"*Spero che non è il pollo,*" he said in jest, nearly certain that
it was lamb and not the rooster which had been shredded into
the sauce.

"*Come?*" the old man asked.

"*Il pollo,*" Michael repeated and imitated the child holding the
rooster in his arms.

"*Ah, il pollo!*" the old man said, delighted. "*Non è il pollo,
capitano . . . Gino! Gino, porta qui il pollo.*"

The child obeyed, scurrying into the room beyond and reappearing almost instantly, the rooster racing, his beak extended, a few feet in advance. The man with the gold chain stooped. There was a flutter of feathers and wings, and the old man's shrill laughter; then the rooster was calm again and suspended above the table.

"A great runner," the man with the gold chain said in Italian.

"A very great runner," said the old man. "Very swift."

"An old pal of mine," Michael said. "*Il mio vecchio amico.*"

"Old and clever," the old man added. "And very strong with the hen."

"Only too old," Michael said, "*Solamente troppo vecchio per la pasta.*" It seemed a huge joke. The captain was a wit, a comedian, a friend.

Michael could feel the warmth of the welcome spread inside him. It was hard to imagine the old man lying stunned on the hillside. He belonged here, and Michael felt himself also belonging. That was the essence of it. He became conscious of the room in its entirety: the stone walls decorated with faded, stiffly posed photographs, with a picture of the Madonna framed in wood; the heavy dun-colored curtains hung over the single window, the purple hyacinths, the individual faces around the lamp, the ceiling blackened with smoke; the old man, the patriarch of the family, eating his pasta with an aluminum spoon. It was like a painting which he himself had done and in which nothing was out of place; and these were not strangers around him. They were totally unlike strangers. He tried to explain that to them as he was leaving.

"*Amici,*" he said. "*Tutti in questa camera sono mi amici—*" He was peering at them, smiling, shaking hands again, trying to make the words seem adequate. He was saying goodbye to Angelina's parents, to her grandfather. They had gone with him to the door.

"Goodbye, *capitano.*"

"Goodbye, Angelina—"

"My father says for you to come back and see us again."

"I will try very hard . . . I will try my best."

He walked slowly into the lane and began climbing toward the house where the terrace was. The lane was empty. He could hear the click of his boots on the cobblestones; and it seemed that he was still in the room, still drinking the wine, still hearing the voices and the laughter—Angelina closer to him than the others. Then he could see himself greeting the major and getting into his jeep and heading toward Naples; and Angelina was suddenly and incongruously beside him in the jeep, or she would appear miraculously when he went alone to the place where it was parked. He had nearly reached the end of the lane. This was the doorway they had gone through to the terrace. He walked through it and was abruptly aware of the noise from the guns, seemingly louder than before, but that was caused by the darkness. In a few minutes he would find the major, but he wanted a last look at the terrace and out beyond toward the farm. It was invisible, however. The flickering glow from the mountains was too high to silhouette it. He had a sudden image of Angelina climbing over the wall, as a child, picking the fruit from the fig tree. No, it was over, he thought; the day was over—

"A cigarette, *capitano?*"

His head turned sharply. For a moment she seemed no more real than a shadow.

"I think I must be dreaming," he said.

"You do not wait for me?"

"Maybe I wait without knowing it—"

"I wish to say goodbye better than in a room full of people," she said. "I think if you feel this you will wait. I think to myself you will wait here."

"You are very wise, Angelina. More wise than I." He could see the large eyes and the lips tilted upward.

"You like me, Mike—do you not?"

"I like you very much—"

"And you do not wish to leave?"

"No," he said and bent just a little to kiss her lips. Her body pressed against him all at once.

"We will pretend," she said. "We will pretend you are a soldier going away, but not forever. We will pretend we know each other for a long time, every way there is to know." She drew back slightly. "Or maybe we do not pretend, maybe—" Her eyes searched his. "Maybe you will tell me I can go with you."

"No, Angelina," he heard himself say. "I can't ask you."

"But why, Mike—why? You can find a room for me to live near where you are. You can bring me food. I do not eat very much. I do not have a great stomach, you can see. It is easy. You are a captain. Why say you cannot do it? You are afraid?"

"Yes—perhaps I'm afraid."

"Oh what? Of me—that I will bring trouble to you? But I will not. When it is finished we say goodbye, and I go back to my family. Maybe I go there or another place, and my family will be sad I leave them, and maybe not so sad. They will understand. I will give you my love, Mike—and you will take me to a nice restaurant in Napoli, and we will laugh. I will show you—"

"Suppose I gave you my love, Angelina—all of mine?"

"Oh, but it does not happen like this. You do not fall in *love* with me—"

"Is it so impossible to imagine?"

"I do not know," she said. "I do not think like this before. You are afraid that you will be in love with me? I do not understand."

"I don't quite understand it either, Angelina. Only I know I can't take you with me tonight."

She stood back from him. "You are a strange man, I think. A brave man who is afraid . . . Or maybe you are too kind. Maybe that is what is wrong. Maybe you are too kind to take me with you. It is a funny thing. For the first time in my life I throw myself at a man who asks for nothing, and it is no good. I will not ask again."

She laughed suddenly and kissed him hurriedly and with tenderness and violence, and he was holding her, his fingers pressing the dark tangle of her hair; then she was walking away. He watched, not knowing whether to call to her, or what exactly they would say to each other if she stopped and let him reach her, or whether she was laughing at him now, or whether the way he had refused her had been a source of deep, even bitter disappointment. It wasn't until she had disappeared that his thoughts turned fully to Ruth and then with a sense of guilt; and Ruth seemed quite close to him and yet of a different world and a different time.

HE had visited the village once afterward. It was in July. There were no longer troops in the area. The line had broken, had pushed on to Rome and beyond, and he was on leave. He had gone laden with gifts: cigarettes, a dress for the mother, candy for the children, and for Angelina a ring with a jade stone and a gold band. It had been in his desk drawer for weeks; and sometimes he had wondered why he had bought it and had tried to minimize its purchase to a trifle; but it was not a trifle, and she would be pleased with it, he knew—she would say it was beautiful.

He had parked his jeep near where the artillery headquarters had been. A child was playing in the doorway. He remembered the major joking with him when he had come down alone from the terrace: "Well, if it isn't Captain Clark Gable. How are things at the front, Captain?"—and now sunlight flooded over the doorway and he felt gay, almost lightheaded, because the village was in a sense his possession.

They would be at the farm, he had decided. They would have moved as soon as it was safe; so he did not inquire at the uncle's house. There would be a delay, and perhaps the news of his arrival would be sent forward. He wanted to make the journey unaccompanied.

The road he found was dusty and he walked at the edge of it, seeing how it climbed across a field and then dropped toward the wooded area where the gun had been located. There were still sandbags piled neatly in tiers. He stood briefly looking at them; but his eyes had been on the dun-colored walls and the red tile roof of the farm, and he knew they were there now because of the wash hanging outside in the sun.

He started up the hillside. The mountains were hazy and

peaceful in the distance. Do you recognize yourself, he wondered, here with presents for children who are not yours, and a ring for a girl who is not your wife? It should be something else perhaps, and yet he could hear himself saying, "It's not made of diamonds, Angelina . . ." "No, but it is beautiful, Mike. *Che bello!* It is a surprise!"

He was nearly at the farm when the mother emerged, carrying a basket of clothes.

"Signora Nardi," Michael called. *"Buon giorno, signora!"*

She was squinting. She had dropped the basket, had shouted toward the house. She was hurrying forward, her face flushed. *Ah—il capitano! . . . Il capitano!"* The father appeared behind her and the old man and the two children. Michael was greeting them, was saying in Italian, "This is for you—and you—" He was handing out the candy, the cigarettes, the dress wrapped in white paper. They were ringed around him. He noticed that the men wore crude aprons soiled with fresh cement, that the father's expression was not quite as friendly as the others; but this was only the fragment of an impression, and through it, through the smiles and the exclamations, Michael knew she was not there.

For a moment he thought she would be in the village—but no, they were telling him, she had gone. They didn't know where.

"She went with the soldiers," the father said with sudden gravity. "It is no secret."

"Not with the soldiers who were here," Signora Nardi interjected. "They left a little after."

"What is the difference?" the father asked. "She went with soldiers—with the Americans."

"It might not have been with the Americans," the old man said, looking sadly at Michael.

"All right," Angelina's father admitted, "maybe she went with the English then. I don't know. I wasn't present." He looked at Michael and spoke slowly, his forehead creased, his hands partly raised in a gesture of futility. "One day there is a great deal of noise, Captain—from 'way across there, from the big road that runs toward Monte Cassino. Everything is moving. There is dust in the air. You can see it from the village, clouds of dust.

And the next day is like that, and the day after, and the Germans are gone—you understand?"

Michael nodded.

"And after that the noise grows less, but it keeps up from the road, and one morning Angelina tells her mother that she wants to look at the road—and that is all. She does not return. She has gone with the soldiers. Perhaps someone hides her, perhaps she makes up a story and says she is trying to find some relatives and someone takes her into a truck or a car. . . . We look for her, but naturally it is of no use. She is gone."

"She will send word to us," the mother said. "She will come back."

"She will not send us word," the father interrupted. "But perhaps she will come back—I do not know."

There was a silence.

"I'm sorry," Michael said. "I'm very sorry."

"It's the war," the mother said. "The war is very bad."

Signor Nardi shook his head. "It is from before the war with Angelina."

"Yes, perhaps—but not the same. But I do not worry about her —often, Captain. She will be all right. I pray for her. I say to myself I will see her soon. She spoke often of you. She said you were not like the other Americans."

And Gino had tugged at Michael's sleeve. "I know where my sister is," he had announced. "I know very well." He had smiled brightly. "She is in Rome!"

It seemed a long way back to the jeep. They had insisted that he have a glass of wine, and he had seen where the men were repairing the damage done to the house. Perhaps they knew why he had come, but they had not referred again to Angelina. He had not known what to do with the ring. He had given the small, unpretentious parcel to Angelina's mother. She had promised to keep it safely. Somehow he had believed that Angelina would open it herself.

Then he had walked to the gun pit and lingered there for several minutes, feeling the loneliness of the place; but when he had gone up through the thicket of woods, and had looked at the village again, it had appeared above him and once more like a castle, symmetrical, almost like a childhood vision of a castle rising up in the clear air. That particular view had remained with him more than any other.

And of course the memories were separate: the time on the hillside, the evening after and this day; and yet they were all intertwined. There was satisfaction in them and the reverse of satisfaction; but as the years passed the latter became less dominant. Angelina had become less and less distinct to him, until he could no longer quite imagine himself as the person who had bought her the ring, or as the person who had written cryptically and with a sense of conspiracy to Ruth during that period. He had never mentioned Angelina to Ruth. When he had told her of his two visits to the village, of the family, of the banquet they had given him, and of the old man, he had made the episodes seem more humorous than important. Yet he would have betrayed Ruth, he knew, although in a way which he believed would not have lasted, which had seemed divided from the future and for some reason incongruously inevitable.

In retrospect, however, even this was detached from guilt; and there was something a little ludicrous and possibly a little sad in the image of a soldier carrying a ring to a girl who was not there to receive it. She had become a sort of myth to him, touched with a certain magic and a certain unreality. He had forgotten what she looked like exactly, the exact shape of her face, the sound of her voice; but she was part of his village—and this he did remember, as if he had seen it yesterday.

WAS it right to attach such significance to a memory, to believe that there near the village a pinnacle had been reached, a single moment of complete self-fulfillment? Strange that when he was depressed, when his mind did seek to find refuge, strange that none of the other memories came back as strongly then: neither his marriage to Ruth the year after he had taken the job with Dilks and Stanley; nor their first meeting at the college prom, when they had discovered that they were both almost neighbors at home; nor the birth of his children, Ruth very pale and enormously happy, lying on a hospital bed; nor even his homecoming after the war. These memories flowed together and the ends frayed off into the commonplace; and it was hard to think of Ruth as enormously happy without thinking of her as unhappy, or not *as* happy, concerned with some problem which annoyed her.

The memory of Italy was different. It was isolated. It lifted itself away from the commonplace. At times it seemed to possess a transcendent quality, an ability to rejuvenate, to renew. Perhaps that was its chief importance—and its invitation. He was no longer able to think of the village without feeling that sense of invitation, pulling at him, pulling at him now like a tide. Life and death, he thought—a matter of life or death. Then he was smiling to himself. It wasn't that, was it? It was simply a return to Italy he envisioned—a return with Ruth, his wife—a summer vacation. Ruth would object to the expense involved. There were many things to consider: enough time, for instance. Yet he could see them standing on the hillside together, and he was pointing out to her where the old man had fallen—and he had turned a little to look across the valley toward the village itself . . .

He was closing the checkbook, putting it away, remembering to insert the bill stubs into the folder Ruth reserved for them, remembering to give the desk a semblance of order.

He carried the stamped envelopes into the hallway. It was a school night. The children were already in bed. Mike, Jr., had already passed his thirteenth birthday; Priscilla would be fifteen next August. They were nearly the same height—Priscilla blond like her mother and Mikey freckled-faced, less clever than his sister, but with the large bone structure of an athlete and with his father's brown eyes and hair. We couldn't afford to take the children to Italy, Michael thought, as he had before. They'd have to stay here at home.

He went quietly downstairs and left the bills on the table next to the door. He could hear the wind blowing outside, and he was thinking of what he might say to his children and of how the trip might benefit them—but indirectly and in a way they could hardly understand. Then he wondered what he would say to Ruth—how he would begin.

He entered the combination living and dining room. It looked very tidy, the new chintz curtains drawn across the picture window, the matching stuffed chairs flanking the coffee table arranged at their proper angles, the breakfast dishes prepared in the corner, the ash trays empty and clean except for the one beside Ruth.

She was sitting under a lamp opposite the dining table in a chair more faded than the two by the sofa. A sewing basket was on the rug, a pair of mended socks draped over its top. She glanced up from her magazine. "Well—all finished?" she asked.

"All signed and sealed."

"You saw the dress I returned for Pris—the one I told you didn't fit?"

"Yes, it was credited."

"I wasn't sure they'd get the credit through this month. They're not so prompt in that store. You did see it, didn't you—it was for ten ninety-five."

"I saw it darling. For ten ninety-five."

Her eyes seemed vaguely hostile. He was near the coffee table. He picked up a cigarette and tapped it against his thumbnail. She never failed to question him about the bills, but sometimes he had not been as painstaking as he had been tonight.

"Anything good in the magazine?" he asked.

"Oh—I was reading an article about roses. Here. There's a kind that bloom all summer. I thought we might plant a few bushes out along the fence. We have the azaleas I bought last spring and the flower bed, but the fence looks really rather bare. I was thinking of roses."

"Be nice," he said, "but—"

"But what?"

"But maybe not this year."

"Why not? Why not this year?"

He lit the cigarette. Perhaps this was the wrong time to disclose his idea to her; maybe they should be having a cocktail together on a Friday or a Saturday evening, when the demands of the week were temporarily ended or subdued. This was a momentous disclosure; possibly it required a less mundane setting. Yet it was curious to feel tense in front of your wife—just because she looked tired; more tired, he decided, than hostile or annoyed—her face a trifle gray and lined under the lamp, the eyes a trifle gray instead of bright blue. "I was doing some figuring upstairs," he began, and smiled. Then he said: "How would you like to take a real trip with me this year? This spring. This summer. Maybe the summer would be best and you could still plant the roses, if you wanted to—but how would you like to do something big, something important, different than we've ever done together?"

"I don't quite understand. A trip—a trip where?"

"To Italy," he said. "A trip to Italy. For a month, even longer. How would that strike you?"

She was staring at him. "Why, darling! . . . Why . . . Are you being serious?"

"Of course I am. Don't you think—don't you think it's a nice idea?"

"I think it's a lovely idea, I think it's startling. In fact I'm almost speechless! But how on earth could we take a trip to Italy for more than a month?"

"It could be handled. At least I think it could—"

"How? In what way?"

He stepped toward her. "Well—to begin with, I've put in a good deal of overtime with the firm—over the years, you know. Enough for an extra two weeks at any rate. With my vacation, that would give us five, wouldn't it?"

"And Sam, you think Sam Dilks would give you the overtime—just like that?"

"He might. He might easily if I spoke to him in the right way. And as for money—as for that—we could use some out of the savings account. We wouldn't go on a fancy ship," he added before she could interrupt. "We'd go on a small one. We'd get some kind of a tourist rate. The ship would be part of it. We might come back by plane—"

"And the children? What about them?"

"We'd make plans for the children. We'd hire somebody reliable to look after them here. We'd pay a good salary and we'd have time to find someone they liked. They'd have plenty of friends, even if some were away. We'd make it up to them later on—"

"I'm amazed!" she said. "I'm literally flabbergasted! How long have you had this scheme?"

"I'm not sure how long. I guess it's been in the back of my head for a long time, something we might try to do—"

"Italy!" she repeated. "We used to talk of it, didn't we? You did after you came home . . . But of course it's impossible, Mike. It's completely impossible."

"No, it isn't," he said. "Maybe it was once, when the children were younger—but not any more."

"I never knew—I never thought you wanted to see it again, particularly—"

"I guess everyone who was overseas has kind of the same hankering," Michael said, standing in front of her, the tension growing inside him. "See where he was, what he did—or try to imagine it. See this place or that, this street, how clearly he'll recognize it . . . Like that little village I told you about, Ruth —the one near Cassino. You remember, don't you?"

"I remember very well—"

"I'd like to see it again," Michael said. "I'd like to find out that it's still all in one piece. Probably it hasn't changed a bit, at least not the way towns around us have changed, spread out in all directions, until you can't see the boundaries any more. That isn't true in Italy, certainly not as true. In Italy a village remains a kind of entity, a kind of whole. I can imagine going back to an Italian village after a thousand years and still recognizing it— but I'd like to make sure. I'd like you to be there with me. I'd like to show you the old gray stone walls, drive up to them in a car, instead of in a jeep. We could rent a car . . ." How hard it was to explain, or to imply that one place might represent achievement, and other places . . . He paused, half smiling. "Does it all sound crazy to you?"

"No, darling, not entirely crazy—"

"Maybe it has to do with what a man thinks he is at some special time," Michael said. "I guess even a soldier who was in the jungle, or even in Korea, might have the same notion. It's kind of a universal desire, I guess—but of course you can only speak about where you've been yourself, and Italy isn't a jungle, and it isn't Korea—and it isn't all villages. It's a beautiful country. You'd think it was, I know you would."

"Of course I would, Mike—but that isn't the point—"

"Naples," he said quickly. "You might think Naples was dirty—and it is, but it's beautiful too. And Sorrento. I'll bet you'd think the cliffs at Sorrento were the most wonderful you ever saw—and Rome. I was only in Rome for about twenty-four hours, but it's a marvelous city; and Florence with the river running past . . . Suppose Sam gave me the green light, wouldn't you think it was worth it? Wouldn't you want to go?"

"Certainly I'd *want* to go—"

"But would you think it was worth it?"

"I'm just too surprised to think," she said. "It seems fantastic to me, coming out of nowhere like this. I can't imagine us actually getting on a ship—or a plane. I've always thought that money we've been saving would be for later, later in our lives. That's what we planned, isn't it?"

"I know it is, honey. But we wouldn't spend it all. Two thousand dollars, maybe. That's about what it would cost. We wouldn't be in the lap of luxury, but we'd be all right with that amount. We could pay most of the salary for whoever we hired from the money we wouldn't be spending here."

"Two thousand dollars," she said. "It seems like an awful lot, an *awful* lot!—for five weeks, even if we had them. It just doesn't seem we ought to spend the money—all at once."

"I'll admit it doesn't seem much like us—"

"Why, I'd have to get new clothes. A new dress, a new suit—"

"We could blow you to those, couldn't we? Chalk them up to the spring budget?—"

"I don't know what's come over you," she said. "All these years you've been so gloomy about bills and expenses. You have, you know—"

"Okay," he agreed. "Yes, all right, I have been gloomy, but . . . but I want to do this, Ruth. I want to very much. I'll admit I haven't made enough for any great savings, but we have something over and above, and I'd like to use a part of that now—rather than later." He sat down on the edge of the chair nearest her and leaned forward. "It's occurred to me, darling—I don't know exactly when—but it's struck me that our lives here have—" He hesitated, his eyes intent on her.

"Have what, Mike?"

"Have needed something like this. Something really big to look forward to. Out of the ordinary run. Something we might *long* to do—by ourselves. We haven't even been away like that for ages. A couple of weeks at the shore every summer, but always sharing things with other people, other families. The Johnsons or the Ormonds, the same pattern. We've had a week end or two here and there, but that's about the limit, isn't it?—and sure the children would miss us, and we'd miss them, but don't you think that perhaps we might love them more afterward, that perhaps—"

"That's a strange thing to say," she said. "It sounds as if you don't think we love them now."

"No, not that. Maybe love isn't the right word . . . But be more *aware* of them, and aware of each other. . . . You see, this isn't just a trip I have in mind, not just to get away from it all for a little while, that kind of thing. That wouldn't be the real reason we'd be going."

"What would be the real reason, Mike?"

"Well—to find something," he answered. "A whole different world. Different values, different ways of looking at things." And love, too, he thought: maybe we'd find that we weren't so old and that we could be very gay and impractical and young again and in love with each other.

"It's amazing that you'd have to argue me into a trip to Italy," she said. "It's astonishing! Here I've never been abroad or anywhere really remote—except to your Army camp, and those trips were hardly vacations."

"No," he said, smiling at her, "hardly."

"But I can't help thinking this is all a pipe dream, Mike—that tomorrow or the next day, or next week we'll decide it can't be done, that it was foolish to talk about it in the first place."

"It isn't foolish, Ruth. That's the last thing it is. I'll see Sam Dilks tomorrow morning."

"And suppose he says no. Have you thought of that? Would you want to go for a shorter time?"

"For a shorter time? No, I hadn't thought of it that way," he answered slowly. "I guess I hadn't really thought it all through . . . but no—not nearly as much. If we're to use our savings, if this is to be what it should be, I'd want us to have more than the usual three weeks. I'd want us to have a chance to get our bearings. I wouldn't want us to be aware of time."

"Then suppose—suppose he does say no."

"You think he will, don't you?"

"I think it's very likely—"

"Well," he glanced down at the cigarette, "well, after all, Dilks and Stanley aren't the only people who sell insurance."

"They're the only people you've worked for, Mike." She was frowning, he saw when he raised his eyes. "You wouldn't think of risking your job, would you?"

"You mean I couldn't get another one—very easily."

"Could you? . . . No, I don't want to hurt your feelings, darling. You're a valuable member of the firm and all that, Sam would probably agree—"

"Probably?" he asked.

"Well, you know how he is, compliments don't flow from

him—but I'm sure he hasn't kept tabs on overtime during the years. You've worked very hard, certainly you have—but we have to be realistic, don't you think?" She paused. "I have hurt your feelings, haven't I?"

"No, Ruth. No. You haven't hurt my feelings." He stood up, aware of the sense of deflation that must be evident in his face. "But look," he said. "What if everything turns out, turns out fine tomorrow—would you think the trip would be worth while?"

"Yes—I think I would, dear. . . . All I mean is that we shouldn't make too many plans till we know what we have to go on."

The inflection of her voice seemed abruptly flat. She imagined him failing in the interview with Sam Dilks. He himself had not visualized it clearly—or rather his mind had shied partly away from it heretofore.

"Sure," he said. "But we'll see, shall we? We'll see what tomorrow brings forth. We won't make all the plans tonight." He held out his hand. "Come on," he said, "it's pretty late, isn't it? . . . I guess we'd better be getting upstairs."

He was bending to switch off the lights, listening to Ruth check the latch on the front door. He had only intimated to her his reasons for wanting to go; but that was not wrong, he felt. He had not wished the beginnings of the trip to be shadowed with impressions of discontent. They climbed the stairs together. They looked in at the children and then entered their own bedroom at the end of the hall; and the idea swung through Michael's brain and he could hear Sam Dilks disagreeing with him—and it seemed that more than the trip had become involved.

Perhaps he should have gone to Sam first. If Sam refused him, it might have ended there. He wouldn't have had to tell Ruth. He had approached the whole subject backwards, or too hurriedly. Sam had told him once that he was too impetuous and he had lost his temper with Sam. That was past history, however. Sam would never fire him, Michael thought; he had been with the firm too long. He had anticipated objections—not a warning. Ruth was warning him. Don't risk your job, she had said; but he had not been thinking in terms of risk.

They did not discuss the trip again while they undressed, Ruth's supple but rather spare and angular body reflected by the mirror that hung against the closet wall. Michael felt awkward and inarticulate, and after they had said goodnight he lay in the darkened room with his eyes open and turned toward the ceiling. The sound of her voice surprised him.

"Mike?" she asked sleepily. "Are you still awake?"

"Yes, dear—what is it?"

"I think it would be very worth while—you know?"

"Yes," he answered. "So do I, darling—so do I."

CLAD in a pair of dungarees, an old blouse, and wearing a bandanna tied round her head, Ruth knelt down to push a dry mop under Mikey's bed. The mop scurried in energetic circles, devouring the light film of dust collected from the day before. It was nice to see how the boards glistened, to be occupied with accustomed tasks during the time before Michael would telephone. He had promised to call during his lunch hour, if not sooner. Under the circumstances, he had said, it might be better for him not to use the telephone on his desk from which the conversation could be overheard by members of the Dilks and Stanley staff.

Ruth took the mop over to the window and shook it out, and saw the motes of dust whirl in the February grayness and settle toward the back yard. Mikey's room always needed the most attention. Like his father he was prone to untidiness; yet there was something appealing in the disarray which confronted her each day, appealing, only occasionally exasperating. Priscilla's room was always cleaner.

Ruth stood still and listened. She never paused like this with her tasks only begun, but for some reason today the house seemed oddly empty, almost as if it were listening to her, or waiting. It was only nine-thirty, however. Even if everything went well and Michael should feel free to call her directly from the office, it was still far too early for the news.

She thought of driving him to the station: after the public school bus had stopped outside the house for Mikey, they would drop Priscilla within a few steps of her private school en route to the train. She remembered Michael's turning to wave toward her from the train's vestibule, his briefcase, slightly battered, held in his other hand. It had seemed rather a sad gesture, hesitant instead of triumphant, and peculiarly connected with winter evenings when from the car she would watch him descend the coach steps below the lights strung along the open platform. He had fallen into the habit of walking less briskly than his fellow commuters. Sometimes it annoyed her to see him come forward slowly, as if peering into the darkness. Sometimes the slowness made his clothes appear shabby, his shoulders a little stooped, the briefcase a kind of irrelevancy. But this morning he had smiled toward her from the train, and the smile had been intended to convey the hope of success—and unlike other days she had waited until the train had started before she had backed away from the station.

It was an unusual morning. Italy! she thought again. Was it actually possible? What would he say to Sam Dilks? Michael could be so . . . so ineffectual in the business world. He was secretly afraid of Sam's domineering personality, she sensed, and of overly asserting himself—except illogically, by becoming angry.

She had not recognized these characteristics when she had married him. She had seen him then as a rather lonely, shy person, tall, strong, decent and kind—and quite naive. No, perhaps she hadn't seen him as naive in the beginning. She had been naive herself, at twenty-one; and in a fashion Michael had released her from the confinements of her own upbringing. She had lived much in the shadow of her older sister Emily, wearing Emily's hand-me-down clothes, looking with envy at the gay young men whom Emily brought to the family house. Emily, however, had married a year before Michael had appeared on the scene and had moved to New York City, where her husband was an account executive in a prosperous advertising agency. She rarely saw Emily these days, only at Christmas time, at family reunions when the old attitude of condecension was engulfed in a general air of festivity.

Not that she, Ruth, had been a plain girl; she was a bit taller than her sister, a bit less filled-out, but she had been just as clever—in school, for instance; and when she had moved back to live with her family during the war, the house had seemed altered. She had two small children and a husband overseas—and her father might hint that Michael lacked certain aggressive qualities for the insurance business, as he had when the engagement was proposed; but he spoke from an eminence of semi-retirement, having made his own mark and enough to live on as an investment adviser. She had not believed her father's appraisal of Michael, nor had she envied any longer her sister's New York apartment, nor her sister's husband who was a Navy lieutenant-commander in the Pacific. After all, Michael was a captain then.

She was kneeling beside the tub in the children's bathroom, her hand scrubbing nervously at the ring of dirt on the white surface. Mikey must have used the tub after Priscilla last night. Grace, the cleaning woman, came to the house on Thursday; but this was Tuesday morning, and anyway Grace wasn't terribly skilled—and the house must *shine!* It mustn't be allowed to grow shabby. Her family's house was larger and the ceilings higher; but it was dark and full of Victorian furniture. It never *shone.*

You made compensations, Ruth thought. You did not go back to a decision in the past and say to yourself, "If I had done this or that I might have been wiser." She was extremely proud of her two children. Mikey was a bit more diffident than his sister, he had always needed more protection; but Priscilla's assurance was refreshing and in keeping with her greater age. She had tried to teach them both common sense. Priscilla knew how much her private school education entailed; Mikey knew that one day he would go to a privately endowed college instead of to the state university from which his father had been graduated; but it wasn't necessary to talk to them in terms of sacrifice. They understood. At times Michael spoke to them as if they were younger than they were, but that was an indication of his affection.

What had he meant last night about loving them more, being more aware of them? She was perfectly aware of her children, of her husband. Michael would never be enormously successful in his career, but she was reconciled to that now. It no longer weighed on her mind, as it sometimes seemed to weigh on Michael's—when he became moody and silent, not quite perceiving that his capabilities were limited in certain respects. Then it was best to leave him alone, to let him work out of it of his own accord and—

Ruth straightened. Wasn't that the telephone ringing? She hurried into the hallway and opened her bedroom door. The ringing seemed so strident, so portentous. She snatched up the receiver

"Hello? . . . Oh . . . oh, it's you, Betty," she said. "Yes, a little out of breath. I was cleaning. . . . What?—oh yes, about lunch. But I thought you said tomorrow. . . . No, I don't think I can change it, dear. I'm awfully busy. . . . Yes, tomorrow would be much better. I was counting on tomorrow."

Ruth sat down beside the desk and reached for a cigarette. "Yes, they're all made," she was saying. "Mike helped me hang them on Sunday." She smiled. "Why don't you and Alice stop by tomorrow, and I'll show them off. They really make the room look quite sprightly. . . . No, you shouldn't say that, Betty. You could do it yourself. Honestly you could. Now I really must rush . . ."

It was ten minutes, however, before Ruth replaced the receiver. Normally she enjoyed chatting with Bettina Johnson. Bettina, who had a full-time maid and more leisure, called three or four times a week. It was silly to have believed that Michael was at the other end of the line.

Ruth stood up and thought of the new curtains. Her friends might joke among themselves about how she sought constantly to improve the house; but privately they envied her dexterity, her decorator's eye for color, Ruth had decided. Almost all her friends had more money in the bank—but Bettina couldn't make a new pair of curtains, no matter how hard she tried.

Yet it was pleasant to think of the luxury of lunching at the club tomorrow with the two or three others whom Bettina would assemble. The club wasn't considered as "social" as some further out from town, but the Allens did not aspire toward a different circle of acquaintance—and at least they could afford the membership dues and Mike played his Sunday games of golf there in the spring and summer and fall. She would have a cocktail before lunch, Ruth thought. She might be in a mood to celebrate. Bettina would have two, possibly a third . . .

During the war, when the husbands were all away, Bettina used to give wild parties: wild, wild parties, a lot to drink . . . And there had been that young second lieutenant—what was his name? Arnold something . . . Arnold Kent . . . Yes, that was it—a very brash, disarming young man . . . He had come from Chicago—or was it San Francisco? He was passing through Philadelphia, he had turned up at Bettina's . . . and she, Ruth, had allowed him to drive her home—and they had gone out to the couch on that walled-in side terrace at her family's house, in the pitch dark. She had utterly given in to him, to the most clumsy, obscene advances. Amazing!—with the children, her own parents asleep upstairs! . . . Something almost abnormal, brought about by temporary loneliness . . . She had not seen him afterward. He had telephoned the next day to apologize, to say he was leaving. No one she knew had remembered him, but for a while she had avoided Bettina's parties . . . Strange— she had not thought of Arnold Kent, certainly not distinctly, for years.

A meaningless escapade—unknown to Mike, buried deep in the past. What had recalled it? Surely not Bettina. She had long ago ceased to associate Bettina with Arnold Kent. He hadn't even been handsome. He had been rather short and not more than twenty-one years old. An ugly thing—basically it was only ugly . . .

"I'm distracted," Ruth thought. "Today isn't like other mornings." She realized she was holding an unlit cigarette and put it aside and went downstairs into the kitchen and looked at the clock over the stove. It was not yet eleven. Usually the time passed so rapidly in the course of her routine. When the cleaning was finished, there were the breakfast dishes to be done, and then the laundry. There was always washing to do. She had a machine for this purpose, and except for Michael's shirts and in bad weather a few sheets, everything was washed and when necessary ironed inside the house. Thrice weekly she marketed in the stores along Lancaster Pike (this one had the best coffee, this one the most reliable meat, this one the freshest vegetables). After that, or instead of it, she would undertake the day's particular project—perhaps a dress to alter or mend for Priscilla, or a slip cover to begin (a bedroom chair needed attention next) or the silver coffee service, which her family had given as a wedding present, to polish and polish until it gleamed. Usually she did not permit herself to sit down and relax until mid-afternoon; then in another half hour Mikey would be coming home from school, she would go to collect Priscilla, and there was the evening meal to start preparing.

She prided herself on the food she provided, diligently scanning the newspaper advertisements so that each fraction of a dollar in her budget would go as far as possible; and sometimes Michael suggested that she worked too hard—as if it weren't necessary, as if she made too much of her job, as if her emphasis on details inwardly provoked him. Michael thought in broader terms. The details *were* essential. Someone had to be responsible for them. Among her own circle, Ruth knew, she was considered the most efficient housekeeper of all.

Now, however, she stood motionless in the kitchen, looking at the electric clock, at the sweep of the second hand. Make it run faster, she thought, and her mind slid away abruptly and extravagantly into the unfamiliar. Italy, a trip abroad—a ship, a plane. Was it that important? Should the money really be spent —or was it a whim which she and Michael eventually would forget? Five weeks seemed like a year . . . "Darling, I'm sorry, things didn't pan out today—but I'll try later on. Maybe Sam'll be more receptive . . ."

For a moment anger rose through her. It wasn't fair to propose the impossible. Yet she remembered his voice from the previous evening, its sudden enthusiasm. When she had first met him his voice had been very much like that—not somber, not reticent. Perhaps she had been wrong last night to insinuate the doubts.

She moved over to the breakfast dishes. Michael had surprised her last night. In all the years she had spent with him he had never surprised her more. He was so predictable as a rule. Even his moods of silence were predictable, and hence not overly disturbing. She and Michael never shouted at each other— as Dick and Bettina Johnson did, for instance, even on occasion in public. They might argue now and then; but overtones of bitterness were generally avoided, and it was generally Michael who made amends. Last night, however, he had astonished her. Never for an instant, when he came into the room, would she have predicted that he was going to speak to her about a trip abroad—about nostalgia for certain places . . . Rome, she thought, her heart stirring toward the word . . . A city for world travelers.

How quiet the house was—and tomorrow Bettina Johnson and Alice Ormond were coming to admire a new pair of curtains. Tomorrow morning she would work with greater resolve. She would have everything looking perfect, no matter what happened at the office. She glanced down at her hands. The skin was a little rough, her bare forearms lightly discolored, there was a smudge of dust on her blouse. She wondered vaguely if she stooped a bit at the end of the day, as Michael did when he got off the train.

She was lifting a plate from the water and putting it carefully in the rubberized rack on top of the sink. "I wish I was at the office now," she thought. "I'd know what to say to Sam Dilks. I wouldn't be afraid of him." She began working more swiftly. She felt suddenly alone in her white kitchen with the freshly washed walls. It wasn't like her at all to feel alone.

THE offices of Dilks and Stanley were on the seventh floor in a small group of buildings known as Insurance Row. Actually the name applied more to the past than the present, many of the firms having moved to more modern locations uptown; but Sam Dilks, the senior partner, had not chosen to move, and the offices were not greatly altered from his grandfather's time. Insurance Row had an air of solidity which Sam believed advantageous. Solidity was attached to the stone pillars on the façade, to the marble corridors, even to the measured pace of the elevator with its green plush seat in the rear.

From his desk in the corner of the long, rectangular, sparsely furnished room Michael could see the door leading to Sam's private office. The door was closed; the frosted-glass panel, lettered discreetly with Sam's name, was softly white—like the light globes hung from the ceiling. Sam was conferring with Harold Stanley; a half hour earlier Harold had been summoned. A half hour earlier Michael had been about to rise and walk toward the glass panel himself.

He wished he had not delayed. It was already mid-morning. He should have gone in to see Sam right away, instead of occupying himself with the purely routine report left over from the previous day. Yet he had thought: it's best to get this done, to let Sam finish with his mail, to wait for a lull.

Five others were in the room. Occasionally a chair swiveled round, but the voices seemed hushed and without emphasis. Near Michael Josephine Selmer, whose service with the firm predated his own, was typing out the report. She had a pinched studious face and the enigmatic expression of one who knows many small secrets and who can keep them indefinitely; but humor was not one of Josephine's attributes and Michael had long ago given up trying to joke with her. He watched her fingers strike sharply against the keys; and the room with its central strip of faded Oriental carpet, with its walls half plastered and half paneled in oak, with its old-fashioned coat racks beside each of the six desks, seemed bleak and ancient and yet comfortable. It was the sort of place which could use a bright young man. That had been Sam's phrase eighteen years before.

Michael straightened his necktie. I mustn't be nervous, he told himself. He hadn't been nervous eighteen years ago. Sam had wanted to hire him on the spot, hadn't he? Sam's offer had been the best he had found; but sometimes Michael had wondered why he had chosen the insurance business. His father had been a doctor, a general practitioner who had lived in an old stone farmhouse far beyond the country club and in an area still undeveloped. Dr. Thomas Allen, however, had struggled constantly to make ends meet. He had been a frail, preoccupied man, with a somewhat sardonic wit, who had suggested that medicine was not the most lucrative of careers. He had died suddenly of pneumonia during Michael's final year at the state university, and Michael's mother had sold the house and, with the annuity left to her, had taken a two-room apartment in the city. She was a gregarious woman. She had always wanted to live in town, Michael had realized, but she had not revealed this wish to her husband. She had been unfailingly good-natured with him, catering to his small eccentricities, to the laboratory crowded with books and vials which he had set up in the cellar. "Your father's doing his research again," she would say, smiling. "We'd better not bother him." And once Michael had driven his own son out past the old house and past the stream below it, where he had played alone as a child; but the stream had looked oddly unsheltered and disappointing and the house rather forlorn. Mikey had not been overly impressed.

Michael saw the door at the end of the room open and close. Harold Stanley emerged, glanced toward the sound of the typewriter, sighed and seated himself—a bulky man, gray haired, polite, slow in speech, slow in the gestures of his hands. It would be much easier to approach Harold than Sam, Michael thought; but Sam made the decisions and everyone knew this,

Harold included. Sam's son, Bryan, just out of Princeton, would one day take over the firm.

Michael rose. He walked past Josephine Selmer and past Harold Stanley and stood beyond them in front of the closed door. He touched his tie again and then rapped lightly on the glass panel. The sound seemed muted, almost obsequious against the crisp, clear strokes of the typewriter.

"Yes? Who is it? . . . Oh, it's you, Mike. Come in." Sam was sitting behind his large mahogany desk, his back toward a row of bookshelves, ornately bound volumes climbing in tiers to the ceiling.

Michael closed the door. "You got a minute, Sam?"

"Why—something come up?"

"No, this is personal . . . It can wait till later if you want—"

"No—no, I've got nothing pressing here," Sam said, shuffling through a pile of papers, rearranging them. "Nothing that needs doing in the next five or ten minutes. What's on your mind?"

Michael walked stiffly to the desk. "I've got something I'd like to ask you," he said quite casually, watching the fingers tap the papers together and then looking at the eyes framed in black-rimmed spectacles.

"Sure," Sam said.

Michael drew up a chair. Sam's face was sallow but firmly featured and surprisingly young for a man close to sixty. He had on one of his dark business suits, conservatively tailored, a shirt with starched collar and cuffs protruding just enough so that part of the gold links would show.

"It's about my vacation this year." Michael cleared his throat. "It's about a plan I've been thinking about for some time."

"Isn't it a little early to be thinking about vacations?"

"Yes—maybe. But not this one, Sam."

"Oh?"

"This is a special one," Michael said. Sam's eyes, slightly magnified by the spectacles, scrutinized him.

"Oh—is it?"

"I'd like a little more than the three weeks this summer, Sam."

"I guess we all would, wouldn't we?"

Michael thought of the Florida trips which Sam took with his wife each year in addition to their summer holiday; but these were always excused, although for the senior partner they need not have been, under the heading of business, broadening the name of the firm; and admittedly they were brief and admittedly Sam worked as hard or harder than any of his employees.

"I guess we all would, Sam. Only—well, this is important to me."

"Just how long do you want?"

"Five weeks, about five weeks in all—"

"Five weeks!" Sam interrupted with an expression of bland surprise. "That's a pretty big order, isn't it?"

"Yes, I realize that."

Sam smiled indulgently. "Where would you go in this five weeks?"

"Well—to Europe, Sam. To Italy. You know I was there during the war. I've always had a desire—a great desire to see it again. I thought it would be a nice trip for Ruth . . . A real change." The words sounded lame and tense. Michael saw himself riding on the train into town, rehearsing what he would say. I'm going to fail, he thought. Of course he'll say no.

"A trip abroad, ay?" Sam said. "Well, that's something we'd all like to think about, I guess, if it were possible. Helen and I have the same notions now and then. Paris—you know Paris clothes always appeal to the women. And Italy, gondolas in the moonlight. But as I tell Helen, it isn't for now. Business just won't permit it. What's the name of that hotel in Venice that's supposed to be so good?"

"I don't know," Michael said, "I never got to Venice."

"No? Well, it doesn't matter . . . No, Mike, I'm afraid, much as I'd like to tell you to go ahead, I'm afraid the five weeks are out. If I gave you five weeks, everyone else would be after me, wouldn't they? I can't make exceptions. You know that as well as I."

"It wouldn't have to be an exception, Sam . . . I've put in a lot of overtime here. If you totaled it up, it would come to a good deal more than the extra two weeks I'm asking for."

Sam took off his glasses and rubbed the bridge of his nose and put the glasses back on. "All of us work overtime occasionally. Maybe you have more than some of the others, but occasionally we get off early. I've never put in time clocks around here. I don't believe in 'em, and I've never kept track of overtime, or undertime. I'll bet you haven't either, Mike. Be honest."

"No, I've never kept actual track of it, but—"

"But now you want two extra weeks so you say you're entitled to them." Sam chuckled. "Well, I can't blame you for asking, Mike. That's your privilege. Look, why don't you do it this way, if you're so set on going?—fly over and fly back. You'd still have time to see Italy."

"It would be too hurried," Michael said, feeling the moisture starting in the palms of his hands. "I wouldn't want to do it that way. The extra time would make all the difference. We'd be running every day otherwise, trying to see too much, not seeing enough. I don't just want to see Italy again. I want to be there. I want to show it to Ruth. I don't want us to be here for a couple of days and there for a couple more—and then only a few left. I thought of flying home, but going over on a boat— a chance to rest and get ready. I thought of it coming into the harbor at Naples, coming slowly in . . . But maybe that wouldn't be necessary. We could forget about the boat, I guess. But a week, Sam. Even an extra week would make a great difference. To me it would. We wouldn't be doing this again for years—maybe not ever. You could chalk it up to sick leave, couldn't you—something like that? I didn't miss more than a day or so last year."

"Neither did I." Sam was no longer smiling. "You know we don't have retroactive sick leave in this office, Mike. No, you plead your case very well, but that's it. And I must say, without meaning to butt into your affairs, that a trip to Europe—well—"

"Well what?" Michael said.

"Well, maybe it's a little farfetched for a fellow in your circumstances. You think it over. I'm afraid I've given you the best suggestion I can offer."

Michael stared at him. "I'll take the extra week," he said, "without pay."

"How's that?"

"Without pay," Michael said.

"Now don't fly off the handle with me, Mike."

"I'm not flying off the handle. I'm simply telling you that I'll take my three weeks vacation and an extra week that won't cost you a damn cent, and I'll make up for it when I get back, or before I go, or whenever. I'll give you the damn overtime—and if that isn't agreeable to you, Sam . . . if that isn't agreeable— you can find yourself another boy."

Sam put his finger tips together. "There's no need to get excited," he said quietly with a half smile. "I didn't say anything about time *without pay*. At least I don't remember I did. . . . No—no, you can have the extra week under those terms, Mike, if you like. This office isn't a sweatshop. It'll be an agreement between you and me. You just tell me when you want to go and I'll arrange it. We'll call it a month, shall we? Which would you like, May, June, July?"

"Whichever is most convenient," Michael said.

"We'll call it May then. May should be nice in Italy."

"Yes, it should be," Michael said, and knew that he had lost, had compromised himself—that perhaps he had been tricked into anger, that Sam had measured the past against the present and had handled his request with ease. He could not reverse himself now, Michael knew, but as he went into the outer room he was aware of relief. The extra time had seemed so important. Some of it had been gained. A strange thing to compromise yourself for. A single week. Yet the week in itself was not all that mattered. In Sam's office, Michael realized, he had had the odd, desperate feeling that in reality he had been pleading for his life.

At lunch time he telephoned Ruth.

She answered the ring immediately. He was surprised at how breathless she sounded. "Yes, I know you couldn't call earlier How did it go, darling—how did it go?"

He craned his elbow against the booth. "It went all right, honey. We didn't get the five weeks—but we got a month."

"Really?"

"Yes. Really."

"Why, that's wonderful—perfectly wonderful! He gave you a whole month?"

"Yes," Michael said without hesitation. "He gave me a month free."

SHE was on the station platform to greet him that evening. He saw her face bobbing against the flow of commuters. He was struck by the welcome. She always waited for him in the car, unless a crisis had developed in the house during the late afternoon—the winter day the furnace had broken down, the day Mikey had fallen off his bicycle and was in bed with a concussion. Seeing Ruth he was reminded incongruously of those times: something had gone wrong; and more remotely and then with sudden recall he remembered days when they were first married, when she would detach herself from the older wives waiting in the cars and come forward like this on another platform to tell him hurriedly and with laughter what she had done in the long interval since morning.

"Hi!" he said, and took off his hat and kissed her, seeing her eyes bright in the lights strung under the peaked roof. "What's the news?"

"Oh, I've been so busy, darling—all afternoon. But you know what I decided this morning—just about an hour before you called?"

"No." He smiled. "What did you decide?"

"I decided that even if we only had three weeks, we could do it. But the month is so much nicer."

"Yes," he said. "It is. Much nicer."

"And I composed an ad for the paper, for the woman we talked about to look after the children, and I called that Mrs. Mullins, you know the employment agency; and I told her what I wanted and she said it might cost fifty dollars a week. Imagine! But she has someone I can interview next Monday."

"Should be the Queen of Sheba," Michael said, and Ruth laughed. He was helping her into the Chevrolet sedan, walking around to the other side, his feet sliding in fresh-falling snow.

The other cars were beginning to back away, their tires spinning. A pair of headlights probed at him. Michael got in and pressed the starter button. Ruth was saying, "And I got out the atlas this afternoon and looked at the map of Italy—and I found those pictures you sent me of Naples and Mt. Vesuvius. They were in a box up in the attic with the letters you wrote. I remembered just where I'd put them, in that corner in back of the crib—under the eaves. And really it is lovely, isn't it, darling. The Bay of Naples. And Capri—do you think we might go to Capri?"

"Sure," he answered. "It's only about an hour from Naples. Maybe less now. You can take a little boat."

"You were there, weren't you?"

"Yes, once—for a few hours. The Air Force had a rest area on Capri. Very swank, the Air Force." He watched the light ahead of him go from red to green. Someone was jabbing at a horn.

"Imagine us on the Isle of Capri," Ruth said. There was a note of hysteria in her voice; but no, it wasn't hysteria, it was joy. Then it changed into the question he had been expecting: "What exactly did he say to you, darling?"

"Oh, nothing much more than what I told you already."

"Yes, but that was on the telephone, and you were rushing. Wasn't he angry? Didn't you have to argue?"

"Well, a little," Michael said, keeping his eyes fixed on the billowing exhaust from the car in front. "I asked for the five weeks and we settled on a month. We made a deal, Ruth."

"What kind of a deal?"

He shifted the car into low gear. "Well, I said I'd make up for the extra time, work a little harder, that's all."

"I'll bet you'll have to make up for it."

"It won't be so bad—"

"Did he boil it down to hours, night work—that sort of thing?"

"No. No, he didn't."

"You didn't obligate yourself to him, I mean too much—"

"No—it wasn't a favor. It was an agreement we reached."

"What did he say about the overtime you've put in up to date?"

"Oh, you know. That it counted, but that it didn't apply retroactively. It did help, though. I wouldn't have been able to ask for anything if I'd been a newcomer. Anyway—" he began and glanced at her and was surprised to see that she was leaning back, not staring at him searchingly as he had believed. "Anyway," he said, "we shouldn't say too much about it, I mean to our friends. Sam'll arrange it at the office—tactfully, I guess, but we don't have to go into a lot of details with other people."

"I won't say a word, darling. I'll just say we have a month's vacation this year, and that you fixed it up. Is that all right?"

"That's fine," he said. "Actually I don't suppose anyone'll be too curious. A month's holiday after all these years doesn't exactly come under the heading of largesse." He settled his spine against the upholstery. The road curved past the more pretentious houses on the hill. "Have you told the children, Ruth?"

"Yes—"

"How did they react? Were they sad about it?"

"I wouldn't say sad. They seemed sort of astonished."

"Did they want to go along?"

"They didn't say so. And during May, of course, they'll still be in school. They'll have that to occupy them—and I called Mother and told her and she said she'd drop by and see them every few days and that they could spend week ends with her, if they wanted, and I said they might do that once or twice with the woman we hired. I've been meaning to ask you, though—how did you happen to pick May?"

He was turning into the driveway.

"I didn't really pick it, Ruth. Sam did."

He saw her nod. "I thought maybe so," she said, but without apparent slyness. "Still it's a good month for us to be gone, all things considered."

"I didn't object to it. The summer's apt to be pretty hot in Italy . . . Some parts, Rome especially . . . May's a beautiful month." He switched off the engine. "I don't think we could have done much better."

He was getting out of the car. He felt more tired than he had on the train. I mustn't let it be spoiled, he thought. The mention of the week without pay would have spoiled it. Ruth would have seen through to the defeat. He could hide it from her, juggle the figures around. Perhaps she would never know, or would not find out until the trip was over, and then she wouldn't care—provided the trip turned into the adventure he had planned. But he shouldn't think of the end of the trip this evening, and he should erase Sam Dilks from his mind. Sam wouldn't broadcast the altercation; he would lose his advantage. Maybe the thing wouldn't come up. No one coveted a May vacation; and except for Sam and Josephine Selmer and Harold Stanley, whom he and Ruth did not see socially, Michael had been with the firm longer than any of the others. If anyone asked questions, he would refer them to Sam. Only if it became unavoidable would he explain the whole agreement to Ruth.

Mikey was squatting on the floor in front of the television set when they entered the living room. He had on a plaid shirt and blue jeans and sneakers. He glanced at his father and stood up and Michael put his hand on his son's close-cropped brown hair.

"How's the old boy been all day?"

"Fine," Mikey said noncommittally.

"How's the picture?"

"Not very good. I've seen it before. I was just sort of looking at it until you came." He reached and twisted the knob and the screen became blank. Michael could see Ruth going toward the kitchen, could hear Priscilla rattling a pot or something on the stove.

"What do you think of your old man going to Italy?"

"I don't know, Dad—"

"Pretty big deal?"

"Yes, it sounds like one."

"It does to me too . . . Here, let's sit over on the sofa and I'll tell you about it." Michael was aware of the disappointment in the face with the brown eyes and freckles. "We won't be gone long, you know."

"Mom said a month."

"Yes, that's right—a month." There was a pause. "You know we'd like to take you with us, Mike. I hope you do—take you and Pris abroad, but—well, it just isn't in the cards this time.

This time has to be just for your mother and me."

"Sure. I know—"

"You think it's selfish of us to make plans like that?"

Mikey fingered the sleeve of his shirt. His eyes were lowered. "No," he said, "not selfish."

"I think maybe you do. It'd only be natural for you to feel that way, wouldn't it? . . . But some day, Mike—when you're married yourself and have your own children as grown up as you and Pris—some day then perhaps you'll want to take a trip, and it won't be possible to bring your children along. Maybe you'll want to get away for a while by yourselves, you and your wife. But it won't mean that you don't love your children. It won't mean that at all."

"No," Mikey said.

"It'll mean that you'll want to get away, and then come back more full of life than when you started out, able to do things better. Your job, everything. I don't want to make too big an issue of it all with you—but I want you to understand. . . . You see, Italy's the only foreign country I know much about. Because I was there in the war. I'd like to show it to your mother. Maybe some day I'll show it to you." He forced a smile. "Or you'll take *me* there, and we'll explore it together. . . . So . . . so, is it okay?"

Mikey looked up. "Sure, it's okay . . . I really didn't think it was selfish." The disappointment still hovered in his face.

"No, but you feel a little left out. I know how you feel, I'd feel the same way if I were thirteen." He hesitated. "But to change the subject rather abruptly, do you know what I was thinking of coming out on the train—other than what I've just been saying?"

"No," Mikey said, turning slightly, drawing his foot up on the sofa. "What were you?"

"I was wondering what I might bring you back from Italy. You know they make wonderful things out of leather. A fine belt or a wallet—but they didn't seem unusual enough to me—and then I thought of a ship model, one to go with that collection we started upstairs in your room. Only this would be more elaborate, more rare, than any we've made ourselves. I thought it should have parchment sails, and some small brass cannons sticking out along the sides, and rope ladders going up the masts to the crow's-nests . . . an upraised stern—"

Mikey grinned, either because the description seemed a trifle juvenile, or in genuine anticipation, Michael could not decide.

"Like a caravel," Mikey said. "Yes, I'd like that very much."

"That's it. That's the stuff. Like a caravel. The decks would be all planked, miniature planks . . . It'd be very nicely made."

Priscilla came out of the kitchen. She moved with a slightly exaggerated yet awkward assurance, as if only recently aware that her body had changed from plumpness, was becoming slim. He looked toward her admiringly. Some day, he thought, she would be quite beautiful.

"Hi, Daddy."

"Hi, Pris," he said. "Come on over here. We were just beginning to discuss navigation, your brother and I. What do you think of it? What do you think of the trip?"

"Why, I think it would be very good for you and Mother.'

"Do you now? That sounds like a sensible pronouncement."

"No, I mean parents need a change from their surroundings every so often."

"Do they indeed?" he asked, smiling at her. "And how about the children of these parents?"

"I'm not a child, Daddy."

"No," he said. "I know you're not . . . and I know you'd like to come along, too—wouldn't you?"

"Of course I'd like to come along, Daddy. But Mother says—'

"What does your mother say, Pris?"

"Mother says you can only afford to take her this year," Priscilla answered.

Michael watched her closely. There was no resentment in her voice. It was as if she were merely stating a fact. "Oh," he said. "Yes, darling. Yes . . . I'm afraid that's the way it is. We can't always do what we'd like to do, can we? . . . But at least we can afford to buy something special for you while we're away. Mikey and I were talking about a ship with parchment sails, an antique model, made by some expert old craftsman long ago. How about a dress for you?"

"A real party dress," Priscilla said.

"Oh, it'd be real from top to bottom. We wouldn't accept any substitutes."

"You know what I mean, Daddy—"

"Sure I do," he said. "I know exactly what you mean. Something with a flaring skirt, off the ground. Something for a dance later on in the summer . . . White—do you think it ought to be white, Pris, with maybe a few rhinestones, or a touch of silver?"

"Yes—that would be lovely."

"And perhaps a green ribbon around the waist?"

"A sash, Daddy."

"Okay, a sash," he agreed, smiling once more. "A fine green sash for a party."

Ruth appeared carrying a tray with a bowl of ice cubes and two old-fashioned glasses. "I put supper off for half an hour," she announced. "I thought we might have a drink to celebrate."

"Just what I was thinking," Michael said, and helped her put the tray down on the coffee table and went to get the whisky. He was selecting the Scotch he had been saving, the annual Christmas gift from Harold Stanley, instead of the half-empty bottle of rye. He turned. Ruth's face was eager and bright against the backdrop of the new chintz curtains. The children had not yet moved.

"You fellows rummage up something nice for yourselves," he said, leaning forward, fixing the drinks, seeing the cut-glass bowl that had not been used since Christmas on the tray. Ruth was saying, "Well, darling, I never thought it would happen. I never did." He could hear the children's footsteps on the carpet, Priscilla talking about the dress, the presents; but for a moment Michael was close to tears.

And later, sitting again on the sofa beside the children, he remembered how he used to read stories to them when they were smaller, both a gap and a bridge existing between past and present so that the intervening years were not as clearly defined. He wished intensely that they could all go abroad together. They seemed more of a family than they had last night or during the previous time scattered rather aimlessly backward, as if in some fashion the prospect of separation had united them. That was his own impression, however, he recognized. The children couldn't help feeling excluded even though they might phrase it differently, Priscilla hiding her emotions more than Mikey. Yet they were not really *excluded*. Ruth would not say they were. Ruth did not feel inadequate toward them—not this evening, not on other evenings, not as he had felt a little while ago. But he must stop thinking about excluding his children and about inadequacy, as if it were some sort of obsession. Slowly the strain of the day slipped from him; and he thought: why—the trip is assured, it's going to come true! He and Ruth would bring home to the children much more than a party dress and the model of a ship. It wasn't feasible to alter the plans; nor should they be altered.

March came and ended. Pete Wadsworth, who was Michael's closest friend at Dilks and Stanley, said, "You lucky stiff—going to Italy!" But Pete had been with the firm only since 1949 and did not seem to begrudge the extra time off, or did anyone else. And Sam would say, "Mike, I wonder if you'd mind glancing over this tonight. Let me have your views first thing in the morning," and Michael would take the policy home and make his assessment meticulously.

"How long did this take you, Mike?"

"Two hours, two hours and a half—"

"Which is it?"

"Two hours and a half."

Sam would smile. "Want to keep a little record, you know. I'll jot it down."

But Michael no longer thought of Sam or of the office as being knotted to the future. The trip was too near. He began counting the days until May. On the train he would find himself staring over the top of his newspaper out the window, not really seeing this particular countryside but smiling at it in a quiet private fashion which his neighbor, had he chosen to observe, might well have considered lunatic. It was an enormously pleasant feeling, hazy and mystical and yet rooted in fact.

They had decided to go both ways by air so that they would have as much time in Italy as possible; and sometimes he would see the plane swooping down toward the airport outside Rome, or himself and Ruth on a restaurant terrace above the sea at Sorrento; and sometimes he saw the village intact, unchanged, the stone walls cresting the hill. It would be there, that was the marvelous thing about it. It would appear around a bend in the road; and he would come face to face with Michael Allen, as if the soldier, who had once tried to rescue a man from intense danger, were an old lost friend. That was the moment of identity he sought to crystallize.

Probably the old man was dead by now, and certainly Angelina would not be in the village. She might be anywhere else, but not at home. He could not envision meeting her, but he knew that he would walk across the hills and fields to the farmhouse. Would they remember him? Of course they would, the ones who remained. Yet it was not essential. The essential part would come when he rounded the bend in the road. He would stop the rented car and, looking ahead, he would feel—what precisely? Perhaps a sense of continuity, from one summit in his life to another—perhaps, for the merest second, a sensation of being immortal. That sounded very pretentious. Yet wasn't it true that a man seeks for his heroism; and wasn't it an evidence to him of something beyond limits? But that was being too serious, and it was foolish to try to analyze the feeling of anticipation. Ruth could not share this; but she would see the hillside where he had done something far less ordinary than working in the offices of Dilks and Stanley. She would be with him in his village.

There would be some sort of small hotel, or an inn, where they could stay for a night, and he would have possibly an afternoon and an evening and the next morning to look and to absorb. He did not visualize lingering in the village. To see it again for that length of time would be enough. A longer stay might make it seem mundane. He would not take that risk. Then they would move on to Naples and Capri and Sorrento, and the rest of the trip, as well as its beginnings, would belong to them both. They wouldn't go at once to the village. They would go toward it gradually and away from it at the same pace. They would spend a week in Rome and another around Florence before they turned south.

Ruth's expectation was different. She talked of having a month free from all her household chores, a month free from worry. She did not refer again to his interview with Sam. To Michael it seemed almost intentional, as if she considered that the time he had gained might be jeopardized through further discussion; but naturally he was not displeased. It showed him, he believed, that the trip had grown to mean a great deal to Ruth.

He noticed that she was less fastidious in her housekeeping, that she was inclined to say we'll let this or that go until later on. Returning home after work he would find travel folders stacked on the coffee table, or a book secured from the library with colored photographs of Italy, or a list of pensions and hotels recommended by the agency Ruth had contacted in town. The village was not included among the photographs or in the hotel guides the agency had on file, but of course it was not a tourist attraction; and when Ruth spoke of Rome and Naples and Florence, he saw an essence of his village there also—as if the first words which he would hear in Italian, whether they were addressed to him or not, would quicken his memory, would serve to recall.

He watched Ruth's enthusiasm increase. "Darling, I haven't had a second all day," she told him one evening at the station. "I went to the travel bureau again and gave them the names of the hotels we chose. I decided to go myself instead of telephoning —and then I spent the rest of the morning and some of the afternoon looking for a new hat. Would you believe it? I spent hours —but I wanted to find just the right one. Wait, I'll show it to you. I have it here in the car . . . There . . . Do you like it, do you think it looks nice?"

"It looks perfect."

"Do you really think so? It cost eighteen ninety-five. More money than I've ever paid for a hat in my life!"

He marveled at how her energies had become focused on the trip, at the schedule she set for herself during the final weeks of April. She arranged most of the details. She interviewed more than a dozen women for the job of looking after Priscilla and

Mikey. She settled on a Mrs. Stevens, a widow with two daughters already married—and then one morning the bags were packed and a taxi was summoned. Michael had talked with his mother the previous evening. "I'll come by tomorrow," she had said, "and see the children after you've gone," and in the bedroom Ruth was calling her own parents. From the hall upstairs Michael could hear her saying, "Yes . . . yes, that's fine. Yes—in a few minutes."

Holding a small suitcase, Michael went down the stairs. Mikey and Priscilla were standing next to the rest of the luggage at the front door.

"Now you fellows take good care of each other—understand?"

"You bet," Mikey said.

"And don't forget about the dress, Pris—"

"No, Daddy."

"Or the ship, Mike—"

Ruth hurried past him and went through the living room doorway. She was talking with Mrs. Stevens.

"We'll send you a cable as soon as we arrive, Pris," Michael said and knew he had said that earlier and that there was a lump in his throat as he stood, listening to Ruth's voice, seeing the children beside the luggage.

Ruth reappeared. She had on her new spring suit, the new black straw bonnet with a half-veil attached to the brim. She was putting on a pair of gloves.

"You have the tickets?"

"Right here in my pocket," he said, producing them, looking at Priscilla, hoping she would smile; but her face remained solemn.

Ruth said, "We'd better get the things out to the sidewalk."

"Yes," he agreed, "we better had . . . No, don't you lift that, Mike. I can handle it. You just get the door."

They were walking across a flagstone path, Michael with the two large suitcases, Mikey holding the smaller one. Since it was early Saturday morning, none of the neighbors were outside. The street looked deserted.

Ruth was saying, "Now, Pris, if any real emergency comes up you know where we'll be, nearly all the places, and you can have a call put through, a transatlantic call."

"Yes, Mother—but we won't have to."

"I don't think so either, dear. But at any rate you know what to do."

"Yes, Mother. I know what to do."

The taxi came into view and backed out of the driveway and pulled up to the curb. Michael put his arm around his son.

"Have a good time—"

"We will, Mikey—and we'll be home soon." The thickness was painful in his throat. "And Pris, darling—you take care of your big brother." He kissed her and then he was helping the driver with the luggage and when he turned Ruth was in the cab.

He had climbed in beside her. He was reeling down the window. "We'll be home soon," he repeated. "Don't forget—" He did not finish. The taxi had started.

He looked out the rear window and waved. The children were close together, waving toward him. He could see Mrs. Stevens on the front doorstep.

"Don't watch them out of sight," Ruth said. "It's bad luck."

He turned slowly. "Okay," he said. "We don't want any bad luck." Ruth's cheeks were brightly flushed. She was sitting up very straight. He put his hand over hers. He was surprised at how rigid her fingers were under the gloves.

"They'll be fine," he said. "Both of them."

"Of course they will be. We've done everything we possibly could . . . You're sure you have the tickets, Mike—"

"Oh God, no!" he answered. "I must have left them there in the hall—on the table."

"What!" Her face astonished him. It seemed contorted, the lips parted in rage, in exasperation. "You didn't—you couldn't have! You—"

"Good Lord, Ruth," he said. "I was only joking."

"Oh," she said. "Oh—of course. I should have known." She sighed and faintly returned the pressure of his hand. "It's just that it sounded so like you for a second . . . And I couldn't have borne it—I couldn't have *borne* going back."

# Part
# T W O

ANGELINA Nardi awoke from deep slumber and found herself gazing through half-closed eyes at the window. For a moment its shape puzzled her. It was longer than the one she had grown accustomed to in the drab room near the Via Roma in Naples. Sunlight never penetrated that window—in the spring, or in any other season. It was always cut off by the wall of the building opposite; but the sun flooded through this one, even though the rays were partly obstructed by the slanting ribs of a shutter.

The sunlight cast diagonal stripes across her bare arm and the white counterpane. It was pleasant to awaken like this from real sleep, and for a minute or two she did not question her surroundings but watched the April sun glimmer against the brass scrollwork at the foot of the bed, making it seem polished, almost like gold. Then she heard the sound of breathing and languidly turned her head and saw the man's profile: the delicately pale skin taut across the forehead and under the point of the chin. Except for the gray hair that was nearly white at the temple, this might be a more youthful face. At any rate it was nicely preserved, elegant, even handsome, and in repose quite peaceful. A fastidious man, an aristocrat perhaps, one with that bearing and knowledge. A man difficult to type, however, not as sure of himself as he would like to appear; but then you had to be wise in the ways of the world to understand that. The uncertainty was not in the gestures of hand or body. It was in the eyes; she had seen it once or twice there; but it was not her business to explain it, at least not this morning.

He had introduced himself the previous evening. She had been sitting at a café table in the Vomero section of town, up above the Via Roma.

"You are alone, signorina?"

"Yes—as you can see."

"You are waiting for someone?"

"For no one in particular."

"Would you object to my joining you?"

"No, I do not think I would object . . ."

She had learned his name—Gerald Newell. He had spelled it out. There was no reason to disbelieve the name. He had said he was an American writer, that he had lived abroad for much of his life, that he had moved recently from Paris and might be in Naples for several months, with occasional trips to Florence where a friend was interested in publishing and translating his newest book. He would be ready to present it within a few weeks. It was to be a long historical novel, he had said, about Pompeii. He wanted to be near Pompeii during the book's completion, and at the same time to live in a city. He had chosen Naples as a result; and there was no special reason for disbelieving this either. Yet he had been evasive about his work, anxious to mention it, and apparently anxious not to discuss it in detail.

"You are a famous writer then?" she had asked him.

"Oh, not famous exactly, my dear. Let us say merely that I have had some success, and that I strive for more."

"I do not know any successful writers," she had told him. "A few who struggle and have no money."

"I envy them on two counts," he had said. "Because they are undoubtedly young, and because they should know you."

"But you are not old—and I am not hard to know."

He had smiled. "In that case perhaps we shall get along very well . . ."

He had spoken in flawless Italian. He had been in Italy many times, he had told her—and this was the apartment which was near the café and which he had rented three days before. He had apologized for the size. It was not as large as he would have wished, but the furniture had appealed to him, the linen, the glass, the silver; and the patio was his and it was sheltered from the street. He might do some writing in the patio, or he would use the desk here in the bedroom and keep the room beyond it for the living and dining area it was intended to be. The whole was not nearly as spacious as his flat in Paris, but one must not complain.

Paris, Angelina thought, idly looking at the profile. Possibly he had lived there, but not in a spacious apartment, unless it belonged to an older woman—that could be. His clothes did not fit into a pattern of extravagant spending. They were not cheap clothes, she knew. They were carefully kept, but when you looked at them closely you saw the small indications of wear. They were a little like his wallet, which she had noticed—the fine leather beginning to lose its sheen and suppleness. Yet the wallet had been far from empty, and he had been generous last night. He had bought for them both a reasonably expensive meal. He had told her to order as she wished.

She looked at him without pity, but without scorn or displeasure. She should be grateful to him, she decided. These past months had not been happy ones. She had even thought of going home again, of going back to the village; but she had lost contact with it in ten years. She had seen her family only twice since the war, and then only briefly—and not since her grandfather's funeral four years earlier. That she should have even considered returning on any permanent basis had made her realize how acutely depressed she had become. She was getting too old for this business, she had believed. She was losing her sense of humor; and that was a frightful, and frightening admission—was it not? Maybe this strange man, who had been kind to her last night, signified a change.

She arose and dressed and went noiselessly from the room and into the alcove of the kitchen. Yes, there was coffee and a percolator to cook it in, and a gas stove with two burners. There was nothing else she could discover. She drew some water from the tap and rinsed it across her face and fluffed her dark hair into order. She found her purse on the dining table and, peering into an antique mirror on the wall, ran a lipstick pencil across her lips, and arranged the belt of her dress and smoothed it over her thighs. She looked quite presentable, she thought. The dress was not cut too low between the breasts as an advertisement. It was plain and dark and trimmed with white. It might easily have come from the shop of a Florentine couturier.

She was turning toward the door leading into the entrance hallway, when Gerald Newell appeared from the bedroom. He was wearing a blue dressing gown, corded with worn satin. He was pushing a hand through his hair.

"You are leaving?" he asked quietly.

"I was going to get some bread, some rolls—some butter."

"Oh," he said. "I . . . I see. I didn't hear you get up. . . . That's very nice."

"You would like something else?"

"No—no, I think that would be very nice indeed . . . Wait a moment." He put his hand through his hair again. "I will get you the money."

"I have enough," Angelina said. "You can pay me back."

"All right. Yes, of course." He was tying the cord around his waist. "I was afraid," he said, "that you were going away."

The apartment was on the ground floor of a rambling but otherwise unpretentious villa on an upper level of the city— an area shaded by trees, with smaller residential streets leading from the central avenue where the shops and the café were located. Gerald Newell had said it reminded him a little of the Montmartre district in Paris. The comparison had seemed complimentary to Angelina, whether it was true or not. She liked the Vomero. It was removed from the hubbub and crowds below; it was cooler when the weather turned hot, and not frequented by as many tourists. It seemed more refined. There were more possibilities on the Via Roma and along the water front with the big hotels, but there was more competition, and the average tourist did not often travel alone. She was tired of the tourists. They used you for a night and then they were gone and you

had to start all over again; and her room had not been a place
to bring a rich gentleman—an old acquaintance perhaps, a native
of the city, or sometimes a foreigner who had had too much
to drink and didn't care where he was—but not such a man as
Gerald Newell, the writer. She would assume that he was
composing a novel, that he had an honorable career ahead of
him still. She would give him that satisfaction while it lasted.
She was glad she had come to the Vomero last evening, glad to be
away from eyes which had spied on her—the greedy eyes of
the two Massolino sisters, for instance, who lived on the floor
above her, who knew when every man arrived and when he left.
She could laugh at them now.

In the bakery the short, stout man behind the glass counter
said, "Ah, it is Signorina Nardi. Good morning. We have not
seen very much of you."

Angelina smiled. "One must eat breakfast occasionally."

"These are very fresh," he said. "These little rolls—"

"Or they were baked yesterday," Angelina said.

The man moved his eyes in an expression of wounded pride.
"No, I assure you, signorina. Feel them. They are still warm
from the oven."

Angelina laughed. "All right. I believe you. I don't want to
burn my fingers. I will take six."

"You have a great appetite, signorina."

"As always," she said and watched him drop the rolls into a
paper bag.

She bought butter and milk at the *latteria* and then on an
impulse a white crock of marmalade from a store which sold im-
ported delicacies on the corner. The postman was emerging from
the villa when she returned. Three wooden shelves, divided into
partitions, had been attached to the wall next to the marble stairs
which rose to the other floors. The writer had pinned his card
below one of the partitions. She drew her thumb across the
name. It was engraved, the way an important person's name
would be, she thought. Above the card there was a single brown
envelope. She drew it out and raised her eyebrows. It came
from a bank—Banco di Napoli. That could be good news or
bad news. She had never received a letter from a bank.

Gerald Newell was still wearing the dressing gown, but he had put a white silk scarf around his neck and had combed his hair and had shaved. He was smoking a cigarette in an amber holder. "I'm afraid I'm not very good at cooking," he said. "I couldn't get the stove to function properly."

"I will do it," she answered. "You don't always have to speak in Italian to me, you know. I am not so fluent but I know English. I learned it long ago."

"No," he said. "I would prefer the Italian, if you don't mind. I am quite at home in Italian. It is a beautiful language, don't you agree? Very soft to the ear."

"It is mine," she said, smiling at him. "I'm not sure how beautiful it is. Here. There was a letter for you. I picked it up."

"A letter? . . . Oh—yes." He glanced at the envelope— sharply, she thought—and put it into a pocket, and she entered the kitchen alcove.

The stove had not been used for a while evidently, but it seemed clean enough. She was calling to him. "There is a little rubber tube here that brings in the gas. It wasn't fastened securely."

"Oh, is that what the trouble was. I smelled the gas. I didn't want to light a match, didn't want to blow myself up just yet."

"It's not dangerous," she said. "There it is fixed." She could hear him ripping the envelope open. "Do you like your coffee strong—or how?"

"Yes—strong," he answered. He appeared beside her. "And what is this?" he asked gaily, examining the white crock. "Marmalade from England. Wherever did you find Dundee marmalade?"

"Naples is full of surprises."

"It reminds me of when I was living in London," he said, "many years ago. Foggy mornings in Hyde Park."

"You were writing a book about the English?"

"You might call it that."

"A good book?"

"Some people considered it so."

"Perhaps I shall read it some day."

"I am afraid not, my dear. I am afraid it has gone out of

print. I have left other examples of my work in Paris. I travel
with only one suitcase, my manuscript, my faithful typewriter.
But I would much prefer to have you read my new book when
it is finished—complete—and translated into your own language."

"Then I shall read it like that some day," Angelina said, spoon-
ing coffee into the percolator. There must have been good news
from the bank. Otherwise he would be less lighthearted. "And I
will say—oh, Gerald Newell! Certainly I knew him—when he
was living in Naples."

"Perhaps you will, my dear. And you will say it truthfully,
will you not? Yes, you will say that you knew Gerald Newell
in Naples. . . . May I ask you a personal question?"

"Of course. You may ask me anything."

"May I ask where you got that ring you're wearing?"

Angelina glanced sideways. "It came from my mother," she
said with a smile.

"From your mother? I hardly believe it. It seems more like
a gift from someone else."

"A lover?"

"Yes, if you wish."

"No, it was not from a lover. At least not exactly. But you're
right, it was not a gift from my mother. It came from a soldier
—whom I met once for a very short time during the war; but
he came back afterward to see me with this—and I had gone
away, and he gave it to my mother for safekeeping. She gave it
to me. I went to see her after the war was over."

"An Italian soldier?"

"No—an American."

"He must have been very fond of you."

"Who knows?" Angelina said. "It was very strange to get
a ring from him. . . . He did a very brave thing once. He saved
my grandfather's life."

"He did?"

"Yes. My grandfather was a very old man, and he is dead
now, but one day there was a great bombardment and my grandfather was frightened and tried to leave the house, you know—
and he fell down, and he was all alone in a field. He would
surely have been killed, but this American saw him and ran

toward him—oh, from quite a distance below the house—
and he saved his life."

"And you met him then, that day?"

"Yes, right after—and that evening we had a party for him in
my uncle's house, where it was safe. He was from headquarters.
He was on a tour of inspection when he saw my grandfather."

"A young man of courage," Gerald said a trifle impatiently.
"Too bad you had gone away when he returned."

"Yes, possibly—"

"May I see the ring?"

"Certainly." She took it off and held it across to him.

"It's really quite exquisite," he said dryly and then: "You
know this is the first thing I noticed about you. I said to myself
there is a young lady of culture."

"Now you're making fun of me."

"Ah no—quite to the contrary. Culture does not come from
books entirely, Angelina—from study and learning. Culture
is an inner awareness of things—of courage for instance, but
of beauty more especially. Culture and good taste are nearly the
same to me. One is merely the manifestation of the other. The
most learned person, if he has no taste, can be gauche in the
extreme."

"I wouldn't know about that," Angelina said. "I wear this
because sometimes I believe it brings me luck."

"Perhaps it has, Angelina."

"Perhaps—"

He dropped the ring into the palm of her hand, gently,
but as if he were discarding it. "The luck depends somewhat
on how much money I have—is that correct?"

"Yes, somewhat. I will admit."

"You would be very unwise not to admit it," he said, his thin
lips pulling back, his eyes studying her. "But you will not be
disappointed in respect to money. We will strike a fair bargain.
If you stay with me, during the times when I'm writing and
when I'm away, you will be completely free to do as you
wish. Completely. But when I am here you will come to me each
evening, at six o'clock promptly, and we will have a drink
in the little garden—and then we will go out to dinner. Some-

times to a hotel, or an expensive restaurant; sometimes to the local café, according to how I happen to feel. Do you have other clothes?"

"Yes—a few."

"Well, you will get them today and bring them here, and I will decide what else you need."

"You are most generous," she said tersely.

"No, please—you mustn't take offense. I'm merely talking of business. You have not made such an arrangement before?"

"My affairs are my own, thank you."

"Of course," he said. "I shouldn't have asked. I respect a desire for privacy—and possibly you are wondering why I should want to do this: to have you come here at such and such an hour every evening, to take you out here and there. I suppose it's an indication of conceit, but it is also because I am a collector—no, an admirer is a better word, and admirer of beautiful things. Surely you don't object to being called beautiful."

"No—"

"Well?" he asked. "Well, Angelina?"

"I will think it over," she said.

"For how long?"

"Until this evening."

"You have—that is, do you have any complaints about last night?"

"No, there are no complaints."

"Good," he said. "That much is settled, and it is fair enough—and we will think about breakfast now. Italian coffee, and English marmalade—and here, why here are croissants! I will call them croissants because they are made like the French. The continental breakfast, as it is termed, and an international one—and our first breakfast together."

"Yes," Angelina said with a sudden quick smile. "Our first together."

Yet she felt ill at ease, seated opposite him at the dining table. The wood seemed as smooth as satin. There was a medallion of inlay work in the center under the crystal pendants of a chandelier. A fruitwood chest stood in the corner, the sides curving into the shape of a lyre, the top surmounted by two painted china figurines, a man and a woman inclining toward each other in the simulated attire of ancient court dress and in the postures of a minuet. The curtains, edging the glass-paneled doorway leading to the patio, were of green brocade, and although partly faded and tarnished made the room seem lush and gave to it a faint odor of must.

He was watching her eat, she decided, visualizing her as his companion at such a hotel as the Excelsior. She imitated his manner, breaking the roll into discreet segments, half expecting that he would criticize her, that he would make some polite but derogatory comment. He was really a prig, she thought: a man of refinement, yes—but also of affectation. She disliked the idea of being scrutinized—she had not been as conscious of it last night—and of being told how to dress, when precisely to appear. Her relationships with other men had not been on this basis. A certain freedom had been attached to even the poorest of them, a certain gaiety, give and take; and there was an artist whose name was Luigi Bertoli who made no demands on her at all without her consent to them, but Luigi Bertoli was almost penniless, and among his friends matters of business were not involved.

This man was clever, though, Angelina knew; and if he were actually the writer he professed to be, she might excuse the rest— it would be nice to dine at the Excelsior with a personage of some distinction; or if he were an admitted and calculated fraud about his work, she might excuse that, too. For some reason she did not think he would deceive her about money. It would avail him nothing. She would simply leave. He had the eyes of a black marketer, she thought—a furtive, shrewd quality in the eyes; and yet at times they could plead with her and be unsure. She had known several who dealt in goods illegally procured, but none with the same oddly flattering turn of phrase.

He was rising from the table, dabbing his lips with a napkin. "It was delicious, my dear. My sincere compliments . . . And now you must excuse me. I must get to my desk. A writer must never sacrifice punctuality. You can leave everything where it is. I will perhaps have a snack later on. I never eat much lunch. One must watch one's figure—even a man." He brought out his wallet. "Here—this will take care of the breakfast, and this is a little extra. I am not in the habit of giving more than I promise, but in this case I would like to make a small exception."

Angelina took the two bills. "In that case," she said, "I accept."

"Until this evening then?"

"Yes, until this evening."

"At six o'clock—"

"Yes," she said tentatively, "at six."

He bent and kissed her hand and pressed it lightly, and then, looking rather thin and frail in the blue dressing gown, went into the bedroom and closed the door.

He put on a pair of slacks, a shirt and sweater and took the typewriter from its worn leather casing and lifted it to the desk. A peculiar instrument, the typewriter. It was like a piano, capable of great music, if you knew the right chords and harmonies. Otherwise there were discords, gibberish, failure.

He unlocked the drawer and drew out a sheaf of notes. They had been compiled nearly a year ago in a library in Paris. Jottings for a novel. An idea. Ancient history—Pompeii, the carnal city on the Mediterranean. It had been done before, but given the proper time and atmosphere, Gerald Newell would produce a masterpiece. And what would they say then in London, in Paris—and in Duluth, Minnesota? The prodigal could return to any of these, and the welcome mat would be unrolled—instead of being snapped out from under the feet. Curious how a constant lack of success kept you on the move. No, it wasn't curious at all.

He glanced at the notes. What did this date mean with the circle around it—and this sentence here? Small matter. He would visit the Naples library if he needed to verify details. "Oh yes, I read Italian. I am an expert in languages"—and in women, all types of women . . . She is unattached, he thought. Last night I believed the ring might mean an admirer here in the city, a lover she might have quarreled with; but the war is far in the past and the brave American soldier long since departed. She evaded my questions, but she spoke of him with almost no regret, with the knowledge of her kind that yesterdays have very little bearing on the present. She will be here tonight— she will come to *me!* I can forget the ring.

He put a blank sheet of paper into the typewriter.

"My dear brother," he wrote and looked with wry pleasure at the old-fashioned salutation. It was so much less prosaic than the "Dear Gerry" he received from the house in Duluth.

"Well—here is the bad penny turning up again, this time in Naples, a long way from Minnesota, but then I am sure you will not consider distance in this respect a disadvantage." That would make his brother William's wife, Vera, smile. How true, Vera would say—but he still has his gift of gab. Quite a detestable woman, Vera—even at the age of twenty-five, and now she would be fifty-two or three. "I am writing, however, not in a spirit of remonstrance, but to tell you that my semi-annual share of the family trust has been duly forwarded, and as always it is promptly acknowledged. I know that the sum may seem relatively small to you, but my life is more simple, and since the trust is all I can positively depend on at this time, I am grateful to you, as administrator, for facilitating with the bank at home my change of locale. I stopped at the Banco di Napoli the day before yesterday and told them where I could be reached. I am always pleased when the money arrives. As you will remember there have been occasional delays.

"I do not mean to imply that I am without expectation. Indeed I am embarking on a new work, and I have high hopes that my novel, 'The Burning Embers,' will be sold to my old friend, Carlo Biasetti, the famous publisher in Florence. I expect to see him early in May."

It was partially true, wasn't it? The manuscript of his novel was also locked in the desk: the novel written sporadically over five years but finished in 1938—the only book he had ever completed. American publishers had turned it down as had the British and French. He had translated several chapters into French, and he would translate a half dozen into Italian, and he would take these and the English text to Biasetti, to whom he had a letter of introduction. The letter came from a French countess whom he had met: "I wish to present to you Gerald Newell, an

American writer . . ." He need not tell Biasetti the date of the novel's completion. It applied to the court of Louis XVI and Marie Antoinette, the fading of the grand manner of life under the eternal stroke of the guillotine. The lie he had told Angelina was insignificant; she would not question it. The guillotine and the volcano were quite similar. He *did* have a manuscript to present.

He would greet Biasetti cordially and yet with aloofness. They would discuss art together. Biasetti would ask him to have lunch. He would stay in Florence for several days while the manuscript was being read; and he would have time to revisit the Uffizi Gallery, to wander through the high-ceilinged rooms and confront once more the Renaissance. How delightful to have lived through the intrigues of that era, when the artist was fully appreciated! He would have been a painter: not like Michelangelo —Michelangelo was too virile, the strength overwhelmed you— but like Del Sarto, with his magnificent colors and textures as soft and clear as a woman's skin. Del Sarto, the perfect painter; and now they daubed with their paints, they did not understand.

Would he take Angelina with him? Would she see herself mirrored by Del Sarto? He would have to explain things to her, and you explained these best to yourself. Such a trip might be too expensive. In addition to the apartment rental it would be difficult to afford the accommodations she would expect from him. Without her he could economize—and, of course, there was the chance she would leave him. Others had left him. Others had refused even his money . . .

He began to type rapidly. "I have at present most pleasant quarters in a villa. It belongs to the Contessa Marcioni. She has let me have the top floor for my studio. From where I sit I can see the whole sweep of the Bay of Naples, glimmering in the sunshine— and always the inspiration beckons. It is like the sailboat I can see out in the bay, a seemingly motionless speck of white, but eventually it will reach land . . ."

He went on typing for a while and then dipped a pen into the purple ink he had bought and signed his name with a flourish. The letter might make them jealous. It might make Vera briefly discontented with her large family, her limited life; but he would not think any more of her.

He pushed the heels of his hands into his eye sockets and rubbed the palms across his cheekbones and stood up and put another cigarette into the amber holder. He glanced at the bed. Here last night had been real beauty—the generous thighs and the large breasts that were heavy and yet firm, vibrant and alive. An ancient beauty, not so much of the present day with its trends toward slimness, the slim silhouette, or the exaggerated artificial contour. The French set styles for slimness, because the French were slim to begin with, but the beauty which had been here was not exceptional to Italy. The sun nourished the Italian, and the languid air, and the beauty ripened and then faded. Italian women grew quickly old. In another year Angelina would look differently. It did not matter, though, what happened in another year.

He crossed to the window and stood suddenly poised, his arm half raised. She was there in the patio. She had moved an iron chaise away from the shadow of the wall. She sat reclining, with her head tilted back and her eyes closed. He tiptoed through the bedroom and out past the dining table, and when he lowered the handle of the glass-paneled door, she turned.

"Angelina—" he said.

Her lips smiled. "You thought I had gone?"

"I assumed you had—"

"I wanted to enjoy your terrace for a little," she said, stretching her arms, her mind filled with the pleasing, far-off sound of the typewriter. "I can give you my answer, Gerald. I have decided I will stay here with you, for as long as you wish."

THE airliner had begun to descend and land was visible below the edge of the wing. That would be the beach at Anzio, Michael told Ruth—and then through the whir of the nearest propeller he was pointing at Rome. The plane seemed to catch in the air. The city spun round slowly and they could see separate buildings and streets and for an instant the dome of St. Peter's before they settled back in their seats and waited for the wheels to strike the runway.

He watched Ruth's hands clasped over the safety belt; but the jar was almost imperceptible. "We're down," Michael said. "You can open your eyes."

She smiled at him. "Don't make fun of me, dear." They were rising with the other passengers, moving toward the door.

A warm breeze blew across the runway. Inside the administration building there was a babble of voices and queues of people standing in line—a plane for Amsterdam being announced in Italian, another one for Cairo. Michael was identifying the luggage, unlocking it for the customs official, and next to him a woman with a cream-colored suitcase was leaning forward and speaking hurriedly in French.

A porter stood behind Michael. He had taken possession of the luggage. "This way, sir . . . This way . . ." They were following him to the bus that would take them into the city. The bus was crowded. It seemed like any other bus, except for the shrillness of the horn; but then they were passing the orange-gray ruins of an aqueduct, and a man on a motor scooter, and the small darting foreign-made cars and a cart drawn by white oxen; and there were villas on both sides of them flanked by cypress trees, and the sky had its special soft blue. Michael heard the sudden pealing of church bells in a large paved square, the

91

sound seeming to come from the city itself. He felt his heart quicken.

He was helping Ruth out of the bus. They were in a taxi climbing the Via Veneto, passing the sidewalk cafés: bright awnings hung over tiny round-topped tables, waiters in white jackets hurrying with trays of exotic-looking drinks in stemmed glasses. He did not recognize the street particularly; yet he had the impression if he walked up to that table, or that one, and explained how he had come back to Italy, a welcome would be offered with understanding, with affection, with humor.

The taxi turned off the Via Veneto and stopped in front of the hotel—not an extravagant one like the Grand or the Hassler, which the travel bureau had said were expensive, but not a cheap hotel. Later they would stay at more modest places; but the first few days, they had decided, would be as luxurious as the budget would allow.

They were shown to a room with high windows which opened above the street. Michael pushed the panes wider and stood listening to the stir of the city: the muffled noise of traffic on the Via Veneto, the clop-clop-clop of a horse's hoofs, pulling a carriage along the street below, the distant chiming of the bells. He went over to one of the twin beds on which Ruth lay outstretched.

"Tired, darling?"

"Exhausted," she answered. "Aren't you?"

"No, not especially. I guess I'm still sort of keyed up."

"It's nice to be tired—and to be able to give in to it," she said. "Just to be in a nice comfortable room after all those hours in the plane. I didn't sleep very well, you know."

"No. I didn't either."

"I wasn't exactly nervous—but I kept thinking, suppose we fell."

"Well, we didn't," he said with a smile.

"No, and I suppose it was all very safe—but this is such a nice room, Mike. I didn't expect it to be so big or quiet. I guess I expected a lot of confusion at first."

Michael laughed. "Oh, there'll be some of that before we're

through, darling. The Italians are old hands at promoting confusion."

"Yes, but it was so easy," she said. "They hardly looked at our baggage."

"Maybe we aren't the sinister type. They asked me if I had any cigarettes, and I said—oh, about a carton—and they let it go at that. One-carton-Allen, they said to themselves. There's an honest fellow for you."

Ruth smiled. "You are happy, aren't you, dear?"

"I am. I admit it."

"I was watching you there by the window. You looked so—so pleased."

"With myself?"

"No—just pleased, pleased with everything."

"I was," he said, "and I am—and we'll have a wonderful time here. I know it. I can feel it. It's hard to explain, but just driving in from the airport gave me the greatest sense of pleasure. I thought we might do a little exploring this afternoon, and this evening we'll sip a few apéritifs and we'll find a real fancy restaurant. I'll ask the man at the desk for the name of one when I go down to send the cable."

"Yes, of course, the cable," Ruth said. "I'd nearly forgotten. That's proof, isn't it—how relaxed I am?"

"I can't think of a better one."

"Really," she said. "I haven't thought of the children since last night. Then I thought wouldn't it be awful if we plunged down into the sea and left them. Did you, Mike? Did you have any such notions?"

"I don't believe so, darling. I guess I was thinking more about today."

He stood up from the bed. "I'll go down to the desk," he was saying, "and send the cable and have a few words with the man down there about restaurants, and maybe I'll stroll out and buy a newspaper or something. You just lie here and rest, and I'll be back in half an hour. How about that?"

"All right, Mike. I guess I do need half an hour—and then a bath, a nice hot tub."

"That's something I'd better investigate for you," he said. "The Italians are apt to be a little miserly in the hot tub department. Plumbing didn't used to be one of their chief accomplishments. Wait a second." He went into the bathroom. "*Acqua calda*," he said, "that's the one we want," and turned on the tap. "No, by God," he called, "I'm maligning them. The *acqua calda* is positively steaming out in a flood. Not like the old days at all. . . . Want me to leave it on?"

"No, I'll get it when I'm ready."

"Okay, we'll save it for you." He re-entered the bedroom and leaned and kissed her.

"Don't be gone too long, Mike."

"No," he answered grinning. "I'll be back for the *bagno*— the bath."

In the lobby he was referred to the concierge, a black-uniformed saturnine man sitting behind an upraised desk on a stool. Michael wrote out the cable: Arrived safely. Lots of love to you all.

"You can send this right away?"

"Of course, sir. Right away."

"Today," Michael said, smiling.

"Of course today," the concierge said without amusement, with the air of having been affronted.

"We were also thinking about restaurants," Michael said, eying him. "Do you have any you like to recommend?"

"For an American?"

"Not necessarily—"

"You are American, are you not, sir?"

"Yes, but not necessarily in the stomach when I'm in Rome."

"Ah, then it is different," the concierge said with less dryness. "You would like a restaurant—where the Italians go?"

"By all means. And perhaps for tonight, a place with a terrace and a view."

"Ah!" The concierge brightened. "I understand. I know of such a place. Not very far from here. The Villa Villardia, in the Borghese Gardens. You can walk, if you wish. Look—I will show you." He clambered down from the stool and went to the door. "See—like this. To the end of the street and then to your left—

to the top of the Via Veneto and then through an arch, like so, then straight ahead."

"*Sempre diritto.*"

"*Sì, sì!*" The concierge's face creased into a smile. "*Sempre diritto.*"

"We'll try it," Michael said. He pulled a dollar bill from his pocket. He had already changed a traveler's check for Italian currency at the airport; but the dollar bill, he thought, would not go amiss. "Here, this will help you send the cable today."

The concierge chuckled. "I do not understand before that you make a joke, signore. The cable will go at once."

Michael walked toward the Via Veneto. There was a huge circular newsstand on the corner; but since it was Sunday the stand was closed and the slanting green shelves were empty. He thought how pleasant it would be to cross over to a sidewalk café and sit at one of the round tables under its awning. The table he chose was half in shadow, half in the sun, and until the waiter appeared he sat listening to the conversation of his neighbors gusting past him in the breeze.

"*Uno vèrmut,*" he said to the waiter, because he wished to order something a little foreign, something he could sip slowly and savor.

"*Sì, signore.*"

Apparently the café was a focal point for Sunday gatherings. Michael watched the greetings being exchanged, the heads inclining, the lips forming into laughter. The men and women were elegantly dressed; they seemed eminently civilized, mature and graceful. He thought of Ruth in the hotel room, on the plane— her rage in the taxi leaving home, when he had tried to joke about the tickets, rage against an imagined blunder. For a second her face had shown hatred. He had never seen quite that expression before; but she had been all wound up, leaving the children—leaving the small area she so effectively controlled. It was wrong to single out one fleeting reaction, distorted out of focus. Here they were on the threshold of their adventure. He remembered her reaching out once during the night to hold his hand . . . Perhaps it had been best to come by air. A ship might have brought more of a sense of arrival—but not the same swift change . . .

He was reluctant to leave after he had finished the vermouth. He wanted to stay a bit longer, to listen, to observe; but he was recrossing the Via Veneto, noticing the broad archway at the top of it, and then the flower stall—all kinds of spring flowers on display, tulips and lilac branches and violets.

The violet stems were wrapped in cones of silver foil. He was selecting a bunch, was paying for it; and a young woman brushed by him. She was holding the arm of a young man. Her face was partly averted. For a moment he noticed only that she was tall and pretty—with dark hair.

"*I violetti*, signore," the woman at the flower stall reminded him.

"Oh yes," Michael answered. "Yes . . . Thank you—"

He heard the girl laugh and say something softly to her companion. She was a short distance from him, walking with the unhurried pace of the other strollers. How odd, Michael thought—how very odd . . . He was staring at her and remembering a child's voice: "I know where my sister is. She is in Rome!"

He was taking the bunch of violets from the flower woman. The girl had on a sleek black and white print dress. He could see her long legs move against the tight skirt. Then a group of people intervened and he was staring at a man with a Homburg hat and a pair of yellow kid gloves.

Michael imagined himself chasing after her, jostling through the crowds; but she must have stopped midway between him and the next intersection, which he could see plainly because he was on tiptoe and because it was a little below where he was standing. He followed after her, keeping away from the curb.

This was where she might easily be, on a Sunday, if she were in Rome. For a few seconds there seemed to be no enormous coincidence involved—except that this was the first day, the very first. Evidently on Sunday, however, well-to-do Romans paraded along the Via Veneto. The expensive clothes did not surprise him. She would have succeeded as someone's mistress, and the man with her might be any number of things: a friend, an actor—they made a great many movies in and around Rome, didn't they?—or even the cousin who had been to the United States. His mind raced to a dozen conclusions. In Cairo they said if you sat on the porch of Shepheard's Hotel, while it still existed, you would meet eventually everyone you knew from all over the world. Shepheard's Hotel and the Via Veneto had something in common—

He saw her ahead of him in front of a shop window, her face in profile, a round gold medallion hanging from the lobe of her ear. He halted. He was about to speak when she glanced at him directly. The eyes held no trace of recognition. They were nearly as large as Angelina's, but they were not hers. Yet they had the same look of disdain which he had seen once or twice; and for a moment he could not realize the mistake he had made.

She had returned her attention to the window. She was pointing, was talking to her escort. Of course it wasn't Angelina. The resemblance had faded completely. He remembered her more clearly than he had for years. Even assuming that she had changed, she could not be this person. This was a total stranger.

Michael walked beyond the two of them, feeling absurd. How could he have been so mistaken? He had not been thinking of Angelina. She had been only vaguely connected with his thoughts last night on the plane. Angelina and Ruth meeting each other—but it would not happen, there was no real chance that it would, and if it did there was nothing to hide, or be ashamed of—not really. He was not going to Italy to see Angelina; that was ridiculous. Yet now she seemed close to him. She was this girl approaching, or one in the distance. He had the odd sensation that if he looked a little more sharply into the crowds she would appear.

He had reached a point where the Via Veneto curved downward toward the wider area of a square before he realized how foolishly he was behaving. Then he stopped and saw the violets in his hand and turned and began retracing his steps. The girl in the print dress had disappeared. He went by the flower stall. The woman behind it had a scraggly growth of hair above her upper lip, he noticed. She smiled at him and nodded and he went into the Via Ludovisi where the hotel was. The street was relatively free from the crowds and he walked through the shade of trees planted at intervals along the pavement. Perhaps the gift had reminded him of Angelina; but no, that was very farfetched.

He entered the hotel lobby. The concierge grinned at him, but Michael did not pause. He was in the elevator, its slow climbing faintly reminiscent of Dilks and Stanley. He was conscious of the elevator boy looking at the bunch of violets.

He rapped on the bedroom door, but there was no response and he opened it hastily and went inside.

The blinds were drawn. The semidarkness startled him, but then he saw that Ruth was still on the bed and that a blanket half-covered the slip she was wearing. She was sound asleep. It touched him to see her sleeping so peacefully, her head sideways against the pillow. He stood for a moment looking at her and then put his hand gently against her cheek. Her eyes opened.

"Goodness!" she said. "You frightened me."

"Did I?"

"I was dreaming . . . I thought you were out . . . How long was I asleep?"

"Not long, darling. Here, I brought you these."

She sat up. "Oh—they're lovely, Mike." She pressed the violets against her nostrils. "Wherever did you find them?"

"Just around the corner from the hotel."

"They're so fragrant—"

"Maybe they should have been roses," he said.

"Why—why roses?"

"Don't you remember we were talking about roses when we first started to plan the trip?"

"Were we? Yes, that's right we were. I'd forgotten . . . I had the strangest dream, Mike. I dreamed we were on the plane, going home I think, and one of the engines had smoke coming out of it, like cigarette smoke—and I was crawling out on the wing to see what the trouble was. . . . It was rather terrifying," she said lightly, gazing down at the violets, fluffing the blooms apart.

He had seated himself beside her. Her lips smiled toward him suddenly. He had leaned forward—had taken her into his arms.

LATE that afternoon they were in Babington's tea shop at the foot of the Spanish Steps. They found it quite by accident and were intrigued by the black-beamed ceiling and by the half-British, half-Italian accents of the waitresses, and by a man in a close-fitting pinstripe suit and with a pallid ascetic face who said to his companion at an adjoining table, "Actually, old boy, this is the only place in Rome where one can get a decent cup of China." They were drinking the China tea and eating British muffins near the stately grandfather clock; and when they went out into the piazza a fountain was splashing water into its oval basin, and children were balancing themselves on the stone coping and the great sweep of the steps was pink and mauve and the double towers of the church at the top, where the sun hit, were a light hazy yellow.

They wandered along the Via Condotti, the narrow street where the expensive shops were. Many were shuttered closed for the holiday, but here and there from the sidewalk they could admire gold-embossed leather, the sparse elegant displays of jewelry against black velvet, and in a window Michael saw a dress that would be perfect for Priscilla, but Ruth said it was probably too costly; there would be plenty of time for choosing the dress.

Afterward they walked over to the Tiber and stood beneath the chestnut trees and watched the river pursuing its ancient course under the white bridges. It was a lazy hour of day, and Michael forgot the few minutes of searching along the Via Veneto. They seemed no longer related to him.

In a taxi he and Ruth climbed to the Borghese Gardens. They were watching a Punch and Judy show set up in front of a tent, and small rowboats circulating in a pond with an old columned temple on an island in its center. They were in a glade surrounded by tall trees and lined with ferns and flowers, and by the time they had gone back to the hotel and changed for dinner, it was growing dark.

They drove to the Villa Villardia in a horse-drawn cab and mounted an outside stairway to the terrace. They were escorted to a table next to the balustrade and lit by candles in hurricane holders.

"You would like cocktails, sir?"

"Yes—martinis, I think. That suit you, darling?"

"That would be fine."

"Two martinis then," Michael said.

"Two martinis American-style—okay?"

"Is there a difference?"

"Oh yes, sir—you must know: the American martini is mostly with gin, the Italian with vermouth." The waiter was handsomely slender with a white starched collar and bow tie. He spoke with a slight air of condescension.

"All right, the American type then," Michael said and watched the waiter move to another table whose occupants were apparently known to him, where he bowed and leaned attentively to remove the woman's wrap.

Ruth had turned toward the balustrade. "Your friend at the desk was certainly right about the view, darling."

"Yes—wasn't he?"

"There's St. Peter's with the lights on it. It looks as if it were floating, doesn't it? Like a cloud. And the other lights—what are they like?"

"Like fireflies maybe."

"Yes, like fireflies strung out as far as you can see." She faced him. "Oh, I do like this place, Mike. I love Rome at night. It's like fairyland."

He smiled. "Glad I argued you into coming?"

"Yes. Only it wasn't an argument."

"No more arguments for the Allens."

"I don't think we argue very much, do you, Mike?"

"Not all the time at any rate—"

"No, honestly. I think we get along pretty well, you and I."

"For an old married couple, you mean?"

"For an old married couple. For anyone married—don't you agree? At least we're not like those people over there. No, don't look around. They're behind you. I think they were on the plane —perhaps not. But they're about our age and they're just sitting and not saying a single word to each other."

"Maybe they've been to Rome before," Michael suggested.

"Maybe—but even so, they shouldn't be bored. I don't think I'd ever be bored with Rome. Just from the little I've seen of it, I think I can tell. It has a feeling of life, doesn't it?—as if it had lived for a long time but still stayed young somehow. Can you compare it with your village, are they alike at all?"

"Well, in certain ways they are. There's a great feeling of life there too. Maybe a more fundamental kind of life. No Villa Villardia, though. No nice hotel—"

"Oh, I won't care about that, darling. I want to see your village very much, and the hill you ran up to that old man. I never quite understood why you did it, when you didn't have to—"

"Sort of a foolhardy thing," Michael said.

"I wonder if he'll still be alive," Ruth said. "It would be quite a meeting, wouldn't it? Quite fantastic. I'd love to see his face when he recognized you."

"Or if," Michael said smiling.

"But I think so. Certainly. You don't look very different than you did ten years ago."

"A little balder, wouldn't you say—around the edges?"

Ruth laughed. "Maybe a shade, if you insist. But it's a strange thing, Mike. You look younger to me tonight—than you have, I mean. You looked younger when you got off the plane, there at the airport."

"And this afternoon," he said. "How did I look then?"

She flushed slightly and drew her finger a few inches across the tablecloth. "A lot younger," she said quietly. She raised her eyes. "Did I?"

"Like a bride," he answered.

She smiled, the candlelight glowing against her face. "No, not like that. That isn't true—but it's funny, you know. I did feel a little as if we'd just been married."

The waiter arrived with the martinis; then he was standing at

Michael's elbow and presenting the menu written in Italian. "I would suggest the *cannelloni* to start with, sir. It is a specialty."

"I've never heard of it," Ruth said. "How is it made?"

"With small rolls of pasta, Ma-dam. Very delicate, with meat inside ground very thin and with a sauce."

"It sounds delicious, doesn't it?"

"Oh, very nice, Ma-dam. See I will show you where it is. Here. *Cannelloni*. See, by my finger. That is it . . . And afterward some fish. You see, here is the fish on this line. Ma-dam does not read Italian—no?"

"No. My husband does, though. My husband has been here before."

"To the Villa Villardia?"

"No—to Italy."

"Ah so. Then perhaps I do not need to translate."

"We'll try the *cannelloni*," Michael said, "and the fish—and some asparagus—"

"Ah yes, the asparagus. *Asparagi*. It is almost the same, is it not? Asparagus—*asparagi*. Very little difference between the two. You were here some time ago, sir?"

"During the war," Michael said.

"Ah yes, during the war. Many Americans were here during the war . . . And after the fish, you would like a steak, sir?"

"No, I don't think so. I think the fish will be enough," Michael answered, staring at the long list of only partly familiar words. "But we'd like a salad. And for dessert some strawberries."

"The *fragole*."

"Yes, that's right—*fragole*. And also some wine."

"What kind of wine, sir?"

"A white wine. A—"

"I would recommend a bottle of Iesi," the waiter said. "You know the Iesi wine, sir?"

"I don't believe so. I remember wine from Orvieto—"

"The Iesi is better," the waiter said. "More light. Very nice." He smiled across at Ruth.

"All right," Michael said. "And you can bring us another cocktail before we begin."

"As you wish, sir. Two martinis."

When he had gone Ruth said with a touch of facetiousness. "He didn't seem too much impressed with your mention of the war."

"No, a little contemptuous—"

"Contemptuous, darling?" she asked in surprise.

"Yes, somewhat . . . Wanting to impress the American tourist. That attitude."

"Oh, I don't think so, Mike. He was just trying to be helpful. You should try some of your Italian on him, make him see you've been around—"

"No, not on him, Ruth."

"Why not, darling?"

"It isn't good enough for that. There'll be others I can speak in Italian to, but not this fellow."

"You mean you'd feel self-conscious? Why, that's silly. He can't be more than twenty-four, or five at the most. He just wants to seem older. He wasn't making fun of you."

"Maybe not . . . Still—" Michael paused. "Oh well, I guess it's nothing to get too stirred up about . . . And he did bring us a good martini. We'll have to hand him that."

"And the—what did he suggest, the cana, canal—"

"*Cannelloni*," Michael said.

"That's it. Have you ever eaten it before?"

"No. Never in my life."

Ruth laughed. "What would you have ordered yourself, darling?"

"I'll admit I didn't recognize many old favorites," Michael said, and thought suddenly of the meal prepared by the women in the village. "We used to have various forms of pasta, but I never learned the names for all the different kinds. We didn't eat with the Italians very often. The civilian restaurants were off limits for the most part, but there was a sort of a dive I'd go into occasionally near my office, and have a big bowl of spaghetti or macaroni in exchange for cigarettes or candy, or flour I'd scrounge from the kitchen. It seemed a great treat from the Army bill of fare, but it didn't have any elegant title—and the wine was red and bitter except for one bottle of Orvieto the *padrone* had in his cellar, or rather the one he brought up for me . . . It was my birthday, I remember. The Italians are great for birthdays, anything that promotes a festival. It was a pretty bleak room, but I was there that night with about five or six other men from the post and we had a fine time celebrating. I remember we even had two kinds of wine. I must have written you about it, didn't I?"

"I don't just recall—"

"Well anyway, that's about the extent of my knowledge of Italian food. I think our young friend would have dropped dead if I'd asked him simply for spaghetti. I'll have to bone up on the menus, so we can order in style."

The waiter, however, was only a minor intrusion. The food was excellent, the wine in its bulbous-shaped green bottle beaded with cold, and the strawberries served in white wine and sugar. The restaurant had no connection with the past and as they walked back to the hotel through the gardens, Michael was aware of this. They walked slowly, close to each other, not needing to talk very much; and he knew that Ruth was happy, quietly so but without reservations. He remembered her earlier in the afternoon, her feet bare, her slip a trifle rumpled, her hair cut short now after the fashion of the times instead of more luxuriant and shoulder-length as it had been when he had married her; but her eyes had been wide and surprised and full of sudden desire. Not like a bride, not quite like that, but for a moment bride and wife had joined together in his mind.

A night breeze stirred through the trees and across the grass, and the Via Veneto when they reached it was alive with lights; but he did not feel compelled to explore it or to accept its invitation. The city could wait for them until morning.

They spent a leisurely day sightseeing. They stood like miniatures in the great dusty arena of the Colosseum, tiers of ruined arches rising to surround them, while a guide explained that it was through this dark tunnel that the lions had come, and through this one that the Christian martyrs had advanced into the scrutiny of a pagan emperor in a marble chair. Later they were in the vast stone coolness of St. Peter's, and walking among the columns outside, past the fixed rigid dignity of a papal Swiss guard.

They had lunch at the hotel to conform with the half-pension plan they had established with the management, the continental breakfast of coffee and rolls and one other meal being included with the price of the room. They had tea and cakes at a sidewalk table outside Donney's on the Via Veneto and afterward they wrote post cards for the children. They chose Ernesto's for the evening, because the concierge had described it to Michael as typically Italian, more so than the Villa Villardia. They would find few Americans at Ernesto's. Alfredo's, which also specialized in Italian cooking, was more popular with the visitors perhaps, the concierge said, but it was a little more expensive.

Ernesto's was furnished with wooden chairs and tables. Next to their own a celebration was in progress, and the room was noisy and full of smoke. Evidently the celebrants had just arrived, the men sitting on one side of a long table, the women across from them.

Michael was ordering—rice with mushrooms, the local wine; and for a few minutes, listening to the voices next to him, he was nearly oblivious of Ruth. He watched the hands gesticulating. There was a sudden burst of laughter, everyone speaking at once. Michael found himself trying to decipher the words. He felt suddenly at home, as if the city had become personal again, as if the tourist who had stood in the Colosseum and walked with awe through St. Peter's had been almost like a stranger. The wine was brought, red wine in a carafe. He had filled Ruth's glass.

"Maybe it's a wedding party," he was saying. "Maybe they've just seen the bride and groom off and these are the in-laws making a night of it, having their one big spree of the year."

Ruth smiled. "I wish they'd be a little more quiet. It's really deafening in here, isn't it?"

"But it's nice. They've probably saved up for this. I like to see them enjoying themselves. The Italians know a lot about that. Look at that fellow there with a napkin tied round his neck, like a great gourmet. A natural comedian, don't you think? If I were an artist I'd like to paint him right here in this setting. The small moustache, the heavy jowls, the big soft eyes. If I were a good artist I'd make him seem a little grotesque, but not conscious of that. Not in the least embarrassed. I think he must be a kind man and he has about a dozen grandchildren, and I can see him at home with the *bambini* climbing all over him."

"I can hardly hear you, Mike. What about the grandchildren?"

"Climbing over his knee—pulling his moustache. He'd be brushing them aside like a big kindly bear."

"I imagine so," Ruth said. He was aware of her annoyance, as if it had abruptly intruded between them. He noticed she had not touched her wine. He was refilling his own glass. The voices next to him seemed less loud. He looked at Ruth and she smiled at him again, but it wasn't a full smile. It was slightly reticent and for a second, he thought, slightly supercilious.

"You don't like it here, do you?" he asked.

"Why do you say that?"

"It's true, isn't it?"

"Well, I don't like it quite as much as the place we were last night, if that's what you mean."

"You want to leave—find another restaurant?"

"Of course not. Of course I don't want to leave. We've given our order, haven't we?"

"Yes, but that doesn't matter. We can countermand it, say we've decided to go some place else—"

"Don't be silly," she said. "That wouldn't make any sense. I like it here. It just doesn't appeal to me as much as the villa what's-its-name, the Villa Villardia. Do you think it should?"

There was another burst of laughter behind him. "No—no, maybe not—"

"It is a contrast, though—a complete contrast."

"You don't think it has more life?" he asked.

"What?"

"More life, more real gaiety."

"Of a different kind, darling. But wouldn't you find the same thing at home where—where a bunch of middle class people, let's say, were out on a spree?"

"Aren't we middle class people, Ruth?"

"Well, yes, I suppose we are—but not exactly. I think our tastes are a little more sophisticated than that. Don't you? I mean, what's so hilarious about a man with a napkin tied around his neck? Isn't he just making a fool of himself?"

"No, I don't agree. A fool is someone who steps out of character and behaves absurdly, but this man isn't like that. Not like someone who needs a prop or a trick costume or a funny hat. He's just being himself, having a good time—"

"I think you're sentimentalizing him," Ruth said. "Now don't look angry. Please don't look angry. I'm not criticizing you—but I noticed something about you, last night with that waiter. You thought he was being fresh, or disparaging—"

"Yes, I did. I know he was."

"But he wasn't. It was only because he didn't quite fit into some picture you had, some picture you've evolved, it seems to me. You like the Italians, and that's fine. So do I. I want to because I know you expect me to—and I love Rome, I told you that. But you mustn't expect *all* Italians to be friends and interesting wonderful people. That's what I'm trying to say."

"I don't expect them all to be friends, Ruth."

"Yes, I think you do. I think that's just it, and you'll be disappointed—"

"Disappointed?" he asked.

"You'll be put off. Little things will put you off. We're foreigners to these people, Mike. I'm a foreigner, you're a foreigner. If you think they'll accept you as one of them—no, let me finish, I've been thinking about this—you'll make a mistake and you'll be disappointed."

"I did belong to them once," Michael said, "but it isn't that I want to be accepted." He paused. "That's not entirely true . . . but I have an affinity for these people, Ruth, a sense of affinity—for the smoke, the wine, the laughter, even the smells—"

"They remind you of the past, darling."

"Sure, that's right."

"But this isn't the past. This is today. You're not in the Army any more. You didn't just save someone's life—"

"I wish you wouldn't say I saved someone's life," Michael said. "It wasn't nearly that definite. There were just the two of us in a sort of confusion and turmoil, and we managed to get out together. It was like putting your hand in fire and pulling it out and seeing that it wasn't burned. I don't know, I suppose when that happens to you, you feel fantastically lucky, as if you'd been born under some amazing star. You feel in control of

everything. For a few minutes you feel supreme, up in the clouds
—and everyone around you then is a friend. But of course it
doesn't last very long. You're back on the ground pretty quickly."

Ruth was only partly listening, it seemed. A violinist had come
in from the street. Ruth watched him as he went by their table
and stood beside the others. Evidently he was known to them.
He was grinning, beginning a melody, plucking at the strings.

The waiter came with the rice and mushrooms. Michael re-
filled his wine glass and held up the empty carafe.

"*Un' altro, per piacere.*"

"*Sì,* signore. *Subito.*"

"*Una celebrazione?*" Michael asked, nodding toward the group
nearby.

"*Sì,* signore. *Una grande celebrazione.*"

"A—a wedding?" Michael asked. "How do you say wedding
in Italian? *Uno matrimonio?*"

The waiter smiled. "Ah no, signore. It is not a wedding, a
*nozze.* It is—anniversary, a wedding anniversary, for the woman
there and the man—the large man."

"The one with the napkin?"

"*Sì,* signore—the one with the napkin." He looked at Ruth.
"The signora would prefer another wine, another kind?"

"No, this is very nice. I don't drink much wine."

"As you wish, signora—but now for the rest of the meal. You
would like some veal perhaps, and some little peas—*piselli?*"

"*Sì, il vitello con piselli,*" Michael answered. "*Il vitello è buono
stasera?*"

"*Stasera,* signore, *il vitello è magnifico.* You speak well, signore.
*Parla molto bene.*"

"*Come un' americano?*"

"*No, come un' italiano. Veramente!* The accent is good, very
good."

"*Spero che il vitello è migliore,*" Michael said and the waiter
laughed. "They are the same, exactly the same," he said in Italian;
and Ruth said, "Why, that's wonderful, darling. That's an actual
conversation."

But the restaurant was more crowded now than before, and the
noise was greater; and he was groping through the noise, Michael
felt, groping toward Ruth. The expression of annoyance had par-

tially disappeared; but it was masked, he felt, it was underneath. He caught the slight flinching around her eyes and lips whenever the noise reached a crescendo—and from a long time ago he could hear a girl's voice saying, "Silence! The captain wishes to speak!" For a moment he imagined the room without Ruth, himself here alone at the table, calling to someone else to join him. But it was a distorted image and not right, and it meant too many things for him to wish to pursue it. It seemed to mean that the trip might fail. What a ridiculous way for it to fail in a room full of noise and laughter.

Possibly, like the imagined encounter yesterday on the Via Veneto, this was an illusion. There were bound to be small differences of opinion between himself and Ruth. Maybe they weren't important. . . .

"Darling, you're not drinking too much of that, are you?" she asked lightly.

"No, I don't think so, Ruth."

"I mean think how you'll feel tomorrow."

"Don't worry about it. I used to drink a lot of this. You know what it reminds me of?"

"No," she said.

"It reminds me of rain," Michael said. "Heavy rain falling on the tin roof of a Nissen hut, with the mud outside. An Italian winter, guys playing cards on an Army blanket, and the warmth, the bleak warmth of that hole-in-the-wall place I told you about —did I tell you?—where we used to go. Yes, that's right, I did tell you last night when we were sitting up on that terrace in the moonlight . . . Pasquale, that was his name—the owner of the place. He had a little scratchy phonograph and some records. We used to play them and sing to them—and he had a cat, I remember, a black cat with one white paw, that was very fond of red wine. It used to lap up whatever was spilled . . . But I guess those aren't—particularly—thoughts for a holiday, are they? We'll switch to something else. We'll have some brandy and coffee—then we'll put the show on the road."

He saw her eyes flinch again, almost imperceptibly.

"Couldn't we have the coffee and brandy out in the air somewhere, Mike—at one of the sidewalk cafés?"

"Okay," he said. "Sure. We'll do that." He raised his hand.

*"Cameriere!"* The waiter hurried toward them.

*"Cameriere,"* Michael said to Ruth. "That's a pretty tough word, don't you think?" He smiled self-consciously. Damn it, he thought, I'm drunk, Ruth thinks I am; only I'm not really. I'm just a little disappointed—that's it, a little disappointed.

"Signore—*desidera?*"

"*L'addizione*," Michael said.

*"Come?"*

"The bill. The tab."

"Ah, the bill! *Il conto*, signore."

*"Sì—il conto* then."

"You do not wish something else—some fruit, some cheese, coffee?"

*"Non stasera. Grazie. Tanto grazie."*

"The meal was all right. You enjoy?"

"The meal was excellent," Michael said. *"Eccellente. Ritorniamo un' altra sera."*

He was standing, pulling the lire notes from his wallet. He noticed that the diners next to him were watching, the huge plate of cheeses, the basket of fruit on the table. The violinist was in the midst of a tune. Michael tapped his shoulder.

*"Uno momento,"* he said.

The man turned, his bow upraised. His face was narrow and dark with a stubble of beard.

*"Uno momento,"* Michael repeated and looked across at the man who still wore the napkin over his collar. There seemed to be an abrupt silence, although Michael could hear other voices in the background. *"Buona sera,"* he announced slowly. *"Capisco che è—il suo anniversario."*

No one spoke. Then the man with the napkin nodded politely. *"Sì, signore, è vero."* His eyes were inquisitive, his lips no longer smiling.

*"È desidero che,"* Michael began and realized that the words, unused for years, were escaping him. He would need much more practice. "And I would like to buy you a drink," he said.

*"Come, signore?"* the man questioned.

The waiter stepped forward. "Please," Michael said. "Please would you explain that I'd like to buy some drinks—for the celebration."

There was a pause while the waiter translated and listened to the reply. He turned to Michael. "They say thank you very much, sir—but they have enough to drink."

Michael felt himself balancing as if on tiptoe. "Please," he said, "I want them to understand. It would give me great pleasure."

The waiter was translating again. Ruth said in a whisper, "Darling, for Heaven's sake! Don't make a scene."

"I'm not making a scene, damn it, Ruth."

"Can't you see you're disturbing them?" she asked. Her eyes were wide and frightened.

The waiter was saying, "They say thank you, they are very grateful. But they do not wish any more to drink."

I'm not that drunk, am I, Michael thought? Do I seem like some obnoxious person who staggers up to a strange table in a bar?

"A cognac," he said. "Surely a cognac, or a strega—" He stopped, feeling Ruth's fingers against his sleeve. "Oh, all right," he said. "Okay, never mind."

The man with the napkin arose and held out his hand. Michael reached across and took it. The palm was slightly moist. The hand was withdrawn; the man sat down again.

"*Auguri*," Michael said. "*Buona fortuna!*" Then he was straightening, gripping the rung of a chair.

He turned. It must have been funny, because they were laughing. He could hear the laughter, and the waiter said near the doorway, "Your money, sir. You forget your change."

Michael looked at him. "You keep it," he said. "You buy yourself some cognac—will you?"

He walked into the street with Ruth. He had the impression that the room behind him was perfectly quiet, that the violin music had not recommenced.

"I'm sorry," he said, but she did not answer him. They were walking to a taxi stand. Michael was fumbling with the latch on the cab's side.

"Albergo Eden," he said thickly to the driver.

"*Come*, signore?"

"Damn it to hell," Michael said, his voice rising. "Can't you people speak your own language? I was here, do you understand?—during the war. *Durante la guerra!* Now listen to me. I want to go to the Albergo Eden. The Eden Hotel!"

THE room was still in semidarkness when Michael recovered consciousness. Something very bad had happened, he knew, but at first he could not identify it. They had been in a taxicab. He remembered the headlights probing rapidly through narrow streets, as if the streets had somehow become subterranean. At one time they had passed the white cascade of a fountain.

He remembered Ruth crying out, "We're lost, he's taking us in the wrong direction. Make him stop! Make him stop here! . . ." and they had been suddenly on the Via Veneto, walking together. He remembered that, being perfectly able to walk. He had insisted on pausing at a café for a glass of brandy. He remembered that the café had been crowded, that perhaps he had tried to joke with Ruth about her alarm in the taxi; but he could not recall entering the hotel—or yes, there was a dim recollection of the elevator, slowly climbing.

He braced his elbow against the mattress and raised his head. A fine thing to do—an absurd thing! Then he saw Ruth in the faint light from the open window. She wasn't awake. She had been furious. Well, he couldn't blame her.

He lay back. He realized he still had on his shirt and trousers. After a moment he stood up and rummaged quietly for a pair of pajamas and put them on. They made him feel more respectable. He was hanging the trousers and shirt carefully over the back of a chair, when he thought with quick misgiving: the wallet, where was the wallet, with almost all the money inside, the passport, the traveler's checks? The wallet had been in his trouser pocket, hadn't it? It wasn't there now. Perhaps it was in the coat to his suit. He looked frantically for the coat. Ruth must have put it away. He remembered the waiter offering him the change, but no—he hadn't used the wallet then, hadn't brought it out again. He must have paid for the taxi, however, after an argument—and for the brandy. He opened the closet door. There was the dress Ruth had worn—and his coat. He pushed his hands through the pockets. He slid the coat off its hanger and brought it toward the window. It was true: the wallet was missing. He began searching desperately. He looked across his bed, across the floor below it, across the bureau and the desk. There must be another explanation, a simple one. It would occur to him. If he turned on the light he would find the wallet, he thought; but what if the light revealed nothing, and Ruth awoke?

His head throbbed and he was cold now and was trembling. He switched on the bureau lamp and looked across the carpet and the closet floor . . .

"Ruth," he called softly. "Ruth."

"Yes?" she answered, moving. "What is it? . . . What on earth?—"

"It's the wallet," he said. "My wallet. I can't find it. I'm afraid it's gone."

"It's in the top bureau drawer," she said dryly, "in with my things. I put it there. It was hanging out of your coat."

He stared at her. "Oh—was it? . . . Yes, I see—"

"Why on earth would you be looking for your wallet at this hour? What time is it anyway?—only a little after five."

"I'm sorry," he said. "I was afraid I'd lost it, afraid it was gone. I couldn't remember—"

"Coming back here?"

"I couldn't exactly remember."

"I'm not surprised," Ruth said. "Last night was a perfect nightmare."

He crossed the room and stood beside her. "I'm awfully sorry, Ruth. Honestly I am. I—it was all a mistake."

"Do you remember how many brandies you had in that bar?"

"A couple I guess—wasn't it?"

"You had four. You ordered us each one, and I didn't want mine, so you drank them both, and then you ordered two more— and you were talking so wildly—"

"What was I saying?"

"Oh, you were talking about the taxi driver cheating you—how could he cheat a friend?—and about Italians who couldn't speak Italian, and you kept asking the waiter if it was his birthday, everyone should have birthdays. I'm not usually frightened of you when you've had too much to drink, there haven't been too many times, but I was terrified last night. You seemed so confused—and you were angry, you were angry at me for leaving that frightful restaurant. You said I didn't understand, no one understood."

"Were people looking at us—noticing us?"

"No, not especially. You weren't especially noisy. You just kept rambling on in a sort of aimless monotone. You said that the trip had failed and that I couldn't possibly understand why it had. I don't suppose you remember that—or do you?"

"Not much of it—"

"I didn't know what to do," she said. "I didn't know how to get you back here, but it wasn't far—thank God!—and you could still walk. You didn't fall down until you got into this room."

"Where did I fall, Ruth?"

"Oh, halfway on the bed, halfway on the floor; and then you pulled yourself up on the bed and I took off your coat and your shoes and your necktie. I didn't bother with anything else. You told me to leave you alone. I think that was your final statement of the evening."

A silence followed. "It won't happen again, Ruth," Michael said.

"I sincerely hope not . . . You know what I thought of doing? I even thought of writing you a note and packing my bag and going out to the airport, trying to catch a plane. But I was too tired."

"You still feel that way?"

"No, not as much. I don't suppose I would have left anyway. Only I hated what you said about my ruining the trip. Why did you say that? Does it make a particle of sense to you?'

"No," he answered, "it doesn't. It was my fault. The evening was my fault."

There was another silence. "Well, we'd better get some sleep,' she said.

"Yes. I guess that's right—"

"I see you managed to find your pajamas."

"Yes, I found them."

She turned over on her side. "Get the light, will you, Mike? It's against my eyes."

"Okay," he said. "I'll get the light."

He switched it off and in the bathroom groped for a glass of water. His cheeks and forehead felt burning, but his hands were still cold and he remembered abruptly the Italian with the napkin around his neck, the face as if leaping toward him . . .

He lay down again. His mind was somewhat clearer. The wallet was safe. No irrevocable harm had been done, had it? Even if the wallet had been lost, there would have been no complete disaster. He had copied the number from the traveler's checks on two slips of paper, hadn't he? Ruth had one of them. The other was in the suitcase pocket. Most of the money could have been redeemed, and the passport replaced, although there would have been delay and great inconvenience . . . He would be very careful in the future. Strange that Ruth should have mentioned going home. Yet it was probably true; in her anger she had considered leaving.

He tried to imagine himself waking up in the room without Ruth, hurrying to the airport in an attempt to overtake her, but the image eluded him. It was far too melodramatic. A husband and wife, married for seventeen years, didn't just rush away from each other. Not in a foreign country—not at home . . .

He began to think of the village then, at first distantly and uncertainly, but with a gradually increasing feeling of re-assurance. Tonight hadn't happened there. In three or four days Ruth would forget tonight. It would no longer annoy her. She would forgive him. In another week they would be in Florence, and tonight would be still more remote; and when they came south again he would be prepared. They would pass through the village quite calmly. . . .

The room seemed brighter. Perhaps he had been asleep or

dozing. He could hear someone walking along the pavement outside and had a sudden desire to see who it might be, walking alone through the streets of Rome at dawn. The desire intrigued him and he gave in to it and went over to the window; but whoever it was had disappeared. The footsteps were receding, no great urgency in them, but as if someone at this unusual hour, were merely out for a brisk stroll. Michael was vaguely amused at himself, standing there in his pajamas with his hangover. Then he opened the bureau drawer a few inches and closed it and looked at Ruth. She had not changed her position. She was frowning a little in her sleep, her lips tight shut.

GERALD Newell strolled along the Arno River in the direction of the Uffizi Gallery. It was a hot day for Florence, approaching the middle of May; the small cluttered office of Carlo Biasetti, the publisher, would be quite airless at this late morning hour, but here along the river there was the suggestion of a breeze crossing the slow-moving water, rising from the valley where the ancient stone city rested, to the sunlit green of the Boboli Gardens, to the cypress-covered hills beyond. It was strange to think of death on such a day, in such a place; yet apprehension plucked as if at Gerald's sleeve, as he walked carefully and alone among the crowds.

The tourists were increasing in number, he observed—the vacationers, the sightseers, the gawkers: a man in a gaudy American sport shirt and ill-fitting slacks, focusing an expensive camera on the ponderous arches of the Ponte Vecchio. For a moment the juxtaposition of the two was amusing. How incredibly naive the sightseers were! On another day, Gerald thought, it would have pleased him enormously to mingle with them, to laugh privately at their unwariness. He had made his own study of them on this and other thoroughfares. Those two women, for instance, in flowered dresses, who were a little lost and frightened and apart, were like the two he had accosted yesterday. They had been schoolteachers on sabbatical leave, with the savings of a lifetime stored in their fat black purses. They had been infinitely easy to approach: he had followed them into a store, waited until the question of price arose and then discreetly intruded . . .

Of course it was rude to interfere, but the price overheard was far too high. The shopkeeper must have made, inadvertently, a mistake. Wasn't it so? He had argued and bantered with the shopkeeper until the price was lowered, until the ladies in question were surprised and gratified. He had tipped his hat. One must understand about the Italian philosophy of price, he had confided to them. The price varied with the supposed potential of the purchaser. It wasn't cheating; it was like a game. To know the rules required experience. If the ladies could use any assistance from a fellow American who had lived abroad for a while . . . Oh, it was no trouble. He was merely putting in time before an appointment later in the afternoon. It was nice to talk to Americans again after months of hard work finishing a book . . . Where were the ladies from? From Illinois! Well, that wasn't a great distance from Minnesota . .

They had bought him lunch. They were the type who said, "Two against one," when the check appeared in the restaurant which he had suggested to them and where he had ordered an extravagant meal. "But we are in *your* debt," they had said . . . They had giggled nervously and looked toward him with longing when he had said goodbye, the small intriguing adventure perfectly concluded. Sometimes it was more intriguing to concoct a fiction, to become a British novelist, or a person of renown traveling incognito, to skate on the thin ice which years of practice had made secure. How gullible they were, Gerald thought, his eyes greedily following the women in the flowered dresses—but they could wait for a different occasion. Today he was lunching with Carlo Biasetti; and again the apprehension plucked at him, and again it stirred dryly in his throat.

Of course Biasetti would ask him, even though their first conversation had not been overly rewarding—the writer of the introductory letter, the French countess whom Gerald had beguiled for only part of an evening in a Paris café, not recognized at once. Perhaps, however, that was Biasetti's business manner: brusque, enigmatic. In the sociable atmosphere of a restaurant the manner would change. I *am* a writer, Gerald thought, staring at the Arno, his mind moving stubbornly with its slow course. I don't have to pretend; but the stubbornness faltered abruptly, as if unable to maintain its own effort—and death seemed to float slowly past him, as if a corpse were in the river, below the surface, repellent and yet fascinating

He had thought many times of dying, dying obscurely—in his small Paris flat, in the evenings when people were coming home from work, when voices called out cheerily through the labyrinth of streets, alleys, hallways. In Italy, however, the image had receded. In Naples his apartment had not been empty . . .

Near the Duomo, near the intricate monumental bronze doors of the baptistry, he paused in a shop and bought a pair of gloves. They made wonderful leather in Florence. He might allude to the gloves when he saw Biasetti. "It's an affectation, perhaps, but I couldn't resist . . . The Florentine is a superb artisan, a genius." The manuscript had been with the publisher for five days now . . . "Within a week, Mr. Newell—yes, I am sure in less than a week I will have at least a tentative opinion for you." In another half hour or so it would be time to make the telephone call, the polite inquiry. "I have marvelous news for you, Mr. Newell . . . Yes, we like it immensely . . ." That voice and death floating in the river.

Holding the gloves in his left hand Gerald walked through the Piazza della Signoria adjacent to the Uffizi, past Michelangelo's David and the large statues upraised on pedestals, through the long colonnade and up the wide steps to the gallery. In one of the rooms a blond woman, possibly an American, was standing in front of a Titian, her face partly hidden from him, so that only the yellow hair shone against the redder, richer tones on the canvas. The Italian blond and the stranger, Gerald thought; the Italian blond and the interloper. He waited until she had moved away, until a group with a guide had circulated past him; and then he walked with a sonorous, measured tread toward the Del Sarto he had come to admire.

For a minute or two he stood absorbed. The Madonna—peculiar, almost ludicrous in a way to compare the Madonna with Angelina Nardi. Yet the painting reminded him of her, as it had earlier in the week. Perhaps she would laugh at the comparison and would spoil it; but she is my salvation Gerald thought—not the Madonna but the prostitute. How did you tell a prostitute she represented salvation? I'm confused, he thought, I'm growing confused. I am salvation to *her*, not the reverse—she promised to wait for *me*. Yet the painting continued to hold him, the soft somber colors, the luminous eyes. I will buy her a present, he decided. I will make her forget the ring. Why do I think of the ring, when she never mentions it herself? . . . Ah yes, Angelina, look at me with admiration, not with scorn: the man of letters confronts you, he is equal with the artist, he can make or destroy—not you; it is he who can see the power of death, sliding underwater. You must admire me! . .

He had turned. A man had grazed against his arm. "You do not have to crowd," Gerald said in Italian, "there is plenty of room." The man smiled at him uncomprehendingly and Gerald strode out into the corridor.

He felt abruptly shattered and old. In the piazza he paused to light a cigarette, to glance at his watch. The cigarette was still burning when he reached his hotel—a boardinghouse, he thought, in England it would be considered a boardinghouse; but there was a telephone in his room. "I haven't yet decided where I will stay, Mr. Biasetti. Possibly with friends, possibly at the Excelsior . . . No, it would be better if I called you . . ."

He had a sudden vision of himself entering the lobby of the Excelsior, striking his gloves lightly against the desk. "Any messages for me? I'm expecting word from my publisher."

He climbed to his room and closed the door and seated himself next to the window. He brought out his amber holder and meticulously lit another cigarette, the vision of the Excelsior brightening in his mind: a suite of rooms, a balcony above the Arno. He had not been able to afford bringing Angelina with him this time, but . . . He lifted the receiver from its slender pronged cradle. His hand was steady. He leaned back in his chair.

"I wish to speak to Mr. Biasetti," he was saying in Italian. "Yes—in person. Tell him it is Mr. Newell who is calling." He pushed his tongue over his lips.

A voice said, "*Who* is calling?"

"Newell," he answered. "Gerald Newell. New-well, the author." There was no reply. A pulse had begun to beat in his neck, against the figured patterns of the silk stock he wore in lieu of a tie. He waited. Through the window he noticed a corner of the Duomo, the edge of a stone buttress.

"Ah!—it is Mr. Newell," Biasetti said with loud cordiality. "How are you, Mr. Newell?"

"I am quite well."

"You are enjoying Florence, I hope?"

"Yes—yes, I always enjoy—"

"And now you are calling about your manuscript, I suppose," Biasetti seemed to interrupt cordially.

"Yes," Gerald said.

"Well, I have read a part of it, Mr. Newell. Several chapters. A few in English, as well as those in Italian. A great art to be able to translate one's work into another language." The compliment appeared too bland; the voice had a rasping quality, as if the wires transmitting it were at fault. Gerald could see Biasetti in the disarray of his office, the books in paper bindings on the desk—the effete enigma of the face, the small white beard, like a goat's.

"I do not find it difficult, Mr. Biasetti—"

"No, possibly not. Still it is an accomplishment. But now you want a report on your book. You want an honest opinion."

"Yes—an honest opinion," Gerald repeated.

"And I am afraid, Mr. Newell—I am sorry to say that it will not be what you wish to hear."

"No?"

"No," Biasetti said. His voice seemed to rasp into sorrow "You see, we don't often buy works by foreign authors, Mr. Newell—unless they are already published and fully translated, and that is also rare. The work must be very exceptional to merit an investment, you understand—and this—well frankly, Mr Newell, although I like certain sections, the rest was to me over-written. Old-fashioned in style." There was a brief pause. "It's not just my opinion," Biasetti continued. "It is also the opinion of my staff. They have read more of your book than I."

Gerald struck his cigarette with his forefinger, the ashes spilling down on the tile floor. "Overwritten," he said into the mouthpiece. "I'm afraid I don't understand . . . Perhaps you would consent to discussing with me, in your office, the passages you find—you find not favorable. Perhaps we could have lunch."

"That would be delightful, of course, Mr. Newell, but not entirely possible for me at this time. As a matter of fact I am to lecture at the university this afternoon—I am in the midst of preparing an address—and tomorrow, tomorrow I must catch a train for Milan."

"And after that?"

"Well after that, Mr. Newell—I hardly think we can make plans now. I may be in Milan three days. I may be gone longer."

"I see," Gerald said. "Would you have time to see me for a few minutes, before you catch your train tomorrow, or later today—after the lecture?"

"No, Mr. Newell. No, that really isn't feasible. I'll tell you what I suggest, though. I will have my staff prepare a short synopsis of what we have thought of your book. It will be ready for you by tomorrow."

"I would not wish to put you to any trouble," Gerald said, jabbing with his shoe at the spilled ashes on the floor.

"Oh, it would be no trouble, Mr. Newell. You will be in to collect your manuscript some time tomorrow?"

"In the morning," Gerald said. "I believe—I believe I mentioned to you another book I have decided to undertake. Perhaps we can get together on that—at a later date."

"It is possible, Mr. Newell," the voice said brusquely. "Now you must excuse me."

"Yes, of course," Gerald said. He hesitated for several seconds. "A pleasure to have talked with you, Mr. Biasetti."

"Yes indeed, a pleasure for me. Goodbye, Mr. Newell."

"Goodbye," Gerald said.

He listened to the click against his ear and then replaced the receiver and sat motionless, staring at the telephone, wondering why the disappointment should be so acute. Had he actually expected anything from Biasetti? For a moment he had, there in the gallery. But then you were separated from illusions, from the supremacy they afforded. You had to talk to someone, a prostitute, a publisher. You could tolerate a certain number of refusals—losses; but they became heavier. This one weighed like iron.

If Biasetti came through the door now, I would murder him.

He would have a most decorous funeral: a hearse with large wheels and sloping glass sides, driven solemnly through the streets by a man with a black silk hat—two sleek black horses with plumed leather collars surmounted with polished brass. You saw them often in Rome and Naples and Florence. I must arrange to die in a city, Gerald thought . . . but as he stood up and went down the stairs, the river and the painting and the hearse drifted away from him, and he imagined only the terrace next to his bedroom, the chaise drawn out into the sunlight. He was glad that Angelina was not with him now. Perhaps he had not brought her here, because in his mind he had seen . . . He might propose marriage to her. He might say: this is what I have, you will be entitled to half of it, to all when I die. It might easily seem a fortune to her. He wondered if she was on the terrace now. He tried to visualize her there. She had been his mistress for more than a month; a month implied permanence.

He had had no news from her. He remembered her saying, "But you know, Gerry, I can write." Yet he had not requested a letter. He had not wanted her to know where he was staying. It was nonsense to think that she might have left the apartment, that she might have gone away . . . He would be in Naples tomorrow evening.

A cameo in a shop window caught his eye. He was an expert on cameos. He entered the shop and approached the counter She had promised to wait for him—she had promised.

Michael had wandered away from Ruth into the rear of the antique store. It was ill-lighted and musty, but he had seen the two ship models among the chairs and tables piled nearly to the ceiling and the smaller model might do, he decided. He had the feeling that Ruth had grown a trifle impatient with his search. She was much more interested in the furniture on display. He could see her standing, talking to the proprietor near the door. The man was impeccably dressed. He wore a black coat, a pair of striped trousers. His voice had an unctuous quality. He spoke excellent English. The front of the shop was very ornate, more so than others they had visited.

Michael picked up the model and scrutinized it. It didn't

have any guns, but a tiny anchor hung from a cord underneath the bowsprit and there were miniature railings and planks and a raised stern, and portholes hollowed into the sides and parchment sails. They had already bought the dress for Priscilla. It wasn't quite as elegant as the one he had imagined their buying, but it was white and delicate and Ruth had said she could make a sash for it, if Priscilla insisted. Priscilla would be delighted with the dress, Ruth had said; she had none as pretty. Perhaps that was so. Anyway it came from Florence; and as he had purchased it Michael had visualized his daughter laughing, pirouetting in front of a mirror. Now he tried to picture Mikey removing the wrappings from the ship model, touching the two slender masts.

Yet he was listening to Ruth, the words indistinct, coming faintly down the length of the oblong room. For some reason he thought again of her leaving the house in Wynnewood, her eyes turning swiftly from the children. "I couldn't have *borne* going back"—her face momentarily contorted—her eyes filled with anger in the hotel in Rome. He wondered why those particular memories should coincide, why it should occur to him that Ruth had thought little of the children since the first days of the trip. It was hardly true, was it? The children were fine: a letter from Priscilla had been waiting for them in Florence when they had arrived. I'm imagining what doesn't exist, Michael told himself. The night at Ernesto's is all but forgotten—leaving the house is still further behind us. Ruth and I aren't losing sight of each other here in Italy. There have been times when we've been closer to each other than we were at home. He brought the model forward. Ruth turned to meet him, her arm partly extended.

"Darling," she said. "Look here! Don't you think this is the most beautiful sofa you've ever seen?"

"Why yes," Michael answered. "Yes, it's very nice—"

"Look how it's made," she continued. "The owner here says it's over two hundred years old—and all carved by hand, the frame I mean. And look at the color of the satin, Mike. Wouldn't that shade of green, that exact shade, be perfectly lovely in our living room?"

"Yes," he said. "Yes—I guess it would."

"Oh, I wish we could afford it," she said excitedly. "But it's terribly expensive. It's three hundred and fifty dollars."

"It is really nothing for such a piece," the owner interrupted, rubbing his hand across the antique frame, caressing it. "I would crate it for madam. There would be no charge for the crating. I ship all over the world—to many Americans."

"I'm sure you do," Ruth said. "You have beautiful things." She glanced at Michael. "I see you found your ship, darling."

"I think so. I think I have. How much is this, signore?"

The owner took the model and examined it. "This," he said. "This—" He pursed his lips. "For this I will ask only twenty-five thousand lire."

"Why, that's almost forty dollars," Ruth said. "It's not very big . . . Is it worth that?"

"Ah! But it is old, madam—older than the sofa even. See the little ropes, madam—see how each one is tied."

Ruth smiled. "I'm afraid I don't know too much about models. Not a great deal anyway . . . Mike?"

Michael hesitated. "Twenty thousand," he said slowly. "Would you consider twenty?"

The owner smiled and shook his head. "No, I am sorry. There are other stores where one may bargain, if one wishes—but not here . . . Of course, if you wish to buy the sofa, sir, I could make a special price for the two—"

"No the sofa is out of the question," Michael said. "I will give you twenty-one thousand for the ship."

"Let us not argue, sir. Let us say twenty-three thousand and the ship will be yours. But only because I know you could walk all over Florence and not find such another."

Michael looked down at the ship. He felt dissatisfied. It seemed wrong, however, to haggle over Mikey's present. It would be better to pretend to leave; the owner might call them back. Yet they had been to nearly a dozen shops and it was true, the model was less expensive than others they had seen. They hadn't haggled over Priscilla's dress; but that had been in something similar to a department store and the price had been clearly marked. The dress had cost thirty-five dollars, almost forty . . .

He found himself thinking about the sofa then. He wished he could make the sudden grand gesture that would buy it for Ruth—that would change the moment into a surprise.

"All right," he said. "I'll pay you the twenty-three thousand."

The owner beamed. "You make no mistake, sir. It is an item for a collector."

"It is for my son," Michael said.

"For your son, sir—for a child?" The owner seemed astonished.

"No, not for a child. He's almost as tall as his mother—"

"He will take care of it? It is not a toy—"

"He will take very good care of it," Michael said. "Here— I'll give you the money."

The owner took the bills and withdrew. Ruth was silent. Michael was looking at a gilded clock on top of a marble mantle. He had the impression again that he was a long way from Ruth; but the owner was returning with the ship wrapped in brown paper and was counting out the change; and when they re-entered the street and joined in among the crowds, the musty feeling of loneliness began to disappear.

"Well, I'm sort of glad it's over," Ruth said in a comfortable tone.

"Glad what's over, dear?"

"Getting the things for the children, getting it all settled."

"Oh," he said. "Sure . . . Only I wish I could have bought the sofa for you."

She glanced sideways at him. "Don't be silly, Mike—it was much too costly. But the color, the color of the satin gave me an idea. I can match it some day and make a slip cover, or have the sofa at home reupholstered. It really needs reupholstering, or it will in another year."

Michael nodded and took her hand. Another year, he thought. The Duomo confronted them: the vaulting patterns of mosaics, the triangles of stone. They went past it. They had planned to have an evening cocktail further on at one of the tables bordering the immense airy rectangle of the Piazza della Signoria.

RUTH'S thoughts moved idly with the unhurried pace of the small rented car. It was called a Millecento, and at first she had been amused by the size. It had seemed a humorous conveyance, the name rather bombastic; but Michael had been like a child with it, raising the hood, testing the various instruments that were so unlike their own American Chevrolet. He drove it skillfully, however, with a certain pride, his knees angled upward beside the steering column in a way that seemed half comic and half appealing. "No, it's not awkward," he had told her. "As a matter of fact it feels fine."

They had used the car for three days. They had driven from Florence to Perugia and then to Assisi and to Orvieto. She had been delighted with each of them—the major hill towns, the ones all the guidebooks had described. They were much larger than his village, Michael had said, the architecture of various buildings was on a grander scale; but then smallness wasn't necessarily a deterrent, Ruth thought, and vaguely compared the car with the village in her mind.

They had spent last night in Rome. The journey from Orvieto had taken only a little more than two hours. This would be their longest day on the road, but she did not feel tired yet. They had eaten a quick lunch at a seaside restaurant below Anzio, where they had spent an hour or so surveying the battlefield. The vastness of the graveyard had arrested her; yet it had looked so clean and well kept—quite peaceful, a breeze blowing across it under a partly overcast sky, the sea on one side, the blue Alban hills south of Rome on the other. The horrors of war could scarcely be revealed in such a place—but she had been glad when Michael had suggested that they move on.

She remembered him suddenly in Assisi offering a package of

cigarettes to the young priest who had served as their guide through the basilica of St. Francis. They had all been standing in a colonnade which ran along one side of the church. Through the arches a view had extended across the yellow-green plain toward Perugia, on top of its own domed hill. The priest had winked at Michael and Michael had winked back, and the cigarettes had been slipped under the black cassock; yet the gesture had touched her, the humorous, solemn fashion in which the gift had been given and received. Money, she had realized, I might have given money. Money would have been a tip, it wouldn't have been as nice. Michael had merely shrugged, however, when she had brought up the subject. "Oh sure, the cigarettes," he had said. "They used to be the medium of exchange. I guess they still are—even with the clergy," and she had not told him that quite unexpectedly there in the colonnade he had appeared to her as a man of the world.

She was pleased with Michael. His temporary silence did not bother her. He had atoned for his one mistake. It might easily have been much worse: a strange city, a strange country—the most understanding wife would have been enraged. Many would have left him alone in the Roman café to his own devices; but she had been afraid to do that, afraid that she might get lost again. Of course now she knew that a great many people in the cities spoke good English, that she need not rely on Michael's Italian, although it had improved. But she had not been aware of that then. She had disliked the feeling of being dependent on a drunken husband. It had been completely new to her—because Michael was, and had been for as long as she could remember, dependent on her—on her help, her advice, her ability to manage, to keep things running evenly. That was true, wasn't it? She hadn't been able to understand him that one evening in Rome. Some kind of nostalgia had taken hold of him—ideas about the war, about the role he had played in saving, or trying to save an old man's life. Somehow she couldn't picture him flinging himself into danger, when it wasn't called for. Maybe it was because she could no longer imagine him living apart from her, from the life they shared and—oh well, she thought, don't be so concerned about it; it happened years ago . . .

She began composing an imaginary letter to Bettina Johnson. "We lived in a *pensione* near Fiesole on the outskirts of Florence. It was terribly attractive and inexpensive. Our rooms opened right onto a terrace overlooking the whole valley, the Arno, the cathedral they call the Duomo, the campanile, the bell tower— everything. We had breakfast on the terrace every morning . . . and while we were staying in Rome we took an excursion through the country just outside and saw the Emperor Hadrian's villa and the baths of Caracalla and the catacombs and the gardens at Tivoli. I didn't care too much for the catacombs. They were dank and gloomy—but, Betty, you'd love the gardens. They're absolutely magnificent, full of all kinds of exotic blooms in deep grottoes and on hillsides, and there are more fountains than you can count, more than in the city of Rome itself, I think, and that's certainly saying a great deal. A cardinal used to live in the villa which the gardens partly encircle. Imagine being the cardinal . . ." Bettina had been to Paris once—before she was married, however. None of the Allens' friends had ever been to Rome.

Ruth could see Bettina reading the letter. Bettina wasn't very good at gardening. She would smile at the allusion . . .

Whatever became of the rosebushes? Ruth wondered abruptly: the roses she had seen described in the magazine that evening when Michael had proposed the trip abroad? Funny, they had gone completely out of her mind. Michael had mentioned them once, hadn't he?—there in the hotel room when he had brought her the violets, when he had made love to her—unreserved, yet practiced love. It had seemed so new, so intense, luxurious there in the room with its casement windows slightly ajar above the quiet street . . . Funny about the rosebushes, though, how she had forgotten all about them. Home seemed so remote. Italy, just driving like this in a foreign car, gave you a feeling of detachment.

"In Orvieto, Betty, we stayed in a lovely little place near the cathedral—and Mike ordered a bottle of the special white wine they make nearby. It was a warm night, but the wine was beautiful and cool . . ." They had really done very well, Ruth thought. Except for Michael's extravagance during that one frightful evening, they had kept within their budget. The gifts for the children might seem a trifle lavish, but the gifts belonged to the trip, would serve to recall it. Tomorrow they would be in Naples. Their hotel would be close to the bay. "I wish you and Dick could see it as we do from our window . . ."

Ruth shifted her position. She became aware that she had said nothing to Michael for perhaps fifteen minutes. They were approaching Cassino now. She tried to remember all she had heard about the monastery: it had been heavily bombed, the Germans had used it for an observation post, many lives had been lost. Michael's village was not too far beyond Cassino. The village must be like others they had passed: groups of gray stone buildings turning against the horizon. From a distance the color had seemed drab, slightly mournful, but of course she had not said so.

She leaned forward. "How much further is it, darling? How much further do we have to go?"

But the road twisted, and the view in front of them was more extended. His eyes were intent on the mountains rising ahead. For a moment he did not answer.

"How much further is it to Cassino, Mike?"

He glanced toward her. "Oh," he said. "Only a couple of miles."

"What were you thinking about when I spoke to you?"

"You mean just now?"

"Yes, just now."

"I guess I was wondering how it all would look, honey. We're getting pretty near some of the old landmarks. I never came by this road, though. We used the old Appian Way, Highway Six. I never came across from the sea."

He was silent again, seemingly withdrawn from her. He seemed suddenly tense; and it was as if he had rebuffed somehow her own private musings, or made them appear inconsequential—almost as if she had been chatting with him at home and found that he had not been listening.

She tried to project herself into his thoughts. Did he visualize an old man lying on a hillside? She remembered him laughing about the episode long ago—talking about it in the Roman restaurant, talking incoherently afterward.

The inside of the car seemed cramped; the air, as they descended, hot against her face. Of course I can understand, Ruth thought. It isn't that I want to minimize an heroic act; yet she found herself wishing, almost furtively, that this day was over, that they were approaching Naples now instead of Cassino. How could you be nostalgic about a time you had spent away from your wife, she wondered? How could you be *nostalgic* about a war—even if you had done something brave?

MICHAEL saw the monastery. The sky was overcast behind it, and it seemed almost higher than he had remembered, but the outlines were more distinct. The walls which the planes had smashed into rubble had been rebuilt. "The Poles took the monastery," he was telling Ruth. "There weren't many Germans left up there, only a few hundred, not many prisoners. The Germans had pulled back off the mountain finally, after months of holding on. They were outflanked. Canadian and British tanks were crossing through the marshes, over there to the right. . . . We're sort of here on an anniversary," he added. "That was also during May."

It was hard to imagine the countryside as having been disrupted by the war; but if you had been a British or Canadian soldier or a Polish infantryman, you would never forget this particular area, Michael knew. It would be minutely recognizable. You would know exactly where the tanks had roared across the marshes, turned dusty and firm in the spring, and this peaceful stretch of road would be filled with strange sounds and smells; and you would remember looking sideways and back at Cassino and seeing the mountain and the ruins, from which the Germans had watched and where they had repulsed attack after attack.

Ever since morning Michael had felt his anticipation growing. He could feel it now in his stomach and in the tips of his fingers. Awakening in Rome, he had thought: this is the day; this evening—barring an accident with the car—we'll be there. The Millecento was running a bit unevenly; but it wouldn't fail them. They had come this far. Even without the car, he felt, they could somehow manage the rest of the distance.

He drove around the shoulder of the mountain. The road was

wide and paved. He remembered it pockmarked and bordered
by craters half full of a greenish scum—the road the same
bleached skeleton color as the town's ruins below the monastery.
The day he had driven through the ruins, after leaving the ring
with Angelina's mother, came back to him—the incredible
slaughter of the town itself, mashed to pieces, like a carcass
which had been picked over, splintered bones rather than buildings. But now the town was alive.

He was dimly aware of the valley floor stretching out beyond,
of the sudden familiar rise of the hills framing the valley. There
was a reddish cast to the fields; they must be full of flowers.
Then he was staring at the face of a woman. She was short and
heavy, wearing a black dress. She was standing at the roadside
as if waiting to cross, and as if she had just emerged from
the gray ruins on the slope behind her. She looked middle-aged;
her lips seemed gray. She was pregnant, he saw. She was
holding a black kettle for water. He could see the rest of the
family behind her; but the street ahead looked more like old
pictures of the American frontier than an Italian town. It
had a raw, garish quality. He could hear the hammers and
chisels, the clatter of stone falling, but he was looking at the
woman again. They had nearly passed her. She stood impassively.
She did not smile or glance into the car; and all up the slope
until it rose almost vertically were the ruins, gray instead of
white, more smooth now than jagged. The nearest family
squatted under an arch. They were cooking, he saw. They were
around a small fire. There were others, other pairs of eyes
further up. They were like cave dwellers, he thought. They must
have hollowed out rooms in the earth. How long had they
been there? How long ago had they returned to their homes?

He drove slowly down the street. The new buildings were
not like the ones they were replacing. They were square and
rectangular and without much grace—and it wasn't like the
frontier any more. For some reason this seemed a strange
parasitic growth, as if an architect had blundered; but it was
new, he realized—the new Cassino, tawdry and amorphous
in the heat.

He glanced at Ruth. "Well, this is it," he said. "This is

Cassino. This was the most destroyed town in Italy."

"I can believe it," she said softly. "It's amazing—"

"You want to get out and walk around a bit? We ought to, I think. We oughtn't to just drive through."

"All right, Mike . . . Maybe for a few minutes."

They were walking along the wide street. A new hotel had been completed on one side, but no one was on the terrace and they did not climb to it.

"There was a big hotel here once," he said. "This was kind of a resort. The Germans had a tank in the hotel cellar, I heard— the tip of the gun barrel sticking out, and the rest of the hotel was demolished, but the gun kept firing. I heard it was still in place when the troops passed through."

They had halted in front of a restaurant with slender beaded chains hanging down over the doorway to keep out the flies. He suggested they go inside. Several Italians were sipping soft drinks and eating ice cream at the counter. The interior was almost like a drugstore at home, as if it had been transplanted, as if it didn't quite belong. He was ordering Coca Colas. It seemed very odd to be drinking Coca Cola in Cassino.

"I wonder what the old ghosts would think of this," he said to Ruth, but he noticed that she had become quiet, that the Italians were quiet, that they did not look at him directly—more from the corners of their eyes.

"I see they have a few post cards," he said. "Maybe we ought to buy one or two."

"Oh, let's not bother, darling. Let's get back to the car."

"It won't take a second," he said. "I'd sort of like to remember being here today."

He was selecting the cards. The backs were faintly yellow. They showed Cassino as it had been before the war. There were none of the ruins. He wondered when pictures would be taken of the new Cassino, if these old cards eventually would be replaced.

He brought the post cards to the counter and paid for them. "A beautiful city—at one time," he said in Italian to the man who had served them the Coca Cola.

The man nodded and half shrugged, but did not reply.

Michael and Ruth went outside.

"Let's not stay any longer, Mike. I have a feeling we're not especially welcome. Do you think we are?"

"No, not very welcome."

"I don't mean that to sound sarcastic," she said, her eyes concerned, watching him.

"I know you don't. I guess they're not overly partial to Americans in Cassino. This is a town we and the Allies helped crush. It saddens me too—in rather a strange way, though. I almost wish they'd left the ruins where they were—as a symbol: death, bravery, utter destruction. It could have been quite a memorial, don't you think?"

"I suppose it could, Mike—"

"Just the ruins," he said. "Nothing else."

They were in the car again. Michael could still hear the hammers pounding against stone, but the noise faded as they crossed the river, the Rapido River, that was more like a slow sluggish stream. To a tank, though, coming down through the marshes to the treacherous narrow bridges, it would have seemed like a river. He remembered stories of men wading into the Rapido in abortive efforts to force a crossing, and when the town of Cassino was rimmed with flame.

"The British used to call this stretch of road the Mad Mile," he was saying. "Someone told me. There were troops dug in all through here, in among these farms—not moving very much, I guess, in the daytime . . ."

He saw the graveyard then and slid by it and stopped. It was small and ill-kept. "I'm curious," he said. "I wonder who's buried there—I'd like to find out. I'll only be a minute."

"No," Ruth said. "I'll come with you."

They walked away from the car. Weeds were growing among the unpainted crosses. The graveyard was very near the road.

"Why, they're Germans," Ruth said.

"Yes," he answered bending forward, "yes, these are German graves."

"Look, Mike, they have the black German cross on the wood."

"Yes," he said. "I see."

"They look—so pathetic," Ruth said. "So forlorn."

"Yes—extremely forlorn."

"You'd think they would have been moved. I mean to some other place where there were other Germans. Why would they still be here?"

"I guess the records were lost. I suppose they didn't have too much chance to keep records."

"But the names are there—at least they have names . . . They're heartbreaking," she said, "all covered with dust . . . Would you mind if I picked a few of those flowers over in the field and put them here? I think I'd like to leave something—"

"Why would I mind, darling?"

"I don't know. I don't know how you'd feel. They were enemies, weren't they?"

"Yes, but that's all over and done with. . . . I guess you can only feel sorrow."

He watched her go into the field and pick the handful of wildflowers. He was struck by the tenderness in her posture as she stooped down. He felt suddenly in love with her, more so than at any time since that first afternoon in Rome, perhaps more than that even. He wondered if she was thinking of Mikey. She seemed wholly engrossed stooping down in the field.

She was putting the flowers on one of the graves in the center of the plot. She raised up and stood in silence looking at the flowers. "They're not very nice," she said. "I'm not sure whether they make it better or worse."

"They make it a lot better, Ruth."

"No," she said, "I'm not sure."

He realized they were looking at each other self-consciously and could not tell why it was, because he felt immensely close to her, as if he should take her in his arms. Then she said: "They're so scraggly. They just make it seem more sad."

Her glance went past him. "Look," she said, "you can see the monastery very clearly."

"Yes—very . . . Sort of looms up."

He looked at the town below. Even from this short distance the impression of newness had partly disappeared. The grayness fitted more against the mountain. The wound did not appear as unhealed.

"They have a kind of dignity to me, these graves," he said reflectively. "They were soldiers, they had to take all the risks. I guess there are worse places in the world to be buried than on the outskirts of Cassino. In a fashion, it's still a shrine."

"They should be moved," Ruth said. "They should be brought back to their own country."

Her eyes had returned to the flowers. He stepped toward her. "Don't worry about them," he said gently. "Let's go—let's be on our way . . . Come on, darling, I'll show you a place that hasn't been destroyed."

Now they were in the hills. The road had narrowed, had become dirt. There were woods on either side, tangles of trees and shade. He was listening to the motor, his mind as if nudging it forward. They came to an intersection. He did not recognize it. There were no signposts. He let the motor idle. Then he thought: yes, I do recognize it, I know how to turn.

They were climbing. They had not spoken for several minutes, and for a while he was once more uncertain. Then, abruptly, he could hear the cough, the soft splutter, of a jeep's engine climbing this same hill long before, and he knew when he reached the top, he would see the village.

It appeared all at once, lifting itself into the overcast. Momentarily it appeared small and foreign, not like a castle at all. He was staring toward it; and then his memory clutched at the way the road twisted downward and leveled and mounted again, at the circle of outlying walls, at the tile roofs and the gray stone, the steeple just to the right near the top of the clustering roofs—and they were all well known to him, each individual shape falling into its pattern. For a moment it seemed that he did not breathe. The overcast was right. This was how he had seen the village first. Only it had been raining then—or had the rain come later?

The magic touched him as if with a wing.

"There it is, Ruth. That's the place. . . . See how self-contained it is. You could look at it from almost any direction, and it would be the same."

"The hill where the old man was—can we see it from here?" she asked.

"No, not from here. It's beyond—over on the other side."

He did not stop the car. He let it slide ahead; but it was as if he had paused, he knew; as if his life had stopped, as if he had saluted some peculiar destiny for the merest second, as if the passage through Cassino had prepared him for this, by contrast, by association.

They drove across the level ground. They were entering the village.

"That's the house where the headquarters were," he told Ruth. "A major was there that day. I know exactly what he looked like—but I can't remember his name." He was peering at the house. "An Irish name . . . Mc something or other." He could hear the major's heavy voice. "Hallahan," he said. "That was his name—Hallahan. He was talking about the fighting in North Africa. He'd seen a lot of the war."

Michael drove into a square and parked the Millecento. He did not recall the square. He must have missed the entrance to the lane into which he had gone with Angelina. He had been looking at the faces of the Italians along the street, the faces bobbing and half turning and moving back to make room for the car.

"There's an inn," he said. "*Albergo*. Let's see what it's like inside."

They walked past a stone trough in the center of the square. A young boy was letting his donkey drink from the trough. The water trickled from an iron tap in moss-covered masonry above the donkey's head. "Not like the fountains of Rome," Michael said to Ruth. "But probably more useful."

He glanced at her. Her eyes were toward the inn, and momentarily he saw in them an expression which reminded him of the evening at Ernesto's. She said, "I wonder if there's any other place to stay, darling."

"I don't know," he answered. "We'll find out."

They went through the doorway. A man appeared in front of them. He was short and thickset. He had an apron tied around his waist.

"Signore?" he inquired politely.

"Do you have a room for this evening for my wife and myself?" Michael asked in Italian.

"*Sì—una camera*, signore."

"May we see it?"

"*Sì*, signore. *Certamente*."

He led them up a flight of stairs. Michael asked if there was another hotel. Ah no, the man said, this was the only one. The village was not very accustomed to visitors. Was the signore American?

"*Sì, sono americano*."

We are complimented, the man said, to have an American visitor. Michael told him he had been in the village during the war.

The man raised his eyebrows. "Ah, during the war!" he said in Italian. "You were with the Army then."

Michael smiled. "Yes—with the Army."

"Did you ever know a major?" the man asked. "A major Hallahan?"

"Oh course," Michael said grinning. "Major Hallahan. I met him at the headquarters. I was only in the village a little while."

"He came to my hotel many times. I am the proprietor. . . . We used to laugh and talk. From all the Americans I remember him. He was a great drinker." The proprietor raised cupped fingers toward his mouth. "Much wine."

"*Sì*," Michael said. "*Molto vino*."

The proprietor was taking a ring of keys from under his apron, was unlocking a door. He had turned toward Ruth.

"You speak Italian, signora?"

"No—no, hardly any."

"I speak not much English, signora," the proprietor said, "but this—this the biggest room . . . One minute, signora." He crossed to the window and unbarred the shutters and pushed them open. "There—can see more." He faced her and smiled as though in apology. To Michael he said in Italian. "We have had no Americans here—for many years."

Ruth had approached the bed. She was wearing a Navy-blue suit and a white blouse. The collar seemed almost luminous in the shadows. She pulled the quilted coverlet down several inches and put her hand against the pillow and turned it over.

The proprietor appeared to understand, "No bugs, signora," he said mildly.

"Bugs?" she said. "I wasn't looking for bugs. But the room is so musty. The sheets are musty and damp . . . Here, Mike—feel them yourself."

He did not move toward her. "I'm sure they're okay, honey."

"No, they're not. Really they're not. The room hasn't been aired."

"I don't suppose they've had too many guests," he said. "The window's open now—"

"But the sheets are *damp*, darling. They'll have to be changed. They won't dry just because the window's open . . . They're almost soggy. Won't you feel them? I'm not making it up—"

Michael stepped over and took a corner of the sheet.

"There—can you feel?"

"I guess they're a little damp, Ruth. Not very." He felt acutely embarrassed. Perhaps the embarrassment made her voice seem louder than it was—slightly hysterical—oddly reminiscent of home, of the immaculate house.

"Is there another place to stay, Mike—or is this the only one?"

"I'm afraid this is all there is." He was still holding the sheet. He could not think of the word for it. The signora, he was saying, wishes to have others—

"*Altri?*" The proprietor came rapidly toward the bed and pulled the top sheet all the way down.

"*Veramente*, signora. No bugs. None."

"*Sì. . . . ma è umido, un' poco di acqua*," Michael said, searching desperately for the word.

"*Acqua*, signore? . . . Water?"

Ruth had started to laugh. "Not water," she said. "These—the *sheets!* New ones!"

"*Ah!*" the proprietor said. "*I lenzuoli! . . .* But nothing is wrong with these. No one sleeps here." He was bundling the bedding into his arms. "*Uno momento*, signora, I will fix."

He left them. Michael could hear him descending the stairs. Ruth was examining the mattress. "It should be hung out in the sun," she said.

Michael did not reply. He was lighting a cigarette. Through the window he could see a portion of the square and the trough. A woman was approaching it. He thought irrelevantly she was no one he knew—that he might be in any of a hundred small villages, that from where he stood he could no longer identify his own.

Ruth had straightened. "You really think we should stay here, Mike?"

"It's up to you," he answered.

"Where else could we go?"

"I don't know, Ruth," he said dully. "I guess Cassino is the largest town nearby . . . There was that hotel we saw there—"

"We couldn't drive into Naples, and come back tomorrow—could we? How far is it to Naples?"

"About fifty-five miles. Two more hours on the road."

"Couldn't we make it in less than two hours?"

"No, we couldn't. Not the way the car's been running."

"I didn't know anything was the matter with the car."

He turned away from the window. "It's not running perfectly, that's all. I don't like to drive it too fast. If we went into Naples, there'd always be the chance it wouldn't get us back."

"You're angry, aren't you? You think I complained too much about those sheets?"

"I guess I thought you didn't have to be as insistent, Ruth."

"Well . . . well, perhaps not. But it was so dingy in here when we arrived. The shutters all drawn and—and certainly I wouldn't want to go into Cassino again. That was so awfully depressing to me."

Don't spoil it any more, Ruth, he thought. Please don't.

"But still it is only for a night, isn't it?" she said. "I suppose we can make out all right for a night. The room seems better now, than it did. It's not as gloomy—and as you say there isn't too much of an alternative."

"No, not too much—unless we want to give it up."

"Darling, I'm not suggesting you give it up. I'm merely trying to think—to think—to find out what other arrangements we could make. If there aren't any, well then that's all there is to it. You mustn't be angry with me. You should make a few allowances.

I'm merely saying we ought to spend the time as nicely as we can. Isn't that right?"

"Yes—sure. Only I was thinking of all the plans we made—"

"Then of course we'll stay," she told him. "Anyway it would be silly to spend hours driving back tomorrow, when we're already here."

They both turned toward the door. The proprietor had reappeared. "*Ecco*, signora. *Ecco!*" He offered two sheets and a pillowcase to Ruth. They were carefully folded and creased.

"Why, they're linen!" she exclaimed in surprise.

"They are from my own room," the proprietor announced proudly in Italian. "Not from the bed, naturally, but from the room. They were washed a week ago and put away."

"What did he say about them?" Ruth asked.

"He says they are fresh and clean—that they've just been laundered."

"They're much better," she said. "Tell him they are a great improvement."

Michael translated: "Thank you. They are very good. They are excellent—"

"You will take the room then, signore?"

"Yes," Michael said. "We will take the room."

The proprietor smiled. "There is a toilet at the end of the hall," he told Michael privately in Italian. "No bath but a toilet. It will be for you, no one else." His glance returned to Ruth. "I am very sure, signore," he said and pointed to the ceiling, "that no water comes from the roof."

THEY walked through the square. They went as far as the house where the headquarters had been but no further because rain was threatening and because it was growing dark. They wouldn't be able to see too much from the summit of the village at this hour, Michael decided. It would be better to wait until morning, when the weather might clear. He saw where the lane led up the hill, however, and went by it and past a butcher's shop where the carcass of a young lamb hung head down from a hook. He did not remember the shop. Possibly it had been closed during the war. Not much meat had been for sale then. He tried to tell Ruth about the white rooster; but his voice sounded flat, as it had when he had explained to her the proprietor's observation about the ceiling, and the story ended rather pointlessly. Had the man been insulted, Michael wondered—or puzzled, or secretly amused?

His own thoughts were scattered and confused. He remembered the closeness he had felt toward Ruth in the German graveyard (that was ironic, wasn't it?—a graveyard) and now she was removed from him again. Or had he removed himself from her? The village would seem dirty to her, and not unusual. She would be wondering what strong appeal it could have. He had no definite conception of tomorrow, going out to the farm. Momentarily he had the impression that it would be altered, that others would have sprung up around it, that he would have to search for the right house. Then he put out his hand and felt the rain, and they were hurrying toward the shelter of the albergo.

Dinner had been prepared for them: a minestrone, a pasta, salad, cheese and coffee. There were four tables in the dining room, two of them empty, the other occupied by the proprietor and his wife, an enormous woman in a dark dress and shawl. The

144

proprietor put candles on either side of the bottle of red wine he produced for Michael and Ruth. The meal was pleasant enough, although not expertly cooked. The Italians, beyond the two empty tables, ate in silence, perhaps as was their custom, perhaps out of deference to their guests. Occasionally the great shadow of the woman moved against the wall, when she arose to remove the plates and to bring another course from the kitchen.

Michael found himself trying to think of things to say: remarks about the food, the trip in the car. He found it difficult to discuss the village. He knew that Ruth was disappointed with it, and he himself was disappointed. He wondered how much his disappointment showed to her and whether it would increase and whether the view through the car's windshield was all there would be for him. Yet he had been in a sort of panic when she had suggested leaving; a sense of panic persisted. Ruth wouldn't understand it. He would not expect her to. Ruth was a practical person, and not a believer in magic. Maybe that was the chief difference between them. Memories were not mysterious to her, were not a source of renewal. Or no, that was presumptuous to believe; but they were not *the* source, the special one, the special refuge. Was it a refuge, though—or was it a myth? Had he been fooling himself all along? Was this the perfect refutation?—this commonplace meal in a third-rate hotel with a husband and wife talking together, as if they were merely casual acquaintances—or worse still, as if they were husband and wife who no longer knew how to approach each other

"A penny for your thoughts?" he asked absurdly.

"Oh, nothing much," she answered. "Actually I guess I was thinking about Naples, darling—how it would be to see the Bay of Naples. You know, the way you described it at home."

They finished their meal and went into the hall at the foot of the stairs. The door was open toward the square.

"I guess you wouldn't like the idea of getting our coats and taking a brief stroll . . . It's just sprinkling."

"No, I don't think so, Mike . . . You go ahead, if you want."

He looked out at the square. "You wouldn't mind if I tried it for a little while?"

"No. I wouldn't mind."

"I mean you wouldn't feel left alone—or anything?"

"No. I have a book in the suitcase. I'll get into bed, I guess and read . . . You won't go into any bars, will you?"

"No, I won't go into any bars—"

"And don't go wandering off into the hills."

She spoke with a trace of humor; yet her voice seemed to warn him. He reassured her. "We'll leave the hills for tomorrow morning. I'll just take a turn around the town and come back."

He walked to where the Millecento was parked and unlocked the trunk and rummaged inside for his raincoat. It was light tan instead of olive green, but it made him remember the trench coat he had worn, and the shadow it cast under a lamp reminded him of other nights when he had walked toward the Nissen hut outside the village where he had been stationed, between Naples and Caserta.

The rain was warm and gentle; and old odors stirred in the air —the smells of dirt and earth and damp stone and age and the fresher smell of wood burning in a stove and billowing down from a chimney. They had nothing to do with progress or change. They came out of innumerable past generations. Wars could alter them for a time and then they sifted in again from their hiding places. They were the smells of peace: an isolated peace perhaps, one away from the cities and the larger towns, but one he could join himself with.

He was suddenly pleased to be alone. He walked without hurrying, and remembered the footsteps outside the window in Rome in the early morning, and the man who had been driving the donkey, laden with sticks, the evening when he had been here in this same spot with Angelina.

He entered the lane which curved upward. He reached out to touch the moss on the walls, grazing it with his fingers. As a child he used to reach up and touch the coping above the landing whenever he went down the stairs in his family's house. It was a gesture which he had thought brought him luck. For a moment he visualized how the light filtered in through the white bannisters, but here it was dark and he did not see the man approaching him until he was almost opposite.

*"Buona sera."*

. . *"Buona sera,* signore," the man said.

Michael could not see his face. He had gone by. Suppose he had
been Angelina's uncle—would they have recognized each other?
It was better to assume that they would have than to risk a conversation, or to make inquiries now, for these next few minutes.
Michael knew exactly where he was going. It was nice to be
anonymous in the lane. The memories made him smile; and then
she was there in his mind, the girl with the black sweater with
the beads of moisture on it. She was walking beside him, holding
his arm, her breast faintly pressing against him through the trench
coat. He remembered how she had walked gracefully and proudly
—the startling dark beauty of her face . . . Of course you will
take me to Naples with you in your jeep . . .

He had reached the top of the lane. It was brighter now. Small
lighted windows shone above him, and then one from the house
where the terrace was. He stopped. He had not expected to find
the house occupied; but surely no one would be out on the terrace in the rain.

He went into an alley almost too narrow to permit passage.
Momentarily it seemed absurd to be trespassing here like a thief.
Angelina had spoken of climbing up from below—but the terrace
was abruptly in front of him, the balustrade across the far side,
just visible. The rubble had been cleared, but in the dim light he
could see no other signs of repair. The fountain, the tree had not
been replaced. The doorway behind him was partly illumined;
otherwise the façade of the house was in darkness.

He went to a corner of the balustrade and sat down. He lit a
cigarette, watching the match flicker in the rain, keeping its glow
and the glow of the cigarette away from the house. He thought
how odd it would be if someone called to him. He did not know
whether he felt more like a thief or a ghost. How many times
had he been here in his mind? This was the center of it. Had he
known that? This was the center of his village—not the hillside,
nor the headquarters room, nor the room where the celebration
had been held, but here.

His eyes strained toward the distance. He could not see the
range of hills, but knew how they sloped against the horizon—and

among those pinpoints of light closer to him was the farm. He sat smoking his cigarette and looking at the lights. He did not yearn to approach them. They were near enough; and slowly the sounds returned—the guns firing, but far off, and another sound which he had not heard: the thunderous rumbling which had shaken the village when the troops and guns and trucks had moved forward; the noise like a whole world revolving, a giant's wheel beginning to spin. Angelina had gone toward the noise and had been engulfed in it, and countless others had gone into the same dusty vortex of sound, rising and turning and spreading out and leaving the village quite stationary. Michael listened. The rain pattered against his coat. This is the center of the world, he thought, the living center. That is its magic—for no one else in the same fashion, but for me.

He stood up. He did not want to stay any longer. He went very quietly to the alleyway and turned and looked back. He could still see himself sitting on the balustrade. He was not sure if Angelina was with him, or how much of her image had surrounded him there. She remained, though. He remembered her even more vividly than during those first few minutes in Rome.

He was descending the narrow street beyond the alley. He recalled Gino, Angelina's brother, darting ahead. He paused. Was this the house, or was it one further on? He thought of Ruth then, but it was not entirely because of her that he did not knock on any of the doors. It was because he did not wish an intrusion, did not wish to confront the puzzled eyes of a stranger, did not wish the spell to break. Later on there would be time for inquiries and talk. Yet as he retraced his steps he thought, suppose she is here in one of these houses—suppose they are all together for an evening, as they were. No, it would be asking too much. It wouldn't be possible; and it was as if he stood on the threshold of discovery and refused it, almost as he had refused Angelina herself, and it was also as if a discovery had already been made.

He walked more rapidly. He was in a section of the village he had never entered before. He could see the silhouette of the church steeple, and there was a sudden fragrance of flowers in the air, but the shadows were very thick and he could not tell where the blooms were. He was in an open area above the square. He could hear the water dripping in the trough and the soft ooze of the rain among the cobblestones at his feet. A solitary figure crossed below him, a man bent over, a coat pulled up to cover his head. It was raining harder. Michael turned up his own collar and went down toward the lighted doorway of the albergo.

The proprietor called to him in Italian. He was in a room to the right, standing behind a counter, polishing a glass.

"You would like a cognac, signore—before you go upstairs?"

Michael entered the room. "You will drink one with me?"

"Thank you, signore. You are kind. A bad night, is it not? No one has come in here tonight except you."

Michael was putting his coat over the back of a chair. He watched the proprietor pour out the cognac. A lamp lit one end of the counter, a few bottles in racks against the wall, the brass coffee urn below them.

Michael raised his glass. *"Buona fortuna."*

*"Buona fortuna,* signore."

"What is your name?" Michael asked.

"Guido Portano, signore."

"And mine is Allen. Michael Allen."

"Yes, I know. I have seen it on your passport, and in the register of course. I am afraid all American names sound alike to me. I remember very few. The ranks I remember better. Major Halla-han. I remember the *major* more than the name. May I ask what rank you had during the war, signore?"

"I was a captain."

"Ah yes, a captain . . . You did not come to my hotel, though, did you?"

"No, not to the hotel . . . But I would like to ask you about another name, an Italian name. You will have to speak slowly so I can understand. I learned a little of your language once, a little has come back to me . . . I understand more than I speak. But do you know in this village—a family whose name is Nardi?"

"Nardi? Yes, certainly. Many are named Nardi here."

"An old man," Michael said. "A farmer. He lived about two, possibly three kilometers from the village—in this direction."

The proprietor looked steadily at Michael. "It could have been

Giuseppe. Giuseppe Nardi." He waited a moment. "Giuseppe is dead now. He died, I think it was four years ago."

"He was very old," Michael said, his eyes intent on Portano.

"He was nearly eighty, signore. . . . There was an American who once saved his life . . . A captain—like yourself . . . You are the same person?"

"Yes . . . Yes, the same."

Portano's head moved forward. "I thought so! . . . Of course in the beginning I do not want to ask too many questions—but I ask myself why an American has come back here. The first American since the war. A small village—not much of a place."

"But it is important," Michael said. "Important to me."

"Yes, I can see that is true. You do something good in a place and you wish to see it again. The major told me about what you did. Giuseppe Nardi himself! Giuseppe has told everyone about the American captain." Portano grinned. "Only in the end I think you became more like a general, and the story was that he had rescued you."

"We rescued each other—"

"No, signore. I know the real story . . . But may I ask if you were looking for Giuseppe Nardi tonight—in the rain?"

"No, not exactly. I wanted to see the village tonight—especially in the rain. The rain was here before."

"It is interesting," Portano said. "All dreams, all wishes are different. You have wished to come back to a small village in Italy— and I, the Italian, think of one day going to New York."

"New York on a day when the sun is shining."

"By all means in the sunshine," Portano said laughing. "I would like to see the tops of the buildings—the very tops. The major has told me often about New York. You remind me of him. You smile like him. Only he would not walk around on a rainy night like you. He would stay here and drink a bottle of wine—with a girl. The major always liked to have a girl with him, not to make love to necessarily, but to talk to."

Michael set down his glass. "Perhaps the major was here with Angelina Nardi."

"Angelina? Angelina Nardi. Ah yes!— Giuseppe's granddaughter . . . Yes, the major was here with her once or twice. Yes—because he asked for her when she went away . . . I remember. It was a mystery where she had gone. No one could tell."

"She did not return then—to the village?"

"I think she was here for her grandfather's funeral . . . Yes, that is so—but not since. I have seen the mother and father, but never the daughter since that day. . . . Angelina—a very beautiful girl, signore, ten years ago."

"Yes," Michael said, "very beautiful."

"I remember her as a child, running through the streets, when the parents came in for the market—a little vagabond, always in some kind of mischief, but harmless, always more amusing than harmful . . . A child and then a woman." He hesitated, his eyes studying Michael. "You will have another cognac, signore?"

"No, thank you. One is enough. I told my wife I wouldn't be away too long."

Portano nodded. "You intend to visit the farm tomorrow?"

"Yes. Tomorrow morning . . . I would like to surprise them."

"I understand . . . and I am sorry—that Giuseppe is dead," Portano said carefully. "But if it is permitted, I would like to ask you something else."

"Of course—"

"I would like to ask if you found what you were looking for—outside. Do you understand the question?"

"Yes, I think so. I think I found—some of it."

"More than a little?"

"Yes," Michael said. "Much more."

He went up the stairs. Ruth was asleep when he opened the bedroom door. The light bulb which hung from the ceiling was still on. The book she had been reading was spread face down on the sheet. He remembered her asleep in the shadowed room in Rome. He tried not to disturb her, but as he lay down she awoke.

"That's you, Mike," she said drowsily.

"Who else?" he asked.

"I'm glad it's you," she said. "I'm glad you're back."

He slid into the bed beside her. For a long time he listened to the sound of the rain.

It had been a tiring trip for Gerald Newell. Ascending in the funicular that would take him to the comparative cool and shade of the Vomero, he could feel the weariness in his slender frame and more especially in behind his eyes: always an insistent pain there when he was tired or annoyed. The crowds annoyed him, pushing and shoving, returning to their homes, now in the evening. The funicular climbed into a tunnel, stopped and started forward again. He had been on it many times and never without wondering what would happen if the cogs or the cables, or whatever held the cars to the tracks and kept them moving, broke. The cars would begin a dizzy nightmarish backward plunge. People would shriek and stare at each other. The speed would increase. He would rise and stand in the slanting aisle. He alone would have the presence of mind to show dignity. Weariness, failure, everything else would be engulfed. Death would be superbly inevitable . . . I am a fool, he told himself. It wouldn't be possible to stand. I would merely sit here, sucked against the seat by the backward rush—my eyes blazing with indignation.

He got off the funicular and was pushed through the crowds along the platform. He watched the Italian who was behind him dart by; and then the crowd lessened and he was outside the station, looking at the trees along the avenue, as if he had not expected them to appear so quickly, as if he had not expected to be where he was.

He walked briskly for a block or two and then slowed his steps. He passed the café where he had met Angelina, where they so often dined together. She was not there now; she would be waiting for him in the apartment. He had sent her a telegram yesterday, after he had telephoned Carlo Biasetti. He was opposite the delicatessen where she shopped for breakfast. A row of round yellow cheeses rested against the glass. A woman was emerging with one of them.

"*Ah!—buona sera,* Signor *Newell.*"

"*Buona sera,* signora." He took off his hat. It was Maria Quinto, a great friend of Angelina's.

"We have not seen you for a week. A week, isn't it? How was Florence?"

"Not too bad," he answered. "Not—"

"You must tell me about it later on. I am in a hurry now. I have to fix dinner for my husband, my family, before I start work."

He watched her cross the street, a large woman in a gray dress, who served behind the bar in the café each evening. He was home, he realized; he was where people knew him by name. He paused in front of the delicatessen. He could see them all then, the crowd dispersed, separated singly or two by two, all going home under the trees. The suitcase tugged at his arm. The manuscript was inside it, unwashed linen, another suit of clothes, the cameo.

Abruptly he wondered why Maria Quinto had cut him off. It wasn't like an Italian to break away like that; but possibly the excuse was valid. He tried to see where she had gone.

He continued walking. Could she have ducked back across the street? he wondered. Suppose Angelina was with someone else, away from the apartment, and Maria Quinto had wanted to warn her. Gerald could heard the sudden rapping of fingers against a closed door: he is here, Signor Newell has returned . . . Angelina nude, laughing. "In a few minutes, Maria, do not bother me now."

He went into the apartment house lobby and across the mosaics of black and white tile to his mailbox. The telegram was not there, nor were the two letters he had written. She must have received them. She would go to the mailbox faithfully. She would hope there would be money inside the envelopes. She would scavenge for money—and now Maria Quinto was hurrying to give warning. On the train he had thought agonizingly of the apartment being empty—a vase of dead flowers on the dining table, a slight stench from the moist stems in the unchanged water.

He approached the door. She never meant to stay, she's

laughed at me, she's gone: my salvation, my luck, everything. He was fumbling for his key. He let himself in noiselessly. Once, earlier in the day, he had thought of surprising her, of making his entrance quietly like this, without touching the bell. He was standing by the dining table under the chandelier. He could hear nothing moving, and the fear rose into his mouth. For several seconds he did not realize that the chandelier was softly lit, that the glass panels beyond him were open toward the terrace.

"That is you, Gerry?" she called.

A shadow moved across the terrace. He heard her steps against the tile. She entered the room.

"Gerry—" she said and stopped. She was wearing the blue satin dress he had given her. "Why—what is the matter?" she asked.

"Nothing is the matter—"

"Why, you look all to pieces!" she said. "What happened?"

"Nothing has happened. . . . You—you got my telegram?"

"Of course, Gerry. . . . You thought I would not get it?"

"I thought—it might have been delayed—"

"Or that I would not be here to get it?"

"No—certainly not."

"But you did," she said. "I can see that." She was looking at him quizzically, her brows lifted. "You thought perhaps I had run away with another person?"

"No," he said with greater firmness. "That's absurd!"

"Is it?"

"I had no such thoughts! It's absurd to joke about things like that—"

Her tentative smile had disappeared. "All right, Gerry—quite possibly it may seem absurd to you . . . We will make no more jokes . . . We will get your suitcase, shall we? I see you have left it in the hall." She moved past him, her nearness both tantalizing him and increasing his anger. This was no way to be greeted; he should have been met with open arms.

He watched her carry the suitcase into the bedroom and put it down. He followed her.

"What *did* you do while I was gone? You stayed here alone?"

"Yes, alone."

"And you went out from time to time—"

"Yes."

"To see someone else . . . Another man?"

"I went out occasionally to see other people, Gerry. An artist I know—an old friend . . . Did you expect me to stay all the time by myself?"

"The artist, he was here—was he? In my apartment?"

She looked at him steadily and with disdain. "No, he was not here—sleeping in your bed, making love to me . . . What's the matter with you anyway? The trip was no good—is that it?"

"The trip was highly satisfactory!"

"I can hear you, Gerry—you don't have to raise your voice . . . The man from Florence, the publisher—he liked your book?"

"Yes—very much."

"He is going to publish it?"

Gerald drew in his breath. "I have every hope that will be the case."

"But he has not yet decided?"

"No," Gerald said. "Not definitely. Not entirely . . . You see, his chief editor was not in town . . . My friend depends a great deal on his advice—so I have left my book in Florence, for the editor to read when he returns. I have brought back only the carbon, the carbon copy—"

"Who is the boss then?" she asked. "The editor or the publisher?"

"Why—usually the publisher—but in this case final decisions are shared. My friend in Florence would not think of publishing a work his editor did not approve of . . . but as I say his opinion was most gratifying to me." Gerald smiled faintly. "It takes time, my dear. Time and patience . . . I've been through it before."

"The editor—he will return to Florence soon?"

"Yes—fairly soon, I believe," Gerald said, his mind becoming more easy with the fabrication. "An opinionated man, I understand. Rather conservative—but we shall see. One must not appear too eager with these people." She did wait for me, he thought; she kept her promise. I should have gone toward *her* with open arms. "You will have to excuse me for being abrupt just now . . . I was a little tired from the trip."

"Yes, the train is always tiring—"

"I could only get a taxi to the funicular, everything was so crowded . . . I really didn't mean to accuse you of anything, Angelina. Travel always fatigues me—that is, when I have to travel alone . . . You will forgive me, won't you?"

"I think I will forgive you, Gerry—"

He reached out and touched her shoulder. "I *am* glad to see you, you know that." His fingers were trembling. He tightened them against the bare flesh, but she twisted slightly, and his hand dropped to his side. "I'm forgetting," he said. "I have something for you—something in my suitcase besides words and clothing. . . . Wait, I will unfasten the locks." He bent down and drew out the small tissue-wrapped parcel, and closed the lid so that she would not see the morocco binding which covered the manuscript.

He straightened. His voice became more urgent. "Here, we will remove the paper—like this . . . See, Angelina—see, it is a cameo on a gold chain, the chain very delicate, because the stone is delicately carved . . . I held it under a magnifying glass. It is perfect, each line clear and exact. . . . You find it attractive?"

Her eyes had softened, he thought. "It is very nice, Gerry. It is very pretty."

"I will put it on," he said. "Allow me." His hands shook against the clasp. "There—now . . . see in the mirror, my dear. See how it hangs—just so! With the blue dress it is exquisite. . . . You do not think it is too—too old-fashioned?"

"No—not at all—"

"To me it is like a precious jewel," he said. "It should be worn without other jewelry, I think—near it, I mean. Without earrings, or . . . but you will know how to wear it best." She turned toward him. "It was not cheap, Angelina."

"Why do you say that?"

"Because . . . because I do not want you to think it is ordinary."

"It is not ordinary—certainly. And I am flattered, Gerry—that you should give it to me."

"It takes a great beauty, my dear, to wear such a jewel."

She smiled at him. "Sometimes you say nice things as well as bad ones." She leaned forward and kissed his cheek; but he said, commanding her. "Not there, Angelina. The lips are for lovers. . . . There! That is better, that is more like it! I don't expect gratitude, my dear, but I expect—I expect *you*. . . . You mustn't hate me. You mustn't tell me stories of what you did not do. You belong to me. I've been tormented thinking about you . . . Open your heart to me, Angelina—your heart!"

It was dark along the Vomero when they strolled toward the café. Gerald walked on the balls of his feet, as was his custom, so that he might seem a fraction taller than the girl beside him. His mind was free once more. He could hear a violin playing under the café's awning. He nodded to the owner, to one or two acquaintances; but when he sat down, he stared with sudden suspicion at a solitary man with a thin, pale handsome face at a corner table. The man had seemed to wink at Angelina. It was only a fragmentary impression, however; and the man left almost at once, passing close by them. Angelina did not glance in his direction.

"That was someone you know, my dear?"

"It could have been, Gerry. I know many people."

"It could have been the artist, couldn't it?"

"It could have been an artist," she answered. "There are many artists in Naples. . . . Suppose he was waiting for me, just in case you didn't come back. Suppose he saw you and went away. Am I rushing after him?"

Gerald peered into the darkness where the man had vanished. "You are not in love with him then—"

Angelina laughed. "What a question! If I was in love with him, would I have waited for you?"

He looked back at her. Her eyes appeared amused. He could find no hidden longing in them. She had made a choice, he thought. She had chosen him—or perhaps the artist was simply an invention. There had been no traces of a stranger in his apartment. He had made a careful, surreptitious search—in the ashtrays, in the wastebasket, in the bathroom, even in the bed with the white counterpane. He had felt positive he could recognize the presence of a stranger, if one had been there in his rooms.

Now he was aware of a feeling of triumph. It spread slowly through him. It was like old times, wasn't it?—something special from the kitchen, a bottle of fine white wine.

"You know," he was saying, "I was thinking of plans while I was in Florence. I was thinking of Paris, Paris in the summer, or early autumn. How would you like a trip to Paris, my dear?"

"You would take me there, Gerry?" she asked in surprise.

He took a sip of the wine. "Why not?—after the work here is finished."

"After you hear from your book?"

"Yes—after that. I know a number of Parisian publishers. One in particular has been after me for a long time. I might do a book for him. I might even show him this one, if my Florentine friend isn't—completely receptive . . . if we can't reach agreeable terms." He paused. "You would go with me, wouldn't you, Angelina?"

She did not answer for a moment. "It is a big question, is it not, Gerry—"

"I suppose it is—"

"It is for the future, I think—not for tonight. Tonight it is enough that you are here. We will make other plans when the time comes."

She managed to smile. She was listening to him prattle on about Paris; but she did not see herself there with him. He was not the same person who had left a week ago. The trip had been an utter failure, she sensed, in spite of what he said. Jealousy alone couldn't have made him appear so vindictive and uncertain. Jealousy came from the fear of losing a man or a woman; but the fear which she had seen in his eyes had not been like that. It had been like the dead fear of having already lost. She had seen it often in Italy in the time of defeat: that lusterless lack of hope; but she had been appalled to see it in Gerald Newell, just for an instant, when she had emerged from the terrace. She did not wish to be enclosed by despair.

Could she have been mistaken? she wondered. She could excuse jealousy if it were modified by humor. His voice had become almost gay. She looked around her, at the crowded tables under the awning. Luigi Bertoli, the artist, had slipped off into the dark.

He would say something sardonic and appropriately insulting the next time she saw him. She would laugh and tell him to mind his own business. But this should be the Excelsior Hotel, she thought, not a small café. They no longer went to the Excelsior, she and Gerald Newell, not as they had at the start. They were more settled now, more domestic; yet she had visualized a celebration tonight—an orchestra playing among potted palm trees. She listened to Gerald's voice. Its gaiety grated against her ears; the awning reflected it downward.

She would not challenge the failure now, however. That would be unwise. She would come to his apartment in the evenings, as she had before—at least for a little longer . . . What a shame, though, that the trip had not been a success. . . .

But Gerald, becoming more loquacious with the heady coolness of the wine, saw her attached to him forever, saw her accepting any offer he might choose to make—saw the Champs Elysées and the glimmering of great restaurants, the Tour d'Argent overlooking the Seine. She was still wearing her soldier's ring, he observed; but she was also wearing the cameo. With a swift ebullience of spirit, and as if he had raised his hand to banish him, he decided that the artist had been a fiction.

A BELL was chiming. Michael rose and pushed the shutters wide so that he could hear it more distinctly. It was a fine day. The sun's rays glinted off the bubbles in the trough and made little bright mirrors among the cobblestones where the moisture remained. He had slept soundly. He felt refreshed and at peace with himself. Perhaps he was relieved that Angelina was not here. Portano would have known if she had returned again. The return of a prodigal daughter would make news in a small village. Portano knew more than he let on. Possibly he had guessed at a love-affair. It did not matter. He and the proprietor understood one another, Michael decided. What he had been told about the old man and about Angelina had merely verified earlier and distant thoughts—but it would be perfectly safe now to take Ruth to the farm. It would be safe to go himself. The search had ended.

Ruth stretched her arms. "It's still there, isn't it?"

He glanced toward the bed.

"The village—it's still there, isn't it, darling?" She was teasing him. She was smiling.

"Still just where it was. No one's stolen it—not even the car."

"You came in so quietly," she said. "Did you find any old friends, while you were walking around?"

"No old friends. I wasn't looking for any in particular—but I learned a little about the family . . . I found out that the old man died some time ago."

She looked at him in surprise. "Who told you that?"

"Guido Portano, the proprietor. I had a few words with him after I came back."

"Oh," she said, her eyes serious. "I'm sorry, Mike. It must have been—it must have been a shock."

"No, not actually. I guess I've thought all along he wouldn't

160

be alive. . . . I learned his name, though. Funny, I never knew his name. Giuseppe. Old Joseph Nardi. Old Joe. I don't know if it fits him or not—sounds a bit odd."

"I am sorry, Mike." She raised her shoulders against the head-board. "I know it must have upset you. . . ." There was a brief pause. "Were you ashamed of me yesterday?" she asked.

"Ashamed of you?"

"When we arrived, when I made all the fuss about the room, I mean."

"No, honey, I wasn't ashamed—"

"I don't know why I did it," she said. "The room wasn't that bad. It just seemed so . . . I was awfully tired, I suppose—and sad. Cassino and everything—and when we were driving along the road, I had a strange feeling that I didn't understand you very well, that we weren't really in accord with each other."

"Now that's a silly thing to say, Ruth."

"I know it sounds silly. It wasn't your fault. You were interested in everything you saw—but I kept thinking of that night in Rome and about the war meaning so much to you, and you seemed miles away from me—and then there was that huge woman downstairs in the dining room, eating and watching us—"

"She wasn't watching us especially—"

"I felt she was. I felt she disapproved of me. Probably—undoubtedly—her husband had told her about the sheets, and I knew if I brought that up, you'd be angry again." She gave him a faint smile. "Anyway, I think I was kind of a flop last night—I wish I'd been with you."

"There wasn't anything special for you to see outside. Only for me there was."

"Did you want me to go with you then? Maybe you didn't—"

"Of course I did—but only if you felt like it. . . . Look," he said gently, "there's nothing to be upset about—"

"I'm not upset. I'm simply trying to explain things to you—to find out if anything is wrong between us—"

"What could be wrong, Ruth?"

"I don't know. Maybe nothing, nothing at all." She waited for a moment. "You still love me, do you, Mike?"

"That's a very foolish question."

"Is it?"

"Certainly it is. I love you very much. I loved you yesterday when we drove through Cassino and you put those flowers on the German grave. I wasn't miles away from you then—and I love you this morning, because you look so concerned—"

"But not last night. You couldn't have loved me last night."

He went toward her. "Darling," he said, "aren't there certain places you'd just as soon see alone—places that mean more to you than to other people?"

"I can't think of any—"

"Sure you could if you put your mind to it. But it wouldn't mean that you wouldn't want to show them to me. The only thing is that I wouldn't understand them quite as you would. I'd see them differently—but that wouldn't interfere with all the years we've spent together." He bent and kissed her. Her lips did not fully respond. *Am I contradicting myself?* he wondered. *Didn't I once believe we could gain something from this place together, even if we didn't see it with the same pair of eyes? Am I saying it wasn't possible?*

Yet he loved her and put his arms around her, and when her lips softened to his, the sense of contradiction disappeared.


The fields beyond the village looked fresh after the rain. The path was no longer dusty; and Michael could see the hill and the farm. Nothing seemed changed. The hillside was still terraced with the stone retaining walls, and squinting against the sunlight, he could see the one he had climbed across. Perhaps the olive trees had grown slightly but they appeared as identical to his memory of them as the mountains along the horizon. He had no trouble in finding the pit where the gun had been. There was still a depression in the earth and strangely enough, or perhaps not so strangely, there were the remains of sandbags. He was showing them to Ruth, and pushing at one with his foot. Gray sand trickled across the toe of his shoe.

The two times he had been here before slid back and forth in his thoughts. They were not as vivid to him as they once had been; but he was satisfied and a little bemused, and it was only when he raised his hand and pointed and said, "That's where we came in, the two of us—right there," that his heart leaped or stirred and that the ragged cheer which had greeted him returned with a quick faintness to his ear.

They were climbing the hill together. He was helping Ruth over one of the walls. She was slightly out of breath. Color was in her cheeks. She was smiling up at him, holding his hand. She was wearing a flannel skirt and white blouse and a pink cardigan, rubber-soled shoes for the walk. She looked suddenly radiant to him, and young, and yet mature, the small lines creasing around her mouth and eyes. A feeling of pride came to him. Momentarily it seemed as if they were both motionless, or somehow balanced, tugging against each other—a man and his wife climbing a hillside like children.

"Come on, old lady," he said, affection and humor in his voice. She laughed. Then she was standing level with him.

"You wouldn't believe how muddy this place can get in the early spring," he said. "There's hardly a trace of the rain, is there?"

"No, hardly a trace . . . It must seem rather odd to you, Mike —being here with me like this."

"Very odd—and extremely nice. It's a little as if I could see us from up above, as if I could see the whole hillside instead of just this part of it. Kind of a queer perspective."

"Where was the old Italian, when you reached him?" she asked.

"Up there—between us and the farm. I remember crouching under this tree, watching the shells hit below the hilltop. Very black. The smoke was black when it lifted."

She seemed to be measuring the distance. "I didn't realize they were so close. . . . You took an awful risk, didn't you? Were you thinking of that?"

"I guess I wasn't thinking any too clearly. I thought he was badly hurt—that he needed help, that once I'd come this far I couldn't very well go back without him. It's sort of hard to reconstruct—but this is where I made my dash through the mud."

"Were you scared, Mike?"

He smiled. "You bet I was scared. I was scared to death."

They went past the spot where the old man had lain. Michael glanced over his shoulder toward the ravine. Then they were on the slope leading directly to the farm. He saw the yellowish enclosure of the barnyard and two figures working inside with pitchforks, cutting into a pile of hay heaped against a stake in the center. A woman came abruptly from the house. She stood shading her eyes. It must be Angelina's mother, Michael thought. She was hurrying forward.

She stopped again. Michael saw her eyes searching him. She seemed much older, her hair more white than gray, the large frame more stooped. Then she spread her arms wide, her elbows slightly bent. "*Ecco il capitano!*" she cried in astonishment.

Michael grinned. "Yes, the captain," he repeated. "How are you, signora?"

"Well—" she said, "I am well—" and something he could not understand. She was looking at Ruth.

"This is my wife, signora."

"Ah—yes, your wife! I thought it might be your wife when I saw you." She took Ruth's hand and Michael's. "I cannot believe it!" she exclaimed to him. "It is hardly possible to believe! . . . You have come from where, captain—from the village?"

"From the village and from a long way—from home."

"It is such a surprise!" she said. "It has been so many years! But I do not forget. Only for an instant I am not sure, because I cannot believe it! I speak too fast for you, Captain—too fast?"

"No, signora—only a little—"

"I remember you speak in Italian, I remember it well . . . So much has happened, so many things. You have heard—have you heard in the village about my father?"

"Yes, they told me, signora—"

"That he is dead—yes, he is dead. It was his heart, did they tell you? Here in his heart. How he would have liked to see you, to be here—but there are only three of us now. My oldest son is in the Army. Only the youngest is here. Gino. You remember Gino—and Angelina is in Naples, I think that is where she is . . . So many things. But wait! I must tell the others." She turned. Michael saw the two men approaching. "Look!" she called, "Look! . . . It is the captain!"

Angelina's father was less altered than her mother. The grip of his hand was still strong, the expression in the dark eyes still a mixture of cordiality and reserve. Michael did not recognize Gino at all. He was taller than his father and very handsome; but suddenly there was a suggestion of Angelina in him, an erectness of posture, a certain grace—a faint suggestion that remained when they went into the house and when the young man stood off to one side in the shadows by the stove.

"You will have some coffee," the mother was saying. "See, I will make it right away. The water is heated." She addressed herself to Ruth. "It is so nice to meet you, signora. We have talked of the captain many times."

Ruth smiled and nodded and Michael said, "My wife only speaks a few words of Italian."

"It makes no difference," the mother said. "You can tell her what we say. Gino will bring us the cups . . . No, not those, Gino. Not those. The ones behind you on the shelf."

The young man was taking down the cups. They were dusty. Signora Nardi was rinsing them off and drying them, setting them carefully on a tray; and Michael was answering questions about America.

"You have children, Captain?"

"Two children, signora. A boy and a girl. They are at home. They are not as old as yours—"

"We wondered about you, where you were, and about your home—but we never thought we would see you! It makes me remember the day when you were here before, the last time, when you brought all the presents, the one for Angelina as well." She hesitated and then added hastily, "She was very much pleased. She was with us for a little while, after the war ended, and for my father's funeral—but then we lost her again. . . . Now and then she writes, and we know she is alive." Signora Nardi frowned. "I had an address for her—but it is not the right one. A letter came back from there. She has moved, I suppose. It has happened before. She will write again and tell us where she is. I do not think she is happy—but perhaps I am wrong . . . She was not happy here—only when she was a child."

The father did not say anything. The subject seemed to be closed.

They were drinking the coffee from cups that were rimmed with a slender border of gold, worn thin, almost entirely faded— fine china, though, nearly transparent. A wedding gift possibly, Michael thought, preserved over the years. He recalled Ruth bringing the cut-glass bowl into the living room at home, when they were about to celebrate with Harold Stanley's Scotch the prospect of the trip. It did not strike him forcibly that he would be unable to find Angelina. He did not want to complicate his memory of her, he decided, or to project it beyond the limits in which it was confined. He was not surprised that there was no address. The references to Angelina had made him feel almost ashamed in front of Ruth; but she had not understood them, and the family would not consider his reasons for visiting them unusual. They would have been offended if they had known he had been nearby and had not come. Wasn't it natural for him to bring his wife to meet them? Weren't the old stirrings and desires and enigmas finally put to rest?

Yet as he went outside, as he was saying goodbye, he won-dered if he would ever tell Ruth about Angelina Nardi—and if the village would ever appear to him again as it had the previous evening.

"You will give my wishes to the others in the family," he said. "We do not have time to see them all. But I wanted to see— especially you."

"Yes, Captain, I will do that," the father said.

"And we will send you something from America—for Christ-mas."

"It is not necessary, Captain—"

Michael smiled. "To me it is necessary." They shook hands then, rather solemnly all around. Halfway down the hill Michael glanced toward the farm. The men had gone, but Angelina's mother was still standing where they had left her near the house.

He was carrying the suitcase toward the Millecento. Ruth was already in the car. Her head was lowered. She would be studying the map he had given her in the lobby. He was thinking of Angelina's uncle, the one who had worn the gold chain across his vest. The uncle had visited the albergo while they were finishing packing. Michael had gone down the stairs to greet him. "I just want to say a welcome to you, Captain. Signor Portano told me you were here. I am sorry the others are out working, I could not reach them. I would be working myself— except that I have a little lumbago, here in the leg . . . You remember the rooster, Captain. Ah! How we have laughed about the rooster! . . ." And he was also thinking of the proprietor. The cognac had not been on the bill. They had argued pleasantly about it. They had agreed that one brandy should belong to Portano and one to Michael. That way they would each have bought a drink for the other—

"Signore! *Capitano!*"

A hand touched Michael's elbow. He turned sharply. He was staring at Angelina's brother.

"One moment please, Captain," Gino was saying in low, urgent Italian. "Can I speak with you?"

Michael put the suitcase down. "Of course, Gino. Certainly—"

"I hear you say you are going to Naples, Captain."

"Yes. Yes, to Naples—"

Gino's brow was deeply creased. He was holding a cap, twisting it. "I am much concerned about my sister, Captain—about Angelina. I think she is in trouble."

"In trouble, Gino?"

"I feel it. I felt it when the letter came back from the place where she was."

"But your mother says this has happened before—"

"Yes, I know," Gino said quickly, twisting his cap. "But . . ." He flushed. "I know what my sister does, Captain—how she lives. I have heard my father tell my mother. Even she cannot disagree. . . . She says it is a way to live—you understand? She blames it on the war—my father on other things. They do not talk about it often, but they would be very much disturbed if they thought that Angelina is in trouble—with the police."

"With the police— You believe this, Gino?"

"I'm not sure, Captain—not sure . . . but I have thought, I cannot help thinking that Angelina is trying to hide. In my mind I see her trying to hide."

"You have no real reason, Gino. It doesn't mean—"

"It may mean nothing—yes, that is true. Angelina may be all right. She has been all right before, but . . . I have not seen my sister for four years, Captain, and this time—this time I think my mother feels it also, that Angelina is in trouble. She would not say it to you. She is too proud." He paused and brought out a slip of paper. "Look, Captain, I have written out the old address in Naples. I have copied it from the envelope. I have not told my mother or anyone. Naturally I haven't mentioned the police— and I haven't said I was coming to see you. I made an excuse." He held the address toward Michael. "Will you take this, Captain? Please—will you go there?"

"I may not have time, Gino. I—"

"Please, Captain . . . Please."

"If I have time, Gino, I will try—"

"It is a big building. Angelina lived upstairs. She wrote she could see down to the street. If you go there someone may know what has happened. It would not take long, just to ask."

"No," Michael said, holding the address. "I suppose it wouldn't—"

"And if you find Angelina, if you see her, you will tell her to write my mother?"

"If I see her—yes, of course I will tell her that."

Gino drew himself up. "I would go myself, but I have no money—and I would not know how to leave . . . You will not forget, Captain?"

"No, Gino. I won't forget—"

"You promise?"

"All right, Gino . . . Yes, I promise."

Michael walked to the car with the suitcase; the soft, slightly crumpled paper inside his pocket. Ruth's head was raised when he opened the door. "What was that all about?" she asked. "That was the boy from the farm, wasn't it? What did he want?"

"He was worried about his sister, darling. He thinks she may be in some kind of trouble."

"His sister?"

"She was with the family when I was first here. . . . Then she went away—off on her own. They think she's in Naples now, somewhere in Naples."

"You didn't tell me about a sister, Mike. Why does he think she's in trouble?"

"Well, apparently she's moved from the place where she was living. A letter was returned from there . . . They haven't had any news for some time. The brother—Gino—has some sort of notion she's gotten involved with the police, but I hardly think so."

"With the police! . . . Why with the police?"

"I don't know exactly why—"

"Was she ever in trouble with the police before?"

"No, he didn't say that . . . It's just because he's worried, I think—and because, since the war, she's lived here and there—I guess in not any too orthodox a style."

"I see. . . . How old is this girl?"

"About twenty-eight or so. Twenty-eight or nine."

"Was she pretty?"

"Yes, she was quite pretty. I don't know what she looks like now."

"Why didn't you tell me about her, Mike? You never mentioned a girl of eighteen or nineteen. I'm sure you didn't."

"Well, it was a much bigger family then. There was another son, he's in the Army now—and there were all the relatives."

"What was the girl's name?"

"Angelina . . . Maybe you heard the mother mention her name up at the farm—"

"I wasn't conscious of it," Ruth said. "You went to the farm the second time you came here, didn't you—"

"Yes—"

"Was Angelina there?"

"No, she'd already left—for parts unknown."

"Did she have anything to do with your coming back, Mike?"

"No . . . I wanted to see the whole family, not just one of them." The car had started forward.

"What do you intend to do about her?" Ruth asked quietly.

"I'm not sure, darling. Gino gave me the old address. He asked me to look it up, to have her get in touch with her family. I said I'd do that, if I had the chance. But I don't really know what I could do, if she is in trouble. If that were true, she'd hardly leave a trail to follow."

"I can go with you, can I—when you go to this old address?"

"Sure, if you'd like—"

The Millecento moved through the square, past the headquarters house. At the crest of the hill beyond, he remembered to look toward the village again, but he did not see it as clearly as he had before. A sense of alarm moved inside him. For the next mile or so, and in the silence, it would not subside.

# Part
# THREE

THEY drove through Caserta and took the road leading away from the great gray façade of the King's palace toward Naples. They had passed the field where the Nissen huts had been before Michael fully realized it. The café where he had celebrated his birthday slipped by them. The town itself seemed shabby. It wasn't until they were beyond it that he remembered how he had kept the ring for Angelina in his desk, how often he had pulled open the drawer to examine the jade stone.

He wished that he did not have her address, that he had not felt it necessary to evade Ruth's questions. The lie, or lies, he had told her might be insignificant; yet they rankled in his mind. How nice it would have been to have had the village entirely behind them, to have seen it just as they had, without changing any of their stay except for the last few minutes. He had expected, or hoped that Ruth would be a little more anxious to share some of his memories; but the memories in themselves had not failed him. They had been there, ready to receive him. He would remember the terrace in the rain and Ruth with him on the hillside, and here and now those two times would have been completely perfect, if only he didn't have Gino's slip of paper in his pocket. He had the feeling that he had climbed a mountain peak, that he had stood away up in the clouds, and returned to find his ascent not truly accomplished . . . Well, he would postpone considering his promise to Gino. Probably nothing would come of it—probably nothing would be required of him.

The wide arc of the bay was flawlessly blue when they saw it from above. There was the water front and the white tiers of the city mounting from it, and Vesuvius off to the left. There were the cliffs along the distant peninsula jutting out toward the silhouette of Capri and, in back of the cliffs, ranges of higher hills, their summits hazy and nearly as blue as the sea. Ruth gave a little gasp.

"How beautiful, Mike—how marvelously beautiful!"

"Better than a small village?" he asked lightly.

"Well—don't you think so?"

"I'll admit it has its points. I guess this is one of the finest sights in the world."

She did not speak for a few seconds. Then she said: "I'm sorry about the village, Mike. I was a disappointment to you there, wasn't I?"

"You shouldn't say that, honey."

"I think I should . . . I keep thinking about what you said about special places, about what went wrong yesterday—and how we seem so close to each other at times, and then far apart."

"Do we seem far apart to you now?"

"Not particularly now—but I keep thinking about this girl—the sister. How did you meet her? With the rest of the family?"

"Yes, they were all in the farm together, the morning the old man was caught out in the open."

"She saw you from the farm? She saw you with her what—her grandfather?"

"They all saw me, I think. Angelina's mother, her father, the two other children. They were all debating whether or not to leave, you know, and the old man ran out first and fell—and when the firing stopped they all came trooping down and took old Giuseppe back into town. . . . But it was Angelina who found me later in the day at headquarters. She came as a sort of delegate from the family, to invite me up to the banquet they'd set out. She spoke English—really quite well. She said she'd learned it from a cousin who'd been in the United States."

"You talked with her quite a lot then."

"On the way to the banquet—and for a little while when it ended, before I left and drove back to where I was stationed, that place by the road I showed you." He hesitated, maneuvering past a pair of horse-drawn carts on the level thoroughfare stretching toward the Via Roma. "I guess one of the reasons I never mentioned Angelina to you, darling—was because she had a wild idea she wanted me to take her along when I left. Away from the village. To Naples, or near it—near enough. That I'd fix things up for her, a place to live—"

"With you?" Ruth said. "Is that what you mean, Mike?"

"Yes . . . That was the idea she had." He glanced at her, expecting to find her face flushed and angry, but there was no sign of anger. Her eyes seemed opaque. He could not define the expression in them.

"And you refused?"

"Yes—I refused her."

"Why?" Ruth asked.

"Well, darling, I don't mean to imply I was any shining example of faithfulness at the time—but it might have been, it might just have been then, because of you."

"It might have been."

"You don't believe it? . . . You think I'm making it up?"

"No, Mike . . . Only it puzzles me why it's taken you so long to tell me that."

"I guess I was afraid to, Ruth. I was afraid you might misunderstand."

"Why, if it was so perfectly cut and dried?"

"Well, you know how it is. You could have invented all kinds of different interpretations."

"Possibly I might have . . . You could have arranged for this place for her to be with you? Would it have been difficult?"

"No, not too hard. I guess I could have fixed it up."

"Others were doing the same thing, I imagine."

"Yes, others were—"

"I don't suppose I thought too much about it," she said. "I mean it didn't occur to me—that you wouldn't come back to me and the children when the war was over."

"That didn't occur to me either."

"Did you think—did you think she might be in the village this time, Mike?"

"No, darling. I didn't. I didn't at all."

"But you wanted to see her the other time, the time in between."

"I thought of seeing her then, Ruth." He smiled. "Only she was gone."

They were entering the Via Roma. The street seemed narrower and more confused than when he had last seen it, despite the absence of military traffic: the clogged, bumper-to-bumper lines of heavy trucks, staff cars, jeeps, starting their convoys from the port. Then the Via Roma had seemed as wide as New York's Fifth Avenue. Momentarily he remembered the sound of a tank's tracks turning, biting into the pavement, a random sound, shredding off—

"Did you ever think of what I might be doing when you were away?" Ruth asked. "How lonely I might become?"

"Yes, of course."

"Did you ever think I'd do anything foolish—myself?"

"No, darling, nothing very foolish."

"How long ago it seems," she said. "Almost as if we were different people."

"We were a lot younger—"

"Ten years younger. More than that in the beginning. . . . Well, I suppose I'm glad you told me about your Angelina, Mike."

"Hardly mine," he said.

"No, hardly yours. That is true, isn't it?"

"It's completely true." But he was thinking about the ring in his desk drawer, and wondering if he should tell her about that; and then they had turned off the Via Roma and were in sight of the esplanade along the sea. The water shone brilliantly, a blue rectangle of it framed below the overhang of a tiled roof. "Don't worry about ten years ago," he told her, and when he looked at her again, she was smiling. It was a queer smile, he thought. It was surprisingly warm and intimate.

MICHAEL and Ruth walked into the Galleria Umberto. The glass dome, partly broken during the war, had long since been repaired and sunlight filtering down nearly two hundred feet cast its designs across the floor. They had entered through the arches fronting toward San Carlo, where they had gone to the opera the evening before. The spaciousness of the Galleria was reminiscent of the opera house; only here there were small expensive shops set into the walls—the shop where he had bought the ring. He glanced at it and went on toward the Via Roma, past the tables arranged outside a bar where troops, speaking many foreign languages, had sipped vermouth in the days when Naples had seen funneled through it the vast, heterogeneous assortment of the military. At this hour of the morning, however, men were drinking coffee at the tables. There was an air of leisurely business. An Italian naval officer in his uniform seemed somehow out of place.

They found the street address on the Via Azuni. Number thirty-five, the slip of paper had said. The façade of the building was grimy, almost black. A vendor, pushing a vegetable cart, momentarily blocked them. The cart was almost the width of the street. Michael noticed the flies on the vegetables. The doorway was high and cavernous. A trickle of greenish slime ran through it, through cracks in the uneven pavement leading back into an open court against which the four interior sides of the building were crowded. In one of the corners a stairway confronted them. They halted uncertainly and then climbed to an upper level, into a hall lit by a single window.

"I don't see an office or anything, or any names on the doors," Michael said.

"No. I should think it was fairly hopeless."

"We ought to try to find someone, I guess—and ask."

He saw the child then, a little boy in faded gray clothes, standing motionless, staring at them from the end of the hall.

"*Buon giorno,*" Michael called. "Hello."

The child did not move. Michael approached him.

"I won't hurt you," he said in Italian. "I am looking for someone. Maybe you can help me. I am an American."

The child continued to stare. The face seemed old to Michael and immeasurably sad. He remembered it suddenly, not this face in particular, but a duplicate—among the bands of children, foraging through Naples in wartime, scavenging, picking up cigarette butts, running through the military parking areas, making off with some item of loot, always pursued.

The child turned abruptly. A door banged shut but opened again. A woman appeared, the child watching from behind her.

"Yes? . . . You wish?"

"I am looking for someone who lived here," Michael said. "Signorina Nardi. Angelina Nardi. Do you know her—of her?"

"No," the woman said.

"You have been here for a long time—you and the little boy?"

"No, not a long time."

A second door opened and another woman appeared.

"What is the matter?" she asked.

"It is an American. He is looking for someone. Angelina Nardi."

"I have come from her family," Michael said. "I knew them during the war. They are not from Naples. They are worried because they have no news of her. They think she has moved from this address."

"Paula Massolino would know," the second woman said. "Paula Massolino knows everyone. I will call her."

"Can I go with you?"

"No, do not trouble, signore. I will only be a minute."

She disappeared where the hall cornered to the right. Michael could hear her wooden sandals mounting another flight of stairs. The little boy continued to stare at him. He was explaining his conversation to Ruth.

"It's a dreadful place, isn't it?" she said. "I don't envy anyone living here."

"There are worse places in Naples, Ruth—"

"It's awful," she said. "I hope we don't have to stay here long."

He offered the woman with the child a cigarette. She took it quickly. Incongruously he wondered if Angelina had ever had a child, and whether this woman had a husband. Probably she did. She was too suspicious for a prostitute. He lit the cigarette and offered one to Ruth.

"No, thank you," Ruth said.

The hall smelled of dust and dampness. In the winter, he thought, the stone would be cold.

"How old is the little boy?"

"Six. He is six."

"You have other children?"

"He is not mine," she answered. "I am his aunt. His mother is inside. She has a cough—you know, in her chest. Not tuberculosis, but a cough. I am looking after her while her husband is at work."

"I'm sorry," Michael said. "I hope she is soon better."

"In a few days, I think."

He remembered Angelina talking of the man with the huge expensive car. Tomorrow he and Ruth had planned to visit Capri. Then they would go on to Sorrento. He wondered how long the smell in the hall would stay with him. This was a wild errand, a senseless one.

He heard the clatter of the sandals on the stairs. Two women came round the corner, and another door opened. Someone else was peering out.

"This is not Paula Massolino," the one with the sandals announced breathlessly. "It is her sister. Paula was not in, but it does not matter . . . She knows Angelina Nardi. She has seen her—less than a week ago!"

The third woman was older than the other two, past middle age. She was shorter and more slender, her head thrusting forward above the bony shoulders. She was bursting with importance. "Yes, yes," she was saying. "Angelina Nardi! I know where she can be found. It is in the Vomero, in that section. I have friends who live nearby. I see them once a week, generally on Sunday. I saw Angelina last Sunday. Five days ago. Five days." She held up her hand, the fingers outstretched. "She was at a café, not far from the station for the funicular. You know the funicular, sir? You understand what I tell you?"

Michael was staring at her. "Yes," he answered. "I understand—"

"Good," the woman said. "Good!" She was describing the café. "I have seen Angelina there several times. Last Sunday I spoke to her. She was with another woman, someone from the café, I think. But she has made an attachment with a rich man."

"She told you that?"

The blue-veined lips parted in a grin. "Ah!—not in so many words. But I have seen the two of them. I hear they go to the café almost every evening. An old man, almost as old as me. A writer of books. A man named Gerald Newell. An American, like yourself. I have asked about him. I have heard she is living in his house. I have not seen it myself, but at the café they could tell you where it is. Very probably they would know—"

"But she was all right," Michael said. "She was all right, when you saw her—"

"Oh yes, certainly all right."

"Her family thought she might be in trouble—"

"Yes, I have heard just now about the family—but it is like Angelina. She would not think of her family. She never spoke of them in my presence. She was always very proud. Like a queen. Angelina Nardi always pretended to be like a queen, even when she was here. Last Sunday she did not want to recognize me. Maybe she was ashamed her friend was not with her. She said he had gone away for a day or so—maybe he has gone away for good." She laughed with sudden malice. "That is the only trouble Angelina Nardi would have—if he has gone away for good. You remember the name, sir . . . Newell, a rich American—"

A man was approaching them: a portly, but muscular man, his sleeves rolled up, his collar loose at the throat. "What's wrong?" he asked huskily.

"This American is looking for Angelina Nardi. You remember her. She lived in this building once—over on the other side."

"Ah yes—the tall girl, the one who put on airs. I was not one of her favorites."

The sister laughed again. "No, not one of her favorites. I know that well."

Michael noticed that a number of others had collected in the corridor, that they were coming forward: dark intense faces, moving along the walls. He could hear the footsteps, the sound of the cough through the open door. He had put his hand in his pocket, had brought out a bill. "Here—maybe you will take this. It's not very much—"

"If you wish, sir . . . If you wish, I could guide you to the café."

"No—that won't be necessary . . . I just wanted to have some news." The faces seemed to press toward him. He had turned away. Ruth was already on the stairs. He followed her, the voices rising all at once behind him: "An American—yes, an American . . . Angelina Nardi . . . It is most strange . . ."

The shrill sound of the woman's voice persisted with him as they crossed through the courtyard—the laughter, certain phrases: an old man, almost as old as me; a café with a green and white striped awning . . . But she was still in Naples; he could find her. It seemed an extraordinary discovery. Momentarily a sense of delight touched it, and something grotesque—the image of a woman selling flowers on a street corner in Rome. This woman with the bony neck and shoulders could be her twin. Or was he putting the two together and forgetting the first?

He was speaking to Ruth. They were passing the vegetable cart. Someone was arguing, juggling a handful of greens.

"Well, if you think you know where she is, what do you want to do—keep on looking?"

"Would you mind a great deal if I tried to finish it up, Ruth?

. . . I was thinking of my promise to Gino."

"Couldn't you write and say you've done this much, that she seems to be perfectly safe?"

"Yes, I could do that, but I wouldn't be positive. I wouldn't be doing all I could, do you think?" He remembered Gino twisting his cap, Gino immensely disturbed and embarrassed. He was obligated to the family. The words were partially honest.

"It's so sordid and messy," Ruth said. "At least that's how it appears to me . . . That little imbecile child—"

"How do you know he was an imbecile?"

"Oh, for Heaven's sake—all right, he was a child prodigy."

They had entered the Via Roma. Ruth halted.

"Well—are you going, or aren't you?" she asked.

He smiled suddenly. The question seemed like such a simplification, as if she had punctured a balloon.

"I don't see what's so funny," she said. "I don't see anything funny at all."

"It just seemed a little silly to me that we should be making so much fuss about all this, on a nice day."

"I'm not making a fuss, Mike. I'm only telling you that I find it extremely sordid and unattractive. I don't find it in the slightest bit funny."

"You asked to come with me, Ruth."

"I know I did. I know that perfectly well . . . But I'm not going any further—not another step."

"You don't have to, darling."

"You mean you've decided not to go yourself then—"

"No, I didn't say that." He continued to smile faintly, as if appealing to her.

"All right then, Mike—all right . . . What do you want me to do—wait all afternoon in the hotel?"

"Darling, I'll only be gone a little while," he said; but the statement seemed vaguely obscene, as if some double meaning would leap out at her. The hint of humor faded from his voice "I just want to stop at the café, make a few inquiries—"

"And find *her*," Ruth said.

"She's not likely to be there now. The woman said in the evening—"

"Or find some old man who's keeping her, some jaded old man who favors a prostitute . . . Well, give them my regards, darling. Keep your promise . . . Only to me the whole thing is—is more than a little peculiar."

She stalked away from him.

"You want me to walk back to the hotel with you?"

"No," she answered over her shoulder. "No, thanks very much. I can find it quite easily."

She walked along the Via Roma, remembering his smile. Why had he smiled? What irony had occurred to him? She herself felt degraded . . . Mike knew this girl during the war, and she turned into a prostitute, and he spent the whole morning looking for her . . . No, I'm not prudish, Ruth thought. It isn't a joke.

Had he known she was a prostitute during the war? Or had he seen her then simply as a young girl, a young woman (the Italians matured so fast) eager to fling herself into the outside world with the first man able to accept her invitation? Possibly that was true; perhaps he still remembered her in that guise . . . He had refused her. I *must* believe that, Ruth thought—and tried to picture him smiling naively, going toward the café, wherever it was, up there on the hill, where the sunlight made the buildings seem as white as chalk—Michael saying courteously, "I wonder if you know a friend of mine . . ." Maybe it was a joke after all. Michael exchanging pleasantries with an old roué— a writer—like an artist with his model. That was a nicer way of describing it—more European . . . I wonder what Mike would say to such a person? . . . He had been perfectly willing to have her accompany him this morning, hadn't he? She had objected. She turned abruptly, her eyes searching among the passers-by, but he was no longer in sight. It would be pointless to follow after him now. In a little while he would return to the hotel. Of course he would.

She walked down toward the sea. The gray walls of an ancient castle jutted out from the esplanade. She was looking at them and then up toward the Vomero where the buildings had the white of absolute purity . . . An Italian prostitute—

and a brash young second lieutenant. Did they have anything in common? Certainly not! Ruth thought. I would never for an instant think of looking for him, no matter what the circumstances. He was not even a passing fancy. Am I jealous of Mike because his own experience might have been better than mine? How absurd!—yet she was thinking, I wish we hadn't gone to the village. That girl saw the rescue, didn't she? I wish he hadn't told me—or did I ask the question? It's curious, this is the first time that fact has really impressed me: she was there in the farm, watching him, and I was not.

How had they said goodbye? Was it in the dark? Oh God, she thought, I'm suggesting all kinds of things. Nothing evil is happening today. Mike and I have quarreled with each other, that's all. When he comes back to the hotel, he'll make amends as he always has before. He was never a very good liar. He wouldn't lie to me about anything important.

She looked at the glimmer of sunshine across the bay. How serene it was. There was a seaside restaurant below her, at the very edge of the water. She and Michael might have lunch there together; and yet she could hear their voices disagreeing outside the squalor of the tenement, disagreeing in other places— and the squalor seemed somehow identified with darkness, with the night when she had been with the second lieutenant whose name was Arnold Kent. She felt suddenly angry again—and confused—and realized that she must look rather foolish standing by the stone balustrade, all alone . . . When would Michael come back to her, she wondered—how soon?

He had not told Ruth that Angelina might be alone, Michael knew; but on the funicular the knowledge had not weighed against him. He had tried to convince himself that he should not be accused. He had not deserted Ruth—he had no idea of deserting her. Angelina was not waiting for him; they hadn't planned a secret meeting. Tomorrow he and Ruth would continue their trip. This afternoon they would arrange to do something nice—an afternoon's excursion.

Now, however, as he stood in front of the café, he was aware of guilt—and foreboding. I should turn back, he thought, I really shouldn't go any further—and then: she will have changed a great deal in ten years. Suppose I don't recognize her. Suppose she has grown fat, and middle-aged, and doesn't recognize me.

He glanced swiftly at the only sidewalk table that was occupied: a quartet, two men, two women, drinking coffee. The women had broad, open faces. They were not looking at him. All at once he was conscious of danger, as if it were waiting for him here and inside, as if it came from Gino's voice in the village square, as if it arose somehow from the village, from an old man lying in a field, from a girl smoking a cigarette on a terrace— from a past that was suddenly out of reach. Perhaps, he thought illogically, this isn't the right café.

A man was behind the counter inside. Michael stepped toward him. The rest of the room was empty.

"You are the owner?"

"Sì, il padrone."

"I am looking for an address," Michael was saying. "The address of a man named Gerald Newell. Do you know him?"

"Yes—certainly. Signor Newell. He is often here."

"Do you know where he lives?"

"Yes, of course. It is only a few minutes' walk."

"You could direct me?"

"If you like . . . I can almost show you the house from the door, where the street turns—"

"He has been here today?"

"No, not today. Usually he is here in the evening."

"Is there—do you know if there is usually a young woman with him? Someone named Angelina Nardi?"

The café owner grinned. "Ah yes—Signorina Nardi." He gave the word "signorina" a slightly derogatory inflection. He came from behind the counter. "She has been with him for some time, you know—"

"So I have heard," Michael said. "If you will just direct me, I won't bother you any further."

"But it is no bother, signore . . . Look, like this . . ."

They were in the doorway. The four at the table had raised their eyes. The owner was pointing with a short, stubby finger. "I am very grateful," Michael was saying, "very grateful to you."

He hurried into the street, feeling the embarrassment again—perhaps he had blushed. All five were watching him, he thought. For the first time he felt ashamed of his search, hurrying along the street like this to a stranger's house. He had the sensation that he was destroying Angelina, making her ludicrous—a middle-aged woman who had made an easy conquest. He should never have mentioned her to Ruth. He should have kept the whole matter private. A note to Gino would have sufficed. Angelina was not wanted by the police, was not in trouble. Of that much Michael was reasonably sure. What compelled him to go on?

He paused. This was the house the café owner had indicated. The walls were white and decorated with a border of green shrubs. Ruth would be interested in the shrubs—an incongruous thought. He mounted a shallow flight of steps and entered the hallway. He felt his heart pounding. Did he want Angelina destroyed, he wondered? Did he want the old memory of her obliterated? Would it make him feel any less guilty, if there was only a trace of recognition, a few casual words? Or was there still inside him the hope that she would be alone? He thought of the ring. He was looking at the double row of mailboxes. It

must be an apartment building. Had the café owner mentioned
an apartment? Michael's eyes fastened on the name—Gerald
Newell, the small letters so decorously inscribed.

He crossed the hallway. This would be the entrance. The
number in the white enameled oval above the door coincided.
He pressed his finger against the bell. He could hear it tinkling
with a soft, muted sound. The door was very thick. Loops of
wrought iron extended from the hinges. Michael waited. He
pressed his finger again on the miniature round button of the
bell. For some reason he thought of home. The bell at home
made a buzzing noise in the kitchen. You could not hear it from
outside.

Someone was approaching. It sounded like a woman: high
heels crossing a marble floor; but the steps seemed short and
rapid. He could not identify them with Angelina. They sounded
more like those of the woman in the tenement—only they were
more brisk, more impatient, more assured.

The door moved inward. It was half ajar.

"Yes—what is it?" The question was in Italian. Michael had
the impression of effeteness, of elegance, of the slender, rather
diminutive figure of a man, a dusky light outlining his high forehead.

"You are Mr. Newell?" Michael asked. He could not tell how
strong his disappointment was. His heart was beating violently.

"Yes, that is my name," Gerald said in English. "Who are you
then? . . . I'm afraid you have me at a disadvantage. We have
met before?"

"No—not before, Mr. Newell. I'm sorry. I don't mean to
intrude, but I am looking—for someone I knew a long time ago.
During the war . . . a girl named Angelina Nardi—"

"You are looking for Angelina Nardi?" The high forehead had
creased into a frown.

"I heard she might possibly be at this address," Michael said.
He had the distorted fragment of an idea that he was selling
insurance, that a prospective client was refusing him admittance.

"Who told you that?"

"It's a long story, Mr. Newell . . . I—maybe if you'd let
me in for a few minutes I could tell you a little of it."

"Yes—certainly, come in," Gerald said. He stood back. "Who on earth told you that Angelina Nardi was in my apartment?"

"She isn't then—"

"No, she is not—she is not here." He advanced ahead of Michael into the dining room. Michael saw the rich brocade of the curtains, the inlaid table, the chandelier, the figurines on the sideboard. Gerald turned and spread his hands. "As you can see for yourself, she is not here."

"Do you know her? Do you know her well?"

"Yes, I know her—quite well. But she is not here now."

"I don't doubt you, Mr. Newell—"

"She comes to visit me," Gerald said. "You understand what I mean to say. We are men of the world, are we not, Mr.—Mr.— I'm afraid you didn't give me your name—"

"Allen," Michael said. "Michael Allen."

"And you say you knew her—long ago . . . During the war."

"Yes, at that time—"

"Well then, Mr. Allen, we will perhaps go out to my patio— and you can tell me how you were able—how you were able to trace Angelina Nardi to this address. . . . It is really amazing! . . . It interests me very much." He was opening one of the glass panels, his back to Michael. "Are you by any chance, Mr. Allen?—no, I will phrase it differently, I will lead up to it . . . Were you a soldier once, Mr. Allen?"

"Yes," Michael answered, his eyes on the thin shoulders, on the white silk of the shirt, on the thin gray fingers clasping the brass handle, jerking it down. "Yes, I was."

"And did you by any chance once give to Angelina Nardi a ring?"

"Yes, I once gave her a ring—" The panel swung out. Gerald seemed to teeter against it. Then he was standing on the floor of the patio, politely gesturing with his arm. "Don't be surprised, Mr. Allen. You see, I have kind of a sixth sense. Perhaps you could call it that. I thought that was who you might be. It came into my mind. Angelina has told me about you."

"She has told you—?"

"In the course of our conversations . . . Here, we will sit

down, shall we?—you on the chaise, and I will use this—this chair." Gerald smiled. "Don't look so surprised, Mr. Allen—don't look so surprised."

Gerald's legs were angled backward, so that only the toes of his shoes touched the rust-colored squares of tile. One knee jiggled constantly while he spoke and listened; but he seemed oblivious of it, as if the jiggling came from habit, or from concentration, and not from nerves. He sat very upright. A blue scarf was knotted above the V in the silk collar. "You must excuse my appearance," he had said. "I'm afraid I must look a bit informal. These are my working clothes—a shirt, a pair of corduroy slacks . . . I was on the point of finishing a chapter when you rang . . ."

Michael watched him warily, with growing repugnance, and yet with a peculiar sense of fascination. The jiggling knee had an almost hypnotic effect, an unhealthy quality—vaguely sensual, insinuating. "So you went to your little village," Gerald was saying. "Yes, yes—I see. I can imagine you going there. I can imagine how you must have felt . . . Nostalgia." He waved his cigarette holder airily. "A romantic concept, isn't it? . . . And then you came here and began looking for Angelina Nardi. How extraordinary that the trail should lead to me. . . . May I ask how long you are staying in Naples, Mr. Allen?"

"Only for another day. We plan to take a trip to Capri tomorrow, and then move on. We—"

"We, Mr. Allen—*we?*"

"Yes, my wife—and myself."

"Your wife, Mr. Allen . . . did you say your wife?"

"Yes—my wife. Is there anything startling in that?"

"No—of course not . . . Only you didn't mention her before. I had assumed—well, I had assumed you might be here—on business of some kind, traveling."

"No—on a vacation."

"On a vacation . . . Yes, I understand. Your wife went back to the village with you?"

"Yes—"

"And you've been married for some time?"

"For seventeen years."

"Seventeen years! Indeed—indeed. This is not in the nature of a honeymoon then, is it?"

"No, I wouldn't say it was quite that."

Gerald crossed his knees, the jiggling ceasing abruptly. He chuckled. "I must apologize to you, Mr. Allen. I had the strangest idea when you came into my flat, that—well, that perhaps you were looking for Angelina Nardi for other than family reasons, if you know what I mean."

Michael flushed, and Gerald went on, leaning forward, "Please, you mustn't be offended, Mr. Allen. It was a natural conclusion to draw—you will admit. A soldier comes back looking for a girl. He goes to a great deal of trouble to locate an address. He finds it—and what else? Perhaps he says to himself, rather a decrepit older man—how can such a man interest a woman? Well, you see what I mean, Mr. Allen . . . I thought for a moment we might be competitors."

Michael contrived a smile. A feeling like sickness had come over him. He was aware of evil, of listening to his own voice instead of Gerald's—listening to lies he himself had half disguised. The man was a charlatan; yet the opinion seemed self-induced, as if it were reflected against himself. I hoped she would be alone, he thought. That was the only reason I came here; the rest was all a feeble excuse. This man represents in his own queer fashion what I was forcing myself to find: Michael Allen, the fraud . . . No, he thought, that can't be it—that's as false as a middle-aged woman with a shrill laugh. I only wanted to find her, to see her again. I would have been satisfied simply to have found her *safe*.

The jocular, bantering voice continued—the polite rebuttals. Gerald was saying, "Of course I can understand your viewpoint, Mr. Allen. It's a little like the Chinese philosophy, isn't it? You save someone's life—no, please don't try to discredit what you did—and you feel a sense of duty to the family as a whole. A pity you won't be in Naples longer. Where are you stopping, Mr. Allen—may I ask?"

Michael gave him the name of the hotel.

"Not at the Excelsior?"

"No, not at the Excelsior. We couldn't quite afford—"

"Don't bother to explain, Mr. Allen. I really think the other is just as nice. A bit old-fashioned, but comfortable. I myself have stayed there once or twice—in years gone by. A pity I can't arrange something for you while you're in town, though. I'm well acquainted in Naples—but possibly the idea would seem a little fantastic."

"Fantastic, Mr. Newell?"

"Under the circumstances, I mean. Your wife—well, would know that I have encountered—shall we say encountered Angelina Nardi? . . . She would know that, wouldn't she, Mr. Allen? I mean you wouldn't keep it a secret from her, would you?"

"No," Michael said.

"I mean if I popped up, let's say at your hotel tonight or tomorrow, you'd have to give your wife some clue as to who I was, wouldn't you? She might easily take offense. She might think—I don't know what—about *me*. Isn't that true?"

"I don't think Ruth would take offense, Mr. Newell."

"Women are curious creatures, though. Sometimes they are amused, and sometimes not. Sometimes they aren't very broad-minded. I mean it's rather a delicate situation." Gerald laughed. "I mean your wife might think me quite a reprobate."

"No, Ruth isn't like that—"

"Well then—perhaps we should leave it open, Mr. Allen. If you would like a cocktail with an aging member of the literary profession, give me a call. I would like very much to meet your wife. It would give me extreme pleasure. I will leave it up to you —for you and your wife to decide."

"All right, Mr. Newell. Yes—thank you." Michael stood up. The conversation had become too devious for him to follow precisely—a maze of conflicting words, conflicting motives. He felt defeated and eager to leave. The writer had no intention of coming to the hotel, he decided; yet the fact seemed to have no real bearing on what they had been discussing.

They had started in from the patio. For a moment Michael imagined Angelina elegantly gowned, seated at the inlaid table under the chandelier, her arms bare, her head raised in an expression of disdain. But she was lifeless, he realized with a sense of horror, she seemed lifeless. She was like a huge doll with glass eyes, like a magnified distortion of the figurines on the sideboard.

"That is where I write," Gerald said, as they were passing the bedroom. "That is my little desk over in the corner. Not much light, but enough." He paused. "You know, Mr. Allen, you haven't asked me a great deal about Angelina. You haven't particularly asked me how she was. You will want to send a note to the family, I presume."

"Yes, I will send them a letter."

Gerald took his elbow and smiled. "She is exquisite," he said almost in a whisper. "She is as beautiful as ever." He opened the heavy door and followed Michael out into the hall.

HE watched until Michael had turned from the side street into the wider avenue beyond. Then he went quickly toward the avenue himself. He saw Michael go past the café, saw him hail a taxi. The taxi disappeared. Gerald began to hum softly, without consciousness of it. He felt tremendously excited. The interview had been eminently successful. He congratulated himself. Only for a moment had he been caught unaware.

So this was Angelina's hero! How amazing—how unexpected! —the sudden premonition that here was the soldier, the suitor, the lover. It was obvious they had been lovers. The embarrassment, the inarticulateness were additional proof. But the wife—what did she know, or suspect? How much had she been told, how much had been hidden from her? Probably she had been shopping this morning—or at some absurd place like a beauty parlor, a Neopolitan beauty parlor, getting her hair waved and her nails manicured—while her husband went prowling about, looking for an address. Probably they had arranged to meet for lunch. "I'm sorry, dear, I'm a little late. I was out walking around. I forgot the time . . ." It was vastly amusing . . . "No, Ruth isn't like that." Ruth—that was her name. What color was her hair? Did she have a pinched face—did she whine and complain? Or was she fragile and innocent? How was she enjoying the vacation in Italy?

Gerald re-entered his apartment. So the soldier went back to his village, he thought—to the scene of his glory, the scene of his crime, his adultery. He went there with his wife; he had admitted that. Fascinating! What illusions did the soldier have, what erroneous concepts of heroism? What boasts had he made? How much did the wife understand? And hadn't he, Gerald, been able to contrive—within the twinkling of an eye—the perfect irony, the perfect negation for the soldier's return? The man obviously detested him. At the end of his long search, he had found not the girl who had kept his ring, but instead—

Gerald nearly laughed. I never once believed I would meet him, he thought; but if I had spent months devising the encounter, I could not have done better. I even had him sit here on Angelina's chaise. That was a stroke of genius.

He almost wished that Angelina had been present; but now that he was home again, now that the pattern of their life was re-established, she would not appear until late afternoon. This morning he had told her he would spend the day writing. When the doorbell had rung he had thought Angelina might be coming back for some reason or other; but it had seemed unlikely that she would have forgotten her key. He had gone to the door, he remembered, thinking that the page in the typewriter was half filled, that if it *was* Angelina she could have observed that he had been busy. A blank sheet of paper could be revealing. Any words were better than none.

He lit a cigarette. Suppose she had been here, though—suppose it had been evening instead of noon. Would I have been up to that, he wondered? Could I have managed an equal subtlety? He half closed his eyes; and it was as if something had caught at his sense of victory and it had tripped. Wait, he thought—wait just a bit, try to remember all that was said . . . But for a moment he could not, and saw in abrupt contrast Angelina rising, walking across the patio. "I will answer the door, Gerry—do not bother." He heard the door opening—and then only a gasp of surprise.

"What is it, my dear?"

He imagined himself calling again: "Who is it? . . . Who is in the hall?"—and could see himself intruding on the quiet, rapturous embrace, inadvertently intruding, holding a glass of vermouth.

I was crazy to say she was beautiful, he thought. I couldn't resist. It was my one mistake . . . Or were there others? His triumph had seemed so complete. He had imagined the soldier retreating, disillusioned, in confusion. He had seen him go by the café, without pausing to make further inquiry, and the retreat had seemed final. But what had they told him at the café? Had they given him another clue? No, hardly that. The disappointment had shown itself too sharply—and if they had known at the café where Angelina was at this hour, Michael Allen would not have come to the apartment. How stupid—certainly that was true. But suppose he hasn't given up the hope of finding her, Gerald thought. Suppose he lied about his stay in Naples. Suppose he plans to return tonight, tomorrow night . . .

He crossed the patio. I could take her away tonight, he reflected. But no—how would I explain such an abrupt move? What if she objected? It was nonsense to consider fleeing off into the night. It was admitting his own inadequacy.

He stood looking through the dining room into the shadows which partly obscured the door. There was another solution, a more intelligent one. I could prevent him from coming back here quite easily, Gerald thought. All I would need to do would be to go to the hotel and find them, husband and wife. Let us imagine I made the wife my ally. We could have a most amusing conversation, the three of us. It might be more clever than what happened here.

He stared at the door. The soldier was tall, with wide-set brown eyes and close-cropped hair—but he was no longer young. He was only relatively young. He had tried to seem so plausible. A sudden fury seized Gerald. I will not brook interference, he told himself—he came too close to me, he tried to rob me, I know he did, I won't give him another chance.

He went into the bedroom and picked up the telephone. "I want to verify a registration," he was saying in Italian. "For an American couple—a Mr. and Mrs. Michael Allen . . ."

He glanced at the patio. The telephone was like the one in Florence; it reminded him oddly of Biasetti. "They are not in their room—but you expect them," he was saying. "Yes, I see . . . No, there are no messages. None at all. I will call later in the afternoon."

Michael noticed Ruth as soon as he left the taxi. She was on the terrace in front of the hotel. There were a few tables with blue umbrellas spread above them, and although the terrace was narrow it was raised slightly above the street level and afforded a glimpse of the water front, of Mt. Vesuvius. She had chosen a table nearest the hotel entrance. He saw her glance quickly at him. He had the impression that she had been waiting there a long time; but he saw that she had changed her dress, that she looked fresh and cool—her eyes cool and a little anxious as he approached.

"Well, Mike?"

He stood awkwardly beside the table.

"Well, did you find her?"

"No, I didn't, Ruth. Not Angelina."

"Oh? . . . What a shame," Ruth said. "You found the café, did you—the place where she lives?"

"Yes, I found those." He seated himself under the blue umbrella. "I found the man she lives with, part of the time anyway. . . . The writer. Gerald Newell."

"Gerald Newell," she repeated. "That does sound quite literary, doesn't it. A nom de plume, do you suppose?"

"I don't really know, Ruth."

"What's he like then?" The tone of her voice seemed cynical, quiet—hurt, he thought, I've hurt her.

"He's rather old. Intelligent. Sophisticated. An American living abroad—"

"He has a nice house?"

"Not a house—an apartment. A ground floor apartment. Nicely furnished, though. A chandelier in the dining room." It was ridiculous to be defending Gerald Newell, Michael thought. His shirt was wet and cold against his chest, but his jacket covered it—and perhaps he could make everything seem casual; perhaps he could hide from Ruth the turmoil inside his mind.

"Really," she said, "a chandelier."

"Yes, a chandelier, and a patio with vines on the walls—French doors leading out to it." He remembered the antique store in Florence. Its mustiness touched him. He wondered how he had looked to Ruth when Angelina's name had been mentioned by the old woman in the tenement.

"He must be quite successful then," Ruth said. "I haven't

heard of him before, though—have you?"

"No—"

"Maybe we can find a book by him when we get home."

"Maybe we can."

"In the library, I mean. It would be interesting to find a book by Gerald Newell . . . Maybe I should meet him."

He did not answer her. "Meet him and Angelina together," Ruth went on. "How funny! I wonder what we'd all say to each other. You could arrange it, couldn't you, Mike?"

He was unable to tell what she was thinking, Michael realized. Possibly she believed the writer, the apartment were inventions.

"We don't know any writers, do we? We could have a party for them," she said.

He saw, or thought he saw what her meaning was. "Ask them in for cocktails?" he said with a faint smile.

"Cocktails—or dinner."

"No, darling, that's nonsense. You know it is. Let's not make a travesty out of it . . . I made a promise. I tried to do what was asked of me—that's all there is."

She was silent for a moment.

"What will you say to the brother?"

"I'll write him of course."

"You could say that his sister is attached to a rich intelligent, sophisticated American writer, and that he doesn't have to worry."

"Yes, I could say just that."

"Would you believe it yourself?"

"Believe what, darling?"

"The part about not worrying—I mean."

"I don't know about that, Ruth."

"Why not?" she asked.

"Well, I'm not sure. I'm not sure what kind of an influence he has—whether it's good or bad, right or wrong. But I can't change it no matter what I think . . . Let's leave it there, shall we? It's foolish to meddle in other people's lives, the lives of strangers."

"Somehow the word stranger doesn't seem to fit."

He shook his head. "No, they are strangers. They seem so to

me. One more than the other maybe—but each of them . . . I can't imagine how they feel, what feelings they have, sad or gay, respectful, contemptuous—"

"In other words you can't imagine what they see in each other," Ruth said, but with less rancor in her voice. It was like something she had said earlier—he couldn't quite recall . . .

He was smiling at her. "That's it exactly. I can't for the life of me imagine what they see in each other . . . Come on, let's forget about them. Let's not waste any more of the day like this. Let's find a really nice restaurant, if we can, and have lunch out. And this afternoon we can do some sightseeing, if you like. We won't go near the Vomero. Maybe I'll show you what remains of Michael Allen in the ruins of Pompeii."

"Or what remains of us both after this morning," Ruth said.

"Yes, old lady—what remains of us both."

She was rising. They had almost reached the street when she took his hand. Her fingers closed lightly around his. "I know just the place for lunch," she said. "I saw it only a little while ago."

GERALD was dressing when Angelina entered the apartment. He had walked over to the café early in the afternoon. The possibility that Michael might have left his name with someone had alarmed him; yet it had seemed an outside chance. He had imagined Michael as too much ashamed to leave his name—or in too much of a rush. A man pursuing a secret quest did not generally advertise himself. At the café Michael could only be identified as an American. Gerald was quite certain of this, but it was essential to be prepared for whatever questions Angelina might ask. He had telephoned the hotel again. The Allens were still out. They were expected for dinner, a clerk had said; they were expected to leave Naples tomorrow. That could change, however. The whole thing could change. He would not depend on a clerk's information. When Angelina returned, he would go to the hotel himself.

His nerves jumped when he heard the key turn in the lock.

"You are home, Gerry?"

"Yes—here in the bedroom." He knotted the cord of his dressing gown and hastily smoothed his hair into place with a pair of silver-backed brushes. The bristles were worn and faintly aromatic. "You are back early," he called. "It's only a little after five-thirty."

"Yes, I know. I was talking with Maria. I spent some of the day with her."

"Ah yes, with Maria." He reached and opened the door. "Come in, my dear, come in. We don't have to stand on ceremony, do we?" She entered the bedroom. She looked sad, he thought—or preoccupied. She put her face sideways to his lips and then disengaged herself.

"I hear you had a visitor today, Gerry."

197

"Yes, a visitor . . . Who told you?"

"I heard at the café," she said, but her voice seemed soft, without recrimination. "I stopped there with Maria for a glass of wine. Who was it?"

"Someone I knew a long time ago in the States," Gerald answered. "A fellow American. I happened to see him the other day in Florence."

"I hear he knew of me. Pietro said he mentioned my name."

"Yes, probably . . . It wouldn't have been strange. I told him of my good fortune—about the place where we met, and so forth. I really didn't expect to see him in Naples, though. Apparently I didn't give him my address. I thought I had, but perhaps not. Anyway, he was up in this part of the city and saw the café and thought he'd inquire. Actually we went to school with each other, years ago in Minnesota. I hadn't seen him since —not until the other day. Rather a dull person, not terribly interesting, but I have to be nice to him."

"Nice to him—why?"

"He's related to a man who has a publishing house in Chicago," Gerald said. "Not too closely related, but nevertheless it's in the family, you might say."

"He looked you up then—to ask about one of your books?"

"No—not today. We didn't discuss literature today."

"What did you discuss—did you discuss me?"

"No, not you, my dear. We talked about old times."

Angelina was silent for a few seconds. "Are you in the habit of discussing me with people you meet by chance, Gerry—with dull, uninteresting people?"

He glanced at her sharply. "No, my dear—I'm not in the habit. I . . . in this case—well, you'll have to forgive me—but he's so proper, so very proper—"

"That you wanted to shock him?" she asked.

Gerald smiled. "Possibly I did, my dear. I'm afraid he came here today, expecting to find sort of a den of iniquity—"

"I see," Angelina said. "Then he was disappointed."

"Oh yes, quite—and quite curious . . . You know, it's just occurred to me—I think that's the reason he didn't announce himself beforehand."

"Possibly it is."

"You're not angry, are you? You don't mind the little joke?"

"No, I don't mind a joke, Gerry . . . What do you plan to do for this man—take him out to dinner, something of that kind?"

"Perhaps not for dinner. I said I might meet him for a drink or two, though, this evening. Actually he's here with his wife."

"With his wife—I see. I suppose she's very proper also—"

"Yes. Yes, I suppose she is. I've never met her, but I suppose she's quite a bit like him."

"Where are they staying—at one of the big hotels?"

"Yes, at the Excelsior."

"At the Excelsior—they must be rich."

"Oh, I don't know how rich," Gerald said. "Just because he's at the Excelsior doesn't mean he's a millionaire." He stepped over to the closet and parted the curtain which hung in front of it. It was amazing how a clever person could endow a fiction with flesh and blood. "What did you do yourself, my dear— while I was working here, talking with someone from long ago?"

"What I usually do, Gerry. I went to see Maria. I played with her little girl, with Carla, for a while—"

"You had something to eat—you had lunch?" he asked, gazing into the closet, trying to decide whether he should wear the gray slacks and the tweed jacket or the dark brown suit.

"Yes, I had lunch."

"Where?"

"Where I eat sometimes. You do not know it. It is a small *trattoria*."

"Ah yes," he said, and brought out the slacks and the jacket. Amazing how the conversation had been manipulated! "You had lunch with Maria?"

"Yes, with Maria. With a few others."

"Friends of hers?" He put the slacks over the brass bar at the foot of the bed.

"Friends of hers—friends of mine."

"Of course," Gerald said lightly. The slacks were freshly pressed. They were of fine English flannel. The occasion seemed to call for elegance. Ruth Allen would be faced with a man of elegance.

"Your shoes are also in the closet," Angelina said. "Shall I get them for you? I imagine you will want to wear the new ones, the ones from Florence."

"No, don't bother, my dear. I'll get them myself—"

But she went past him, and stooped and turned back, the curtain rustling behind her. For an instant he was horrified. In a manner, totally unforeseen, her expression seemed to ridicule him. "Here," she said. "I polished them yesterday. Do they please you?"

He stared at her. The expression had disappeared, as if before he could blink his eyes.

"Yes, my dear . . . Yes . . . Thank you—"

She placed the shoes on the seat of a chair. "You should have bought another pair, Gerry. These are handsome." She stepped toward the door. "I think I will go out on the terrace for a while," she said. "I feel just a little tired."

Through the window he could see her languidly posed on the couch. He could see her whenever he looked away from the mirror. He was knotting his tie, tugging at the lapels of his jacket. Informality and elegance. To be informal and elegant at the same time. He had fitted a pair of gold cuff links into his shirt. He had bought them at Cartier's in New York before he had set out for his European adventures. Once they had implied success. Once they had been like her ring.

This afternoon he had imagined Angelina asking the most implausible questions. He had refuted them all in his mind. He had even pictured himself forced into telling her the truth—and had still been able to banish the soldier. He had seen himself at the hotel, had seen clearly how he would behave: the exact innuendo, the wife aroused, intrigued, suspicious. He had seen tragedy overtaking Michael—tragedy in the Greek interpretation. Destiny. Fate—a wheel of fire, a chariot of gold. Fate descending on the pretended hero, rendering him defenseless. How the mind reeled with the concept!—and now, suddenly, for some unknown reason, she had mocked him. What had she learned at the café? Was it remotely possible that she had encountered her lover after he had left the apartment? I must find out, Gerald thought. I must find him. I mustn't let him get away. He glanced at the telephone . . . No, I'd better not call again. The telephone is useless. I can be at the hotel in a few minutes.

He went out to the terrace. I'm hysterical, he thought. For hours this has been in my brain. It's out of perspective. The only thing is, the only thing is, I must not lose her. I must keep them apart. Of course they haven't found each other yet.

"You must go right away, Gerry?"

"In a moment—in a moment or two."

"I put the Cinzano over there in the corner—and the ice."

"Thank you," he said. He was pouring a little vermouth into a glass. The evening ritual, the beginning of it, might make him more calm. He came toward her.

"Sit down for a minute, will you, Gerry? You seem very nervous."

"Do I? Well, maybe it's because I'm always on edge when I have to talk to someone from—someone connected with the publishing world. They annoy me—many of them."

"This man, I forget—did you say he was an editor?"

"What? . . . Oh no, he's not an editor. He's merely connected, related to the owner of the firm."

"Sit down, Gerry," she repeated. "Sit here, if you like, on the couch. There's room enough. I want to ask you a question."

"What question, my dear?" He continued to stand beside her. "I really don't have much time to linger—"

"It's a very serious question." She sat up and faced him directly. "You can answer it in a second, but I want a truthful answer."

"What question, Angelina?"

"It's about your book."

"My book? . . . My book, did you say?"

"Yes, your book, Gerry. The question is simply this: you don't think any offer will be made for it here—do you?"

He gaped at her. "What? . . . Why—why that's nonsense!"

"You don't think there's a chance—not even a slight chance."

"Why, that's absurd!" he exclaimed, staring at her in consternation. "Whatever put a thought like that in your mind?"

"It is so, Gerry. Tell the truth. All this talk about people being interested in your work—publishers, editors, people connected with other firms—it's all a sham, isn't it?"

"A sham? A sham? I don't understand you, Angelina—"

"I think you do, Gerry. I think you're only fooling yourself. Say what you like to other people—but to me you must tell the truth!"

"I am telling the truth! I have told you! I told you all about my trip to Florence, didn't I? I told you about my hopes—plans . . . that they don't materialize all at once . . . that it's desirable —desirable to keep, to maintain every contact. Surely you understand that." He pushed his hand through his hair. "But yes—I see what's confused you. I made it sound too nebulous, too uncertain . . . but I'm known in many countries, Angelina—in France, in England, in the United States, here in Italy. I'm known to people of influence. . . . Look, listen to me. We'll discuss it all another time. Tomorrow morning we'll discuss it. I'll go over everything with you, step by step. I'll explain how a book comes into being, all the delays involved—how patient one must be. I'll tell you how my first book was published, how long that took. I'll tell you about everything I've written—the successes and the failures. Yes, I will admit the failures. There have been failures—a few here and there—"

"And this book, Gerry?"

"No!" he shouted. "This book is a success! It will be a success! It will bring me a great fortune—and you will wear a diamond tiara, Angelina, and a dress from Christian Dior. Believe me, darling—everything will be discussed." His voice dropped. "I—I never thought you were interested in the details of my work, you know. That's why I've never gone into them with you, except in a casual way. But don't accuse me falsely, Angelina. You must never do that—because I have pride, a sense of pride."

"Yes . . . I know."

"You are sarcastic—"

"No, Gerry. I believe you are a proud man."

"Well then," he said. "Well then, we agree, don't we? And you are proud too, Angelina. I know that—and you are offended because I haven't communicated more to you; but I will, beginning with tomorrow and the next day, and the day after . . . So . . . brighten your face, darling. Make your lips smile for me. There! That is better. . . . I have convinced you, haven't I?"

"Yes, Gerry. I think I am convinced."

"Good," he said. "Tomorrow morning you and I will talk for a long time. Lovers are forever having small quarrels and mending them, are they not? . . . Now I must hurry, mustn't I? I mustn't keep my friend waiting—"

"No." She stood up. "Goodnight then, Gerry."

"Goodnight, my dear—but not yet goodnight . . . I will be back soon, I hope . . . I—perhaps we can have our little talk tonight."

He kissed her and walked rapidly out into the street. The glass windows on the shop fronts seemed overly brilliant, as if the air were cold, almost as if it were winter in another city and the sunlit pavements covered with snow.

But he had escaped, Gerald thought—he had escaped without damage. She had no idea that her soldier was in Naples. She had been piqued, by what exactly?—try to recall—by the fact that he was about to entertain someone without her at the Excelsior, by the fact that he had left her behind when he had gone to Florence? Did she fancy herself as a literary critic? Did she visualize herself discussing books with publishers and editors? How ridiculous! Angelina Nardi, the great critic, who was almost illiterate.

Or had he trapped himself with his own cunning? That was equally ridiculous, wasn't it? He, Gerald Newell, was the tightrope walker who could balance himself indefinitely. He alone was aware of the abyss. Tomorrow morning, tonight—those would take care of themselves.

Near the funicular he paused to catch his breath. Oh yes, he thought, how stupid of me—how my brain whirls. Michael Allen. I still have to deal with him. I will bring him to his knees. She will love me, no one else—she will have no one else to love.

Angelina waited until she heard the door of the apartment close. Then she left the patio quickly and went past the dining table and into the bedroom. She surveyed it objectively, as if it were a room she had entered for the first time: the ornate brass of the bed; the cupboard he had set aside for her, its painted panels suggesting in dim colors a country scene, green leaves, bluish sky, the twining of grape clusters; the mirror in the half embrace of the curving bronze light brackets; the marble-topped bureau which he alone used; the slenderly supported fruitwood table in the corner which served as his desk. She remembered seeing his face in profile the first morning she had awakened here. Only in retrospect, the face seemed more like a mask, as lifeless as the room itself.

She would take only what she had come with, she decided. She had always felt more comfortable in this dress—her plain dark dress trimmed above the breasts with white. She had worn the others in the evenings to please him more than herself; but now, standing in front of the cupboard, she fingered them—the green, the blue, the red—before gently closing the paneled door.

He had not harmed her—not yet; yet the feeling of depression had grown steadily since his return from Florence. These people he sought after, they made her feel unclean. He hurried after them so; he tried so hard to impress them. He was like a pimp running through the streets, trying to sell, to amuse, to entertain. But what he sold had no appeal, or little appeal. She wondered if the empty sound of his voice, his anxiety, amused the publishers—the people of influence.

She put her small suitcase on the bed and began packing it methodically. She did not doubt that if she stayed with him, he would take her eventually to Rome, to Paris, to London; that in order to keep her permanently he might propose marriage; but even marriage would not soften the feeling of depression, nor would it disappear entirely in any new place. It would come back, and each time it would be more sharp. Now it was a feeling like death—or perhaps not like death, but like imprisonment. Maybe they were the same. . . .

Haste was not required, and yet several times she paused and listened to the distant sound of footsteps in the outside hall and did not move again until they had diminished on the stairs. She closed her suitcase and left it and went into the kitchen alcove, lingering there for a moment, her eyes scanning the clean enameled stove. The luxuries it had afforded! She turned and glanced at the dining table and at the porcelain figurines he admired. She stepped to the threshold of the patio and looked at the couch with its two spoked wheels which allowed it to be moved easily, almost without noise.

She re-entered the bedroom and was picking up the suitcase when she glanced at the desk again and at the typewriter beneath it. He kept all his writing in the deep drawer which ran along the desk front, she knew. She had never touched the drawer. She went toward it cautiously.

It was locked, she found; but the wood was old around the keyhole and the latch insecure. Only a slight jar was needed to pull the drawer free.

She saw the manuscript in its leather folder, the title, the author's name engraved in gold letters. She lifted the cover. Here was a section written in Italian, another in French—this would be French—and below, pages and pages in English. There was an almost yellow cast to them. It could not come from the subdued light. It came from age. She leafed through a few pages; she could not read some of the English words, but the smell of age mingled with the smell of leather struck her, and the pages crackled and fell away from her hand.

She wondered what he had given to the publisher in Florence, whether there was such a person. He had spoken of a copy, hadn't he? This was a copy. It hardly mattered. This was what he was trying to sell, what he worked on day after day—these words written long, long ago, translated into this language and that language. The top pages seemed new. She saw the note then, as she was closing the cover—Biasetti's name printed on it. "My dear Mr. Newell: We cannot accept your book for the following reasons . . ." The words were in Italian. She did not read any further. She closed the cover. How thick it was—and how tragic. Except for a pile of envelopes, a few separate scattered pages, the rest of the drawer was empty.

She did not examine them. She pushed the drawer shut, striking her hand against the lock. If he saw me now, he would try to kill me, she thought—or would he merely begin to cry, to weep? . . . There—the drawer was in place once more. The wood hadn't been scarred.

She would go to the café and find Maria. Maria might offer her a bed for the night—or no, that might be too dangerous, too nearby; but she would buy a glass of brandy for Maria and one for herself. "I see you are traveling," Maria would say. "You belong in an institution for the feeble-minded." It would be pleasant to hear that kind of conversation. It would make her smile. She would not linger in the café, however. Gerald might begin to look there—later in the evening, though—perhaps not until tomorrow.

But she would not take the risk of staying in a place where they had been together. Perhaps she would go to the *trattoria* and buy a meal for Luigi Bertoli. He would be overjoyed. The food would please him very much. He would suggest making a bed for her from his paintings, from the canvas. He would begin to describe the bed elaborately; she would laugh. She would never go to the building near the Via Roma—never to that building again.

She took off the cameo and dropped it into her purse. Possibly she should leave it here on the bureau, where he could see it; but that would be cruel, like a slap in the face. If it had great value, she might have decided differently, or she would take it for reasons which he would readily understand; but this was of no great worth. She had seen many stones like it in the stores. The value lay more in the careful selection than in the actual cost. The thin gold chain was of almost no weight; yet to him it had seemed beautiful. Perhaps he would always imagine her wearing it; and in the end, when he knew it was all over, this would flatter him. He would think, at least I've taught her some appreciation of what is correct. But, of course, she would not wear the cameo. She would not want to be reminded.

After a while she would give it away—maybe to Maria, but not until she was sure that Gerald Newell had left Naples. He would not stay long, not under the circumstances, not alone in surroundings where he was known. Probably he would return to Paris. It's strange, she thought, but I think I will feel it when he leaves; I think I will be sure even if I'm not told.

She glanced once more around the room and toward the desk. He wouldn't notice that anything was amiss there. He wouldn't know that his secret had been discovered. Yet as she crossed the room's threshold, she felt as if evil were reviling her—and almost as if she had stolen something private from a grave.

GERALD had gone into the hotel. The Allens were in their room, the desk clerk had said. He had an insolent air— yes, he was sure it was Signor è Signora Allen; they had stopped to ask for mail. He was attending now to a newly arrived couple, was snapping his fingers toward the porter. He had not given the corner of the lobby where Gerald had seated himself a second glance.

The lobby was crowded, but not large. From his chair, with its worn tapestry-covered back and arms, Gerald could watch the elevator door without difficulty. At first the waiting gave him time to settle his thoughts, or at least to think more rationally. Michael was here. That was an enormous relief. That was lucky; and he had been lucky also, Gerald realized, to have had an excuse to leave Angelina when she had started to question him about his book. Tomorrow morning, later this evening, he would be very businesslike with her and in command of himself. Tomorrow morning he would go to his typewriter and compose a letter to himself from Biasetti. It would be most complimentary. It would say that unfortunately—unfortunately the price demanded was too high, but that the book had great merit, that Biasetti was recommending it to a more affluent firm in Paris. The letter would serve a double purpose: it would satisfy Angelina, and it would allow him to broach the subject of returning with her to France. She would not object under those terms, he felt—quite the contrary. She would believe he would prosper. He had been reasonably thrifty since he had met her. Her requirements had not been exorbitant. He might be able to afford a different Parisian flat.

Perhaps he would not have to read the letter at once. He would want to avoid the suspicion of a coincidence. He might let a day or so go by. Always before when adversity had struck at him, he had been able to think, to analyze, to take action. Now his brain was working again. So much for that. So much for that . . .

In regard to Michael Allen and his wife, he would need to be more circumspect. Jealousy had made him wish to take revenge on the soldier, but it might not be necessary. It was essential only to make certain of their plans, to measure wife against husband, to discover how much had been withheld from her. What sort of woman caused a man to wander back into the past, to seek out a girl he had made love to ten years before? He was intensely curious about the wife.

Gerald looked down at his watch. It was nearly seven o'clock. He had been in the lobby more than half an hour. They would go toward the bar, he had decided, away from him. He would have a chance for a moment's private observation. The dining room was beyond the bar. Undoubtedly they were on a half-pension plan—a meal out, a meal at the hotel. Commonplace . . . A commonplace setting . . . He watched the elevator door open, but the Allens were not inside. The couple he had seen at the desk walked on by him toward the street. . . .

Commonplace, his mind repeated. A man betrays his wife during a war. That was far from unusual—but then, ten years afterward . . . Suppose she is rich and dried up, he thought. No, they would not be staying here in that case. They would not need to budget expenses. What, if anything, had the wife been told about this morning? . . .

He was looking again at his watch. Yesterday at this hour, he had been on the terrace with Angelina. A week ago he had been in Florence, and Biasetti had not yet rejected his manuscript. Others had rejected it—not Biasetti. Now he was in an ordinary hotel, where he had stayed once himself, years before. Had he been put here by chance, by a series of unrelated, tormenting events—or was a pattern beginning to emerge?

He sat forward, his mind jumping back and forth. Was there a pattern of inevitability?—rejections, women who had left him before, death floating in a river; a hearse drawn by black, plumed horses; a painting of salvation—and ultimate failure . . . But one moment, he told himself, one moment. Suppose I seemed just as inevitable to *him?* Suppose I am like the voice of his own betrayal? He pressed his back against the worn tapestry, the image he was fashioning for himself, not quite complete— emerging through the sound of Biasetti's voice rasping over the telephone wires, through the sudden memory of the ring's gold band glimmering, half veiled by the shadows which fell steeply across the couch on the terrace.

The elevator was descending. The metal grate moved sideways. Gerald saw a blond woman get off, Michael a step behind her. They did not approach the desk. They turned to their left and went through an arched doorway, in the direction of the bar.

Gerald followed them. The clerk was busy with another registration. Gerald wished he was in the Excelsior lobby. The bar there was more ornate. He would have enjoyed making a grand entrance—to have halted ostentatiously in the middle of a room . . . "Mr. Allen!—well, what a surprise!" . . .

He paused in the archway. The room beyond him seemed bleak. He remembered the partitions of gray, frosted glass enclosing it from the dining area. The blond was quite well dressed, quite presentable. An American housewife on a vacation—merely that? She seemed to be smiling at something her husband had said. Gerald walked up to them.

"Good evening, Mr. Allen—a good evening to you."

Michael was staring at him. He recognizes me, Gerald thought; he recognizes his enemy. "You see I decided to accept your invitation after all—"

"My invitation?"

Gerald made his voice bland. "Of course, I realize it wasn't exactly an invitation, Mr. Allen—more like a suggestion, wasn't it? . . . Still, I decided to accept it in any event. I was passing by your hotel just now. I thought I might find you in the bar. I thought I might buy you a drink—buy you both a drink. This is Mrs. Allen, I suppose?"

"Yes—this is my wife . . . Ruth, this is Mr. Newell."

Ruth was staring at him too.

"May I join you, Mrs. Allen?"

"If you'd like, Mr. Newell . . . Yes, please sit down—"

"I should be delighted," Gerald said. He took Ruth's hand and held it, and then seated himself opposite the two of them. It was marvelous to see them so formal, so properly stiff . . .

"My husband tells me you are a writer, Mr. Newell—"

"Then you have heard about me . . . Yes—yes, I am a writer. I do some writing, not as much as in the past, but enough to keep body and soul together . . . But I see you've just arrived, Mrs. Allen. Have you ordered yet?"

"Yes, we've ordered martinis—"

"Excellent," Gerald said. "They make fairly decent martinis here—if you know what to tell them. You will permit me." He raised his hand imperiously and beckoned to the waiter. He was leaning back, speaking in his flawlessly fluent Italian. "I have made it three martinis," he said. "Very well iced, and with little vermouth and a twist of lemon. This is to be my round, my party, I wanted things to be correct. You don't mind, do you, Mrs. Allen?"

"No, of course not—"

Gerald glanced at Michael. The face was impassive—numb, Gerald thought. I have made him numb. What lies did he tell about this morning? "You know, Mrs. Allen, I really must apologize to you, though, for intruding like this—but when your husband came to my flat today . . . I suppose he has told you all about it—"

"Yes, he told me—"

There were the telltale marks of age around her eyes, Gerald observed. The lips were a trifle thin; discontent could settle around the lips, discontent or a certain resolution. The chin was resolute; but the face itself was not old, not overly made-up. Her eyes were wide now, full of interest, curiosity—yet these were tempered with reserve. "Why, I was quite taken aback. It seemed like such an unusual encounter." He smiled. "And when he told me about you—well, I was eager to meet you, of course, and I was eager for you not to have a—a wrong impression of me."

"I don't think I gave Ruth a wrong impression of you, Mr. Newell."

"No—I'm sure you didn't, Mr. Allen." Gerald shifted his position slightly. "But you see, Mrs. Allen, when you reach my stage in life—you don't like erroneous ideas to be formed. I freely

admit I know this girl, Angelina Nardi . . ." ("What girl—
what girl?" he half expected Ruth to say; but she showed no
surprise.) "This girl, I know her," Gerald repeated. "I didn't
deny it to your husband—but—" He paused. He had forgotten
how he was going to continue.

"You don't have to explain it, Mr. Newell."

"You are most tactful, Mrs. Allen. . . . Your husband said you
had understanding. I wouldn't have come otherwise . . . But—
but I didn't come here to confess my whims, or fancies. . . .
I came to ask about your trip, actually. Italy is very dear to my
heart. I know it intimately. I have often been able to suggest to
my American friends the small restaurant, the out-of-the-way
place. I enjoy being able to give advice. That is the spirit in
which I present myself. I hope you will understand, that you
will—well, overlook other circumstances."

"Certainly," Ruth said. The trace of a blush crossed her face.
She was rather pretty, Gerald thought; she might at one time have
been close to beauty. For a second he compared her with
Angelina: Angelina and himself, Ruth and Michael Allen. I
might even be kind to her, he thought. That is in my power
also.

"May I inquire then, Mrs. Allen—what has appealed to you
most it Italy?"

"Well, I liked Rome very much—"

"Ah yes, the Eternal City! Rome the mother, the wolf."

"The wolf?" Ruth asked.

"The story of Romulus and Remus, Mrs. Allen."

"Oh yes, of course. I read about them in the guidebook—and
long ago at school."

"Rome is so full of culture," Gerald said, smiling to himself.
"But I see our cocktails are arriving . . . Here, allow me . . ."
He watched Michael take the second glass. He is acutely un-
comfortable, Gerald thought—he is afraid of me.

"And after Rome—then what?"

"After Rome we went to Florence, Mr. Newell," Michael
said. "I think I told you that today."

"Yes, you did, Mr. Allen. But what I was asking your wife,
concerned not as much the itinerary of your trip as the high-

lights of it—what she found most striking—"

"I thought Florence was lovely," Ruth said. "We stayed outside the city at a *pensione* near Fiesole. I hope that's the right way to pronounce them. My Italian isn't very good, not nearly as good as my husband's."

Gerald restrained her. "I would say it was perfect, Mrs. Allen."

Ruth laughed. "One or two words aren't a whole language, though, are they? You've been to Florence yourself, Mr. Newell? I suppose you have."

"Yes—often."

"You like it better than Rome?"

"They are very different," Gerald said. "Florence is quite provincial actually—"

"Provincial? How do you mean?"

"I mean—it's a matter of degree. The people in Florence are not so cosmopolitan. . . . It's a little like—well, like the difference between your Philadelphia—I think your husband said you were from Philadelphia—and New York, except that of course the Italian culture is older. Culture is in Florence, the culture of the arts—and culture is also in Rome; but it is on a vaster scale—the culture of empires, enormous undertakings—"

"Maybe you think of us as provincial," Ruth said lightly.

"No, no, no, Mrs. Allen—not at all. I was merely trying to make a comparison. . . . Rome is filled with life. Florence— Florence lives more in the past." Florence, Gerald thought, how had the conversation become so entangled with the city on the Arno?

"And Philadelphia?" Ruth asked, as if she were teasing him, as if his words amused her.

"I'm not too well acquainted with your city," Gerald answered. He took a sip of his martini. "It's of no great consequence anyway. You live in the city itself—or in the suburbs?"

"In the suburbs. But I don't think they look much like Fiesole."

"No, they don't. They're a bit more flat, aren't they?" He raised his glass and set it down. "In fact I think Italy comes as quite a shock to someone seeing it for the first time. I myself remember my initial astonishment—the hill towns, Orvieto, Assisi,

so very picturesque. . . . And even the little villages, Mrs. Allen
—even those." He hesitated, watching her. "I understand you
went with your husband to see his own small village."

"Yes—"

"How did it impress you?"

"Why, I liked it very much."

"And this family your husband—befriended, you liked them
too? Or did you think of them as provincial?"

"No, I didn't think of them like that. They were very nice to
us—very hospitable."

"They had a reason to be hospitable—don't you agree?"

"Yes, a reason—"

"I mean your husband did a very brave thing—a very brave
thing in their behalf, during the war. I suppose they were
pleased to see him again—to meet his wife." She met them,
Gerald thought—she had admitted meeting them. But the conversation was not subtle enough. The woman lacked the in-
telligence to recognize subtlety.

"Well, I don't know how pleased they were to see me. They
were extremely glad to see Mike—"

"Of course they were. Of course . . . I was just wondering if
you shared your husband's fondness for the Italians—"

"I can't say I share it completely," Ruth said, "but then this is
only my first visit."

"Yes, exactly, your first visit . . . So you can understand only
a little about the Italians—how emotional they are."

"Oh, I can see they are emotional people."

"Emotional. Quickly moved. Moved to hate—or to love."
Michael was silent. He was leaning forward slightly; but it was
hard to tell whether he had braced himself, or whether he was
merely an inquisitive spectator.

"To hate—or to love," Gerald repeated. "Both feelings are
intense with the Italians." He looked at Ruth. She seemed
mildly embarrassed, as if he were telling some rather off-color
story. They were both smug. They were both contemptible: the
soldier, the soldier's wife. Was it possible he had not betrayed
her? "Love—hatred—joy—terror, these are all intense emotions
for the Italians. . . . Generosity and the reverse—gratitude. The

Italian remembers the war, sometimes even with gratitude—"

"You were here at that time, Mr. Newell?" The question had come from Michael. Gerald glanced away from Ruth.

"No, not at the time. I was in England during the war . . . but I remember, I have heard stories of our young men, our soldiers here in Italy—bars of chocolate for the children, silk stockings for the young ladies, isn't that so?"

"Perhaps something like that."

"They were the most generous army in the world," Gerald said, glancing at Ruth. "I mean—I mean, Mrs. Allen—here they were in the country of a people they had conquered, who should by the laws of war prostrate themselves, obey every command . . . And here was the American Army lavishing gifts on the vanquished, gifts instead of punishment." The words weren't right, Gerald thought. A note of hysteria seemed to interfere with them. They reminded him of the apartment terrace, of Angelina. They should have been spoken jocularly, with soft innuendo—

"But don't you think that's natural?" Ruth asked. "Americans aren't apt to be terribly vindictive."

The phrase struck Gerald as enormously discordant, as ludicrous. "Of course, Mrs. Allen—I agree with you—but it is not the European way. The European is more sly. Gratitude, yes—he may feel gratitude, but he has learned in a harder school. He has learned that to be generous is occasionally unwise, foolish. . . . He has learned to mistrust the appearance of virtue."

"I'm afraid I don't follow you, Mr. Newell."

"Put it in another way then—in another way," Gerald said. "Take the case of your husband . . . I mean, he sees an Italian lying out in a field—and he rushes out and tries to rescue him. The American conqueror tries to rescue the vanquished Italian. I mean, it is a kind of paradox, isn't it? . . . No, please don't interrupt, Mr. Allen. I have a feeling that your wife may not recognize—may not recognize the heroism involved . . . You see, as a writer it fascinates me . . . The voluntary element. I try to imagine what went through your mind at that moment, Mr. Allen. I wonder if you thought of your wife. Usually a soldier in danger thinks of his home. At least that idea appears in fiction, doesn't it?"

"I don't see how he could answer that, Mr. Newell."

"You don't, Mrs. Allen? . . . Ah yes, I see your meaning." Gerald attempted to smile; yet his throat was dry now, and he thought of Biasetti talking over the telephone and of Angelina quarreling on the terrace, and the elaborate form of his plan was disintegrating. "You feel perhaps I am being rude in regard to what your husband did, Mrs. Allen, but you see—a writer must sometimes be blunt. He is concerned with reactions. . . . I am only saying that what your husband did might have been too generous—and hence unwise . . . But I can readily tell by your expression that you don't agree."

"I'm not sure I do," Ruth said. "Something that happened long ago—"

"Yes—but time is deceptive, isn't it? An hour, part of an hour, can seem longer than ten years. The human brain can distort time, and other things—other things. No, what I say isn't pointless, Mrs. Allen. It concerns you. . . . It concerns especially you."

"It concerns me?"

"Yes—you especially," Gerald said. "We talk of Italians and of how emotional they can become. We talk of generosity and heroism. We talk in abstract terms. We begin abstractly—and we end in personalities." He paused, his hand shaking next to the martini glass. If he tried to raise it, the glass might topple and roll across the table toward Ruth. He imagined her pushing back her chair, the chair itself wedged against the wall. He could see the stain spreading across Ruth's dress. In another second, she could no longer defend her husband; she could no longer be smug and complacent. Or were his assumptions all false? Had there been no betrayal—no adultery? Were they both ready to laugh at him?

He must speak. The wife looked so attentive. "Perhaps," he said, "Mr. Allen would rather I didn't continue."

"No," Michael said, "I won't stop you, Mr. Newell—say whatever you like."

The tone seemed almost flippant. Michael's head was slightly tilted, his brow frowning above the eyes; and for a fraction of a moment it was as if the wheel of fire, the chariot of gold descended in front of Gerald. "Very well then," he said, but his voice seemed to falter absurdly. He was glaring at Ruth. "Very well, Mrs. Allen—I will say what I must. I must tell you that your husband gave to Angelina Nardi, this girl we mentioned—I must tell you that your husband gave her a ring! . . . A ring with a gold band. An expensive ring! She wears it—she wears it on her finger. A ring is a symbol, isn't it? A symbol! Do you understand? A ring symbolizes—" He was standing. A feeling of agony clutched at him, as if he had confessed failure or despair. "I am afraid your husband was too generous, Mrs. Allen—"

The faces opposite him appeared blank. His voice seemed to make no impression on them. "You must understand what I'm saying to you, Mrs. Allen—you must *understand!*"

But she stared blankly at him, and he had turned away—and was walking through the bar, through the archway beyond it. He tried to visualize them sitting at the table, opposite the empty chair. It was as if he could see them in miniature, their ridiculous assurance undamaged . . . He walked through the lobby. A little man, he thought, I am a little man, going out into the street. . . .

He had reached the upper level of the Vomero before he remembered that he had not paid for the cocktails—a trivial matter, impossible under the circumstances; yet it seemed to compound a grievous error, to make it uncouth. He had used a dagger instead of a stiletto—and the dagger had been dull, possibly unavailing. He had not even inquired into the Allens' plans. We should have discussed literature, he thought confusedly—we should have begun in that fashion. I insulted myself in front of them; I demeaned myself. I lost control—at what point, though? I can't seem to recall what we talked about in the beginning— only the insult at the end. All at once he remembered Angelina handing him the shoes—the shoes of elegance, the shoes of sophistication. The insult was directed against those qualities. A tragedy, he thought: something with the attributes of great tragedy—and I spoiled it completely. I showed them only jealousy and weakness. I made it all common. . . .

He left the taxi he had taken in front of the café. He glanced at his watch and at the tables under the awning; but Angelina was not there; nor was she inside when he paused to look in the doorway, to nod to Maria behind the counter. They would not eat at the café tonight—they would go to some other restaurant where they were not known . . . He must discuss literature with Angelina, mustn't he? His book. The single book which must become several—several titles . . . He was nearing the courtyard of the apartment building. I'm exhausted, he thought—I'm exhausted.

He crossed the entry hall to the heavy door and pressed his finger against the bell. Michael Allen had been in this same spot earlier. I won't see him again, Gerald thought; later on I'll think of how to avoid the possibility of ever seeing him. "I won't stop you, Mr. Newell—say whatever you like." Damn his insolence! Was the wife shocked? Was it their smugness which had confused him? Or were they inviolate, husband and wife? Were they roaring with laughter at him now? Were they ordering another round of cocktails?

Gerald pushed against the bell again. The soft sound reminded him of those earlier days, before he had entrusted her with a key, when she would arrive at six o'clock, or a few minutes after. Then abruptly he remembered the evening when he had returned from Florence. He had not used the bell then. He had used his own key, hadn't he? He had thought that she might have deserted him. An odd notion—she had been waiting on the terrace. Perhaps she was asleep on the terrace and did not hear the bell . . . The literary critic had fallen asleep—perhaps she had forgotten the whole argument.

He kept his finger on the bell for a moment longer and then listened. It would have pleased him to have had her come forward to open the door, but she did not hear. He began fumbling in his pocket for the key. Yet when he opened the door, the dining room seemed darker than usual. The doors to the terrace were closed and curtained. Still she might be asleep—

"Angelina!" he screamed.

He was pushing the curtains apart. The terrace was empty. He could see the vermouth bottle in the twilight, the two empty glasses beside the couch.

"Angelina!"

She wasn't here. She wasn't in the bedroom. He went quickly from it and stood in the hallway before he closed the outside door. He turned toward the dining table. He shouldn't be upset, he told himself, he shouldn't have screamed . . . She hadn't expected him back so soon. She might be out for a walk. She might have thought of going to the café—but he would have seen her on the way. She might have decided to eat with other friends, however. That was logical—certainly.

He went out to the patio and lit a cigarette. She did not conceive that Michael Allen was in Naples. That had been established. She would return in a few minutes. He sat down on the couch. A slight fragrance came to him from the upholstered cushions. Was it imaginary—or here, where her dark hair had rested? Michael Allen could not have come and snatched her away. I left him minutes ago—twenty minutes. He could not have arrived ahead of me.

He stood up and paced the terrace and began to hum quietly to himself, but stopped when he became aware of it. He tossed the cigarette aside and stamped on it, and entered the bedroom again and put on the lights. An appearance of order struck him, as if things had been picked up and put down and rearranged. Or was that too an illusion? He listened for a few moments, but could hear no one, and moved suddenly to the painted cupboard and pushed the two panels wide.

There were only the three dresses he had given her. He shoved the clothes hangers along their wooden bar. The wire hangers grated and rattled; and the one holding the green dress fell. What was missing—how much was missing? He was stooping to pick up the dress when he thought of her suitcase, brown and made of something like cardboard. He had seen it this morning, when he was typing—right beside the cupboard. He had seen it every day. Perhaps she had cleaned the room this evening. She might have put the suitcase away—

He surveyed the room, his eyes darting into the four corners.

He began looking for the suitcase systematically and then in unlikely places—in the dining room, in the kitchen, in his own closet . . . I will kill her, he thought. I will tear the skin from her face, I will start with the eyes and tear down. She is a whore, a stupid, bleeding, voluptuous cow of a woman. She is like all the rest. I will find her and kill her. Where has she gone? Not to her soldier—not to him. That is amusing, isn't it? Angelina, if you had been here at noon . . . But no, you had to hurry off, you couldn't wait to arrange this—whatever it may be: an artist, a lover, the wrong lover, the wrong one.

He sat down on the bed and began to sob. She has made me like an Italian, he thought; she has made me too emotional. She has made me common. She has destroyed me. I will kill her.

But he lay back on the bed, the fragrance from the pillow tormenting him. *She* has destroyed me—not Michael Allen. What a superb irony! She has made me think like a criminal—and he saw himself running toward the café, asking questions, offering bribes—or going to the police; but he would not find her like that, and the police would laugh in his face. I would kill her only if she were here, he thought. Death awaits you, Angelina; but you will escape it, won't you? You won't come back.

The sobbing was more loud. In a little while, he thought, I will get up and go into the kitchen and take the small rubber tube from behind the stove and asphyxiate myself with gas . . . Oh yes, I remember it, Angelina—from the first morning we spent together. . . . But don't you see, my dear, if I did that—there would be no one to mourn?

RUTH sat in stunned silence, her gaze fixed on the archway through which Gerald Newell had vanished. She remembered laughing at something he had said about her pronunciation of Italian—the sudden joyful feeling during the afternoon that Angelina Nardi was of no consequence. She looked at Michael.

"You *invited* him here—didn't he say that? You *invited* him, you suggested it?"

"I didn't invite him, Ruth. I didn't suggest it—he came of his own accord—"

"We oughtn't to stay here," she said. The words seemed stifled. "I can't talk to you here."

"No," he answered. "No—all right, Ruth."

She had risen. She was standing in the archway. She was dimly aware that only a few people were in the bar, that another couple was looking at her. She watched Michael pay for the drinks, watched him approach her. He seemed to move slowly, carefully, his eyes intent on her. She wondered vaguely what defense he was preparing.

She stood rigidly beside him in the elevator, and when it stopped she stalked in front of him and entered the room halfway down the corridor. Through the window she could see Mt. Vesuvius, the bay of Naples, the blue fading from it. She found herself staring numbly at the white buildings along the water front. She heard Michael close the door—heard him say, "Darling, you mustn't exaggerate this. You—"

She faced him. "Mustn't *exaggerate* it—mustn't *exaggerate* it? Do you deny what he said?"

"No—I don't deny it."

"You admit you gave this person—this girl—a ring."

"Yes—"

"When did you give it to her?"

"I brought it with me the second time I went to the village, Ruth—"

"The second time? I thought you told me she wasn't there the second time."

"She wasn't. She'd already gone. I left the ring with her mother, wrapped up in a package—"

"And I suppose she came back and got it later on."

"Yes, later on. After the war. Her mother told me that."

"When?" Ruth asked harshly. "When did she tell you?"

"When we were at the farm—"

"When *we* were at the farm—you and I . . . That's what you were talking about, and I was standing right there with you and had no idea what you were saying. Not the faintest idea! You knew that, of course."

"I suppose I did, Ruth—"

"You suppose—you suppose?" A patch of red had spread up from Ruth's throat into her cheeks. "You *knew* perfectly well I couldn't understand."

"The ring was only mentioned," Michael said.

"Just in passing, you mean? My daughter came home—and I gave her your lovely ring. How touched she was, how many memories it brought back."

"It wasn't like that at all."

"No? What was it like then?"

"It was only mentioned. We didn't keep on talking."

"No, you wouldn't want to keep on talking with me in the same room. That would be in bad taste, wouldn't it? So you spoke to the brother and had him come down and give you the address—"

"No, that isn't true—"

"What is true then, Mike? No, go ahead—please tell me. I'm really very interested."

"Darling, I have—I have said what's true. . . . I did buy a ring for Angelina. I brought it to the farm and left it there. I didn't ask Gino for any address. If I'd wanted to be secretive, wouldn't I have tried—wouldn't I have made an attempt to go without you this morning?"

"You ended up going without me. Maybe you planned it that way. I don't know. I'm trying to think. Maybe you planned all along to leave me and go off. . . . Why a ring, Mike? Why did you choose a ring? Isn't that something out of the ordinary? I seem to remember it had a gold band."

"Yes—"

"And this man, this writer, this strange person you ran into, he seemed to think it had considerable value. He seemed quite upset, didn't he? He seemed to think the ring meant a good deal to your friend Angelina. He said she still wears it."

"Yes—he said that. Perhaps she does—"

"A ring is something you give to a person you're fond of, isn't it? An engagement ring, a wedding ring. Those usually mean you care quite a bit."

She paused, twisting her hands together. "This strange man," she said. "You could call him jealous, couldn't you? You could say he was consumed with jealousy, that that's why he came here. Would he be jealous of something that meant nothing?"

"Darling, I don't know anything about his motives—"

"But you know about the ring. You know it means a great deal, don't you—*don't you?* You gave it to her because you were fond of her, isn't that so?"

"Yes, Ruth, I was fond of her—"

"And you had an affair with her—something to make another man jealous. That's true, isn't it?"

"No, it is not."

"And you dragged me into this because you thought you could get away with it somehow—I don't know how. But you thought I'd be the innocent little wife, tagging along, not really understanding anything. Oh yes, what a beautiful country— how lovely it is, how picturesque—and all the time you were thinking of meeting someone else. A prostitute. You'll admit she *is* a prostitute, won't you?"

"Yes—that's probably so."

"A common streetwalker—and you choose to put her ahead of your wife."

"I don't put her ahead of you. Listen to me, won't you? . . .
Just for a moment? . . . All right, I did buy a ring for someone
else—long ago. I bought it because I thought it would please
her, would surprise her—and if she'd been in the village when I
went back to it during the war—"

Ruth's eyes widened. "Yes? . . . What about that?"

"Well, I'm not sure. I'm not sure—but I know that whatever
might have happened then wouldn't have changed my feelings
toward you—"

"Oh, don't talk such nonsense, Mike!"

"I'm not talking nonsense, I'm trying not to. I've thought about
it many times, and I've tried to separate one thing from another—a girl and a village. Maybe that sounds like nonsense to
you, but that's how it is in a way . . . The village, the first day
I was there, represents one thing to me—and the girl, maybe
something a little different—because she was pretty and vital.
But the two can't be separated, not really. A certain kind of love
is attached to both of them, to both together. That first day I was
in the village I loved everyone in it. I loved an old man because
I was able to help him. I loved a little child carrying a white
rooster in his arms, and maybe I was attracted most to Angelina,
simply because she was a girl—but she was part of the day itself,
part of the village, part of the excitement—"

"That's all very pat," Ruth said.

"No, darling—it isn't just pat or convenient."

"It completely contradicts what you've said before, doesn't
it?"

"No, not completely."

"As I recall this is the first time you've mentioned the word
*love* in connection with Miss Italy of 1944, or whenever it was."

"All right—yes, maybe so. But you can't object to my loving
the village, can you? Something made of stone? . . . And don't
you see, darling, don't you understand?—I thought of going
there with you. I didn't think of going alone this time. I wasn't
taking you back to a place where I'd met another girl. Maybe
that's what Mr. Newell downstairs would like you to believe,
for whatever reasons he has—but it's perverted. It's a perversion
of everything. I was trying to take you back to one miraculous

day, Ruth, one day when I had nothing to be ashamed of. Perhaps I was trying to take myself there most of all, but I wanted to see if we could find something—like magic—here in Italy, there in the village. I wanted you to see it with me. And I wasn't so wrong. There was still magic in the place. When we were going up the hill together, there was magic—"

"When Angelina came traipsing down to you—that's what you mean," Ruth interrupted. "You know what I think, Mike? I think you're very confused. . . . I'm beginning to understand you finally—why you brood so much at home, why you've seemed so aloof to me off and on, off and on. Maybe I believe—part of what you've said. But you see what you've done, don't you? You've confused one kind of love with another kind—and you've built up some sort of dream world, some sort of fantasy—"

"All right, Ruth."

"And where am I in this special place of yours? How am I connected with this extraordinary day? I'm absolutely nowhere, am I? Nowhere in sight!"

"Apparently you weren't listening to me—"

"I was listening to you, Mike. I was listening very attentively. It's sad, isn't it? It's extremely sad to come four thousand miles to discover you're nowhere in sight. . . . Do you know what I also think? I think this dream world, this concept you've made up for yourself, has turned you into a failure."

"Be careful," he said. "That's a very cruel thing to say."

"A failure because you idealize or sentimentalize—or idolize the past. An ugly little village is beautiful, and a prostitute is beautiful. That's the miracle isn't it? . . . Certainly, certainly you did something to be proud of when you—I don't know what you want me to say, you always disagree with the terms I use—but when you brought that old Italian back to safety. You yourself belittle it—but whatever it was, or however it was, that was the end of it, it should have been the end. You didn't go on saving lives. You came home to me and your two children. Only it seems you didn't really come back after all. You were still in Italy, playing the hero, making love, and everything else has been on a lesser scale to you—and you haven't faced up to the present, and you've retreated into the past—and that's why you haven't been more of a success."

He thought incongruously of how he had bargained for the extra week of holiday, of how important those days had appeared. "All right," he said, "Try to ruin it as much as you want."

"Maybe that's just what I want to do. I want you to look at yourself and be honest for once—"

"And admit I'm a failure then—or not much of a success? . . . Well, I guess I can't argue with you there. In fact I find it pretty hard to say anything—"

"Oh, don't be so sanctimonious—don't try to win sympathy."

"No," he answered. "All right, I won't. . . . I'll tell you something, though. I never thought we'd reach this point in our lives—here. I never pictured it. I thought this trip would take us away from all the little arguments we've had, all the feelings of discontent. Instead of that we reach the point where we are now, where we see each other as what?—as enemies. I'll admit I haven't been the success I might have been. It's very hard to admit that—but isn't it amazing, that we should agree on that and nothing else?—because I don't agree with the rest. You can't make me admit that one day I spent is a cause for failure. You can't destroy it. . . . So what do we do now—what do we say to each other?"

"I haven't any idea what we say to each other."

"Do we go on saying, admit this, admit that—be honest for once?"

"I don't know," Ruth said.

"Or do we say, let's go down and have dinner, and tomorrow we'll be on Capri, the Isle of Capri, and everything will be fine? Well, it isn't fine. It's just the opposite. Everything about it is wrong!"

"Yes, everything about it is wrong."

"You say it so easily. Don't you realize how serious it is? Don't you realize it isn't just another small argument we can forget about, or partly forget about tomorrow—or the next day? Don't you realize what it is to be told you're a failure, to have your wife tell you that?"

"You've known it for a long time, Mike. It hasn't been a secret."

"How you can say these things—how you can say them. They must have been bottled up inside you for years. I guess I knew they were, though. I guess I knew that's the opinion you had—"

"And I never knew what was inside you," she said, "walking around in the rain—trying to see yourself young again . . . Well, it didn't work out."

"No, it didn't work out, Ruth. It didn't work out for us. You see, to me that's the failure."

"Oh, don't keep on talking in riddles," she said. "I'm tired of it. I couldn't be more tired."

"And so am I," he said, bitterness in his voice. He turned away from her. "I think I'll go out for a while, Ruth. I can't stay here—"

"By all means," she said. "Go out and walk around some more. Certainly that's the thing to do. Of course you'd want to get away from me, you've wanted to all along. Do you think I'll try to stop you? I couldn't care less."

"I don't understand you, Ruth."

"Isn't that nice. You don't understand me, and you think I don't understand you—and it's been going on for ages and ages—"

"Yes, for ages and ages. That's the awful thing." At the door he hesitated. "You—what will you do?"

"Maybe I'll go out for a walk by myself. Maybe I'll be able to think. I'm not helpless, you know."

"All right, Ruth." He paused awkwardly, his hand on the door-knob. "I know you're hurt and full of resentment," he said, "but I haven't deceived you. I haven't lied about the ring."

She looked at him scornfully. "Oh, go on," she said. "Why don't you leave?"

She heard the door close. From the window she saw him emerge to the street below; and once he glanced upward, as if in her direction, before he disappeared. The day whirled in front of her: the squalid tenement; Michael explaining glibly about his meeting with Gerald Newell; Michael at the water-front restaurant joking about the afternoon . . . "All the little arguments we've had, all the feelings of discontent . . ." A prostitute and a second lieutenant—the girl who had seen him from the farm . . . Michael rushing out to rescue an old man from death—buying a ring for a girl, not finding her—ineffectually holding his briefcase, waving from the train's vestibule when the trip was still so uncertain . . . "When we were going up the hill together, there was magic . . ." Michael who had once been betrayed in an ugly, frenzied embrace, and who would never know it. She continued to stare after him. Then with her anger utterly spent and with her fingers against her throat, she burst into tears.

MICHAEL walked along the Via Rome and then away from it, to where the streets were darker, to where they climbed. He had left Ruth, he had left his wife: the realization hammered at him, but not as sharply now. In an hour or two he would go back to the hotel, and Ruth would be there. Sometimes it seemed like that, and sometimes it almost seemed as if the hotel would not be where it had been, as if some force would remove or hide it and he would not be able to locate it again. He kept thinking of the name of the hotel, as if it must be remembered; and then he was thinking of his children and it seemed that an enormous crime had been done against them—and against Ruth.

Could she be right about the past? Had his own search been completely futile? Was it a retreat? He remembered getting drunk in Rome—they don't recognize me, they don't know me as a friend; and he was thinking of Gerald Newell and of getting drunk in Rome, of apprehension, of lives impinging on other people's lives in complicated ways. Gerald Newell had whispered about beauty. Why had he come to the hotel—perhaps to prevent me from interfering with him, Michael thought; but of course it wasn't necessary. I wouldn't have interfered with him if he'd stayed away; if he'd stayed away I wouldn't have had the fight with Ruth.

Possibly, though, from the beginning he had been destined to meet someone like Gerald Newell, someone or something which would distort the past, raise it up in a curious perspective. Maybe the old memories should have been left where they were —the good, the possible evil in them undisturbed. Yet he remembered walking on another evening through the rain, the rain falling gently on his village. He was looking down at the

228

harbor and at the lights strung along it in the dusk, like pearls. Why did she say the village was ugly? he wondered. She didn't have to use that word . . .

He had reached the Vomero, he knew; but when he looked at the length of the broad avenue, he halted. It seemed ridiculous to be standing here under the trees. For a moment he had the impression that the fight with Ruth had released him, that he had provoked it so that he would have a chance to escape. He stood and watched the shadows of strangers moving under the trees; and the emptiness of walking through the hotel corridor came to him, and Gerald Newell was fumbling for words and sipping a martini, and Ruth was putting flowers on a German grave at Cassino; and the avenue stretched out ahead of him, and it was like life and like mystery and longing. I must settle this, Michael thought. Somehow I must settle it—

He heard the short comic blast of an Italian car horn and watched it swerve by. Then he could hear the sound of footsteps and of voices lifted in quick conversation. The shadows, the half-darkness seemed to intensify the sounds. He had no clear plan in his mind; but he would try to send word to Angelina. He would not go to the apartment, would not risk being shut out. He would go to the café. He would make one more attempt to find her and would not think of how he might fail. He was walking past the shops that were closed for the night. He was approaching the café where people were eating under the awning in the warm spring air.

He glanced briefly at the double rows of tables flanking the open door. Then he went inside. Behind the counter a woman was filling small white cups with coffee from an urn. Michael felt his heart beating. He crossed over to the counter.

"Good evening," he was saying in Italian. "The owner, the *padrone*, he is here?"

"Yes—in the kitchen."

"Perhaps you could call him."

"If you wish." The woman smiled. "You are an American—no?" she asked in English.

"Yes, an American—"

"I thought so—because of the clothes. We do not see many

Americans here. They stay down by the big hotels, by the ships. But you see I learn to speak a little English anyway. I learn it during the war. You wish a table, signore?—it is not necessary to call the *padrone*. Any of these—"

"No, not a table," Michael said. "Not right away. I wanted to ask the *padrone* a favor. I wanted to send a message, if it's possible . . . A message to Angelina Nardi. I understand she comes here often—"

"You wish—to send a message to Angelina, Angelina Nardi?"

"If I can," Michael said. The woman's eyes had turned abruptly hard, he noticed. "Do you know her? Do you know where she is?"

The woman slid the cups toward the end of the counter where a group of men stood talking, gesticulating, laughing together. "I think, signore—I think perhaps you were here earlier today."

"Yes, yes I was—"

"And you asked for Signor Newell, for his address."

"Yes, I did ask—"

"And you saw him this morning—and perhaps this afternoon as well?"

Michael stared at her.

"And maybe you have just come now from his apartment."

"I don't understand you, signorina."

"You have come from Signor Newell. He has sent you to find out where Angelina is, to ask questions for him."

"Why on earth would he send me?"

"Because he is clever. Because he knows that no one here would tell him where she is face to face. . . . Not even the *padrone*." The woman smiled shrewdly. "So, you see, signore, I cannot help you."

"But you're mistaken—entirely mistaken! Why would no one tell him where she is? What's happened to her?"

"She has left him—has she not?"

"She has left him," Michael said, his brow knitting, the muscles along his spine drawn taut. "When—when was this?"

"Today—this evening. Do not pretend, signore."

"I promise you I'm not pretending, signorina. I knew none

of this . . . I'm not an agent for Gerald Newell. I'm very glad
she has left him . . . I only met him today, when I was looking
for Angelina—"

"But the *padrone* said you asked for *him*," Maria said stubbornly. "He said there was an American asking for Signor
Newell—and Angelina has said that he was to meet the same
American this evening. So you have gone back to his apartment
with him, and he has seen that Angelina has gone."

Michael shook his head. "No, signorina, no—it's all mixed
up . . . But when, when did Angelina tell you about the
American?"

"A little while ago."

"Then she was here—talking with you here?"

"Yes, she was talking with me here."

"And you know where she is now?" Michael asked. "You do
know, don't you? . . . Please, signorina, please. Look—let me
explain, won't you?" He began to speak of the village then, of
Angelina's family, of the letter they had written—and once
Ruth intruded against the words, but the rebuke seemed faint,
almost lost, almost as lost as the image of Gerald Newell returning to the empty apartment.

"Angelina has never told me of an American soldier."

"It was years ago," Michael said. "I don't know what I can
say to convince you—but I gave her a ring, not very big, but
with a stone of light green jade and with a border, an edge of
gold. Maybe you have noticed it—"

"I may have noticed a ring. . . . Many people wear rings.
Signor Newell could have given it to her, he could have described it—he could have told you about the family. I do not
know much about them myself. Angelina does not speak much
about her family."

"Did she ever mention her grandfather to you—Giuseppe
Nardi?"

"No—no I do not recall it. Her mother, once or twice she
has spoken of her mother—"

"You don't believe me then," Michael said desperately. It was
slipping away from him. In a moment someone would interrupt—

"It is hard to know what to believe, signore."

"But—but suppose it is all as you say. Suppose this is all a story I'm making up. What harm could come to Angelina if you showed me where she is, if you took me there yourself? By the time I had made a report to Gerald Newell, she could be in a dozen different places—couldn't she? . . . She is not tied—"

"No . . . No, Angelina is not tied."

"She will remember me, signorina. You will see I'm telling you the truth—"

"And if she does not remember?"

"Then it will not be Angelina Nardi . . . It will be someone else," Michael said.

He saw that the woman was grinning at him. "I think you are very clever," Maria said. "Nearly as clever as Signor Newell. . . . You have made me very curious, you know?" She hesitated, her fingers brushing the counter top. "All right I will tell the *padrone* that I must go out for a few minutes."

"The *padrone*," Michael said. "He knows where Angelina is also?"

"Perhaps," Maria answered. "But you asked me, did you not? And you must remember, signore, if you try to play tricks on me—you must remember that Angelina is among friends."

UNDER the awning he watched her pause to glance up and down the sidewalk. "Come, it is this way," she said. "It is not far."

Michael walked tensely beside the woman. He had only a vague recollection of talking to her in the café, of how urgent his voice must have sounded; yet the men at the end of the counter had paid little attention to them as they were leaving. On a different evening Angelina might have been sitting there at one of the tables. He wondered when she had left the apartment—exactly when? . . . Suppose Gerald Newell had come into the café before they had gone. Was he waiting for her? She must be afraid of him if she wanted to hide.

Then he was thinking—in a moment I will see her—can it be possible? They were no longer on the avenue. The street they had taken was narrow, and the alley still smaller, but lights shone out at him, and the woman stopped in front of a large window, partially opaque and with gray letters across the glass.

"It is a *trattoria*, a small restaurant, signore. I think this is where she is."

She glanced behind him and opened the door. Michael stepped inside. The air was hot and heavy with tobacco smoke. Angelina was at a crowded table at the end of the room. Her head was profiled to him. He saw the dark hair cut short in wisps above the lobe of her ear, at the nape of her neck; the whiteness and luster of her skin. Her lips were parted. She seemed to be laughing, but he could not hear her over the noise in the room. He noticed the carafes of wine on the table, the flamboyant black bow tie of the man beside her, three or four other men, another woman.

Maria was a step in advance. "*Cara*," she said. "*Quest' uomo—*"

Angelina's head turned. Michael saw the eyes frown and then

fill with surprise. She stood up slowly.

"You recognize me, Angelina?"

"Yes," she said. "Yes—yes, I think—"

"I have been looking for you—at your home—here in Naples—"

"But I am amazed—amazed!" she said. "It is the captain—is it not?"

"It is no one else."

"He is known to your Gerald Newell," Maria announced quietly, watching them.

Angelina looked at her. "He is what?"

"He is known to Signor Newell."

"Only a little," Michael said hurriedly. "It is not important. It's not why I'm here. There are other reasons—"

"Of course there are other reasons," Angelina said, staring at him. "But it is so amazing to look up just like that—to see you! . . . But I forget myself—I forget to introduce. Everyone must listen! This is Signor Michael Allen . . . You would not believe what he has done one day . . ." She was speaking in Italian, going through a list of names. Michael was shaking hands, the men half rising, reaching toward him. He felt suddenly embarrassed, but Angelina's fingers were against his arm. "We will not sit down here," she said. "We will go over to the other corner where the table is empty—" and it was as if she had performed some great diplomatic feat, because they had crossed the room and had taken the two chairs. The noise had lessened. His eyes were on her face.

"It is better here, don't you think—or would you like to go outside?"

"No—no this is very nice—"

"How in the world did you ever find me, how in the world?"

"I went to your home, Angelina. I started there. I've only been in Italy a few weeks—"

"Yes, my home—you said. You have seen my family then?"

"They were worried about you. They—"

"They were worried?"

"They didn't know what had happened to you. They sent a letter to the Via Azuni, but it came back to them."

"Ah yes—the Via Azuni."

"I went there. There was an old woman who said she had seen you—"

"Silvana Massolino perhaps—"

"Yes. I think that's who it was. One of two sisters. It was all confused—a lot of people talking, but I learned about the Vomero, where you'd gone, and about the café—and this morning I came up here, and they told me at the café where you were living—"

"You came to the Vomero this morning—to where, Michael? . . . To the apartment?"

"Yes—"

"How strange! . . . You saw Gerald then, did you—Gerald Newell?"

"Yes, Gerald Newell."

"You had known him before?"

"No—never before this, Angelina."

"Never before," she repeated. "How very strange! . . . I thought maybe you knew him from America. It came to my mind for a second when Maria spoke."

"No, not from America. This was our first meeting—"

"He knew who you were? . . . You told him?"

"Yes—of course."

"And you talked about what—about me?"

"About you—about your family, your grandfather—"

"Ah yes, I see . . . I see. He told me nothing of this, you know. I saw him later on." She smiled suddenly. "You know what he said about you, Mike? He said you were related to a famous publisher."

"Hardly that, Angelina."

"No," she said. "No, but it makes me understand something about him, something about today, other days—"

"Maybe I understand it too, Angelina."

"Yes, perhaps. Maybe you see what kind of a person he is. . . . I have left him—did you know?"

"Your friend in the café told me."

"Ah yes, Maria. Maria was suspicious of you."

"She thought he'd sent me to look for you. When I came

back this evening to look for you again—she asked me right away if I knew Gerald Newell. . . . It's very involved, Angelina. Very complicated. You see, I saw him twice today. He came to my hotel this evening, to the hotel where I'm staying with Ruth—with my wife—"

"With your wife, Mike?"

"I guess he wanted to prove to himself I was married—something like that," Michael said. "I really don't know."

"Did he say something bad about me? What did he say? Did he make trouble for you?"

"Yes, a little trouble—"

"For you and your wife together. He spoke to you both?"

"Yes, to both of us."

"He was very jealous," she said. "He could have thought many things . . . Yes, I see how it could be. It is very sad what he is, and dangerous—to himself and to others . . . He has made a great deal of trouble for you, has he?"

"No—no, not a great deal—"

"Where is your wife? She is in the hotel?"

"Yes, one down by the water."

"She is alone in the hotel?"

"Yes—I think so."

"You have had a quarrel—"

"Yes, a quarrel—"

"It was about me? It was because of Gerald Newell?"

"We shouldn't concern ourselves any more with Gerald Newell," Michael said. "We don't have to worry about him. That part of it is all over."

"It is not a serious quarrel then—"

"No—I hope it isn't."

"But you do not know whether it is serious or not?"

"Right now it doesn't seem serious at all. Right now I'm so pleased—I'm so pleased to see you that nothing seems serious."

"Isn't it all crazy, Mike?" she asked, smiling at him. "Here we do not see one another for—for how many years?"

"Ten, a little more than ten—"

"For ten years, and you find me on a night when I'm running away from another man—and everything is upside down."

"You aren't afraid of him, are you, Angelina?"

"I was afraid of him. I was frightened when I went away from the apartment—but I am not afraid of him here. Only he will be wild with anger, when he knows I am not coming back to him. He will wait for me—and then he will go out and look. I do not want to see him then. But he will not find me, do not worry about that. He knows nothing of where I go when I am not with him—and I will stay with my friends until he has gone far away. . . . But do you know something else that is strange—do you know why I have told Gerald Newell of you?"

"No—"

"It was because of this—my ring. He asked who has given it to me."

"I noticed it on your hand."

"It is very beautiful . . . I have worn it for—not quite ten years."

"No, not quite ten."

"I never thanked you for it."

"Aren't you thanking me now?"

"Yes, I am thanking you. I am making up for the lost time—no?"

"It isn't entirely lost, Angelina. I've thought of you many times."

She smiled. "Also I have thought of you. . . . You think I have changed?"

"No, you are the same—very much the same to me. Have I changed? Do I seem different to you?"

"I cannot tell—exactly. I remember you with your officer's coat and your captain's bars. I do not think of you like this, in a suit—like a businessman."

"It's funny," he said. "I thought of the coat, too, when I was walking around in the village. It was evening after we arrived, Ruth and I—and it was dark and raining a little. I wanted to walk around for a few minutes by myself. I went up to the place where we said goodbye to each other—you know, the terrace, where you stole the fig off the tree when you were a little girl."

"You remember that?"

"Everything about it," he answered. "Everything you said."

"How I wanted to go into Naples with you—and hide in your jeep?"

"That in particular . . . When did you leave, Angelina? How did you leave the town?"

"It was when the soldiers are going—not the ones you knew, not the major. He would have taken me, I think, but I do not wait for him. No, I go out to the big road one day; and there are a thousand soldiers in trucks and jeeps and motorcycles. You cannot see the end of them, or where they begin, and they move a little and then stop and go on again. I have a basket of oranges under my arm to sell, and everyone is giving me cigarettes for the oranges, and I have a basket of cigarettes, enough to smoke for a month. Everyone is saying, why don't you come with us? We are going to Rome—and then they are amazed, because I say suddenly—yes, I will go—and I am in a truck, Mike— but only for a little while, because it is too crowded, and then I am in a jeep with a lieutenant, and then in another jeep with a captain—like you, but not like you because he is English. It is amusing, he is English—and that night I am too far away to walk back; and the next day we are in the mountains—"

"And you are with a major."

She laughed. "No, not with a major—but it is like that. It is very exciting, but we do not get to Rome so quickly. We are in the mountains for days and days—and it is not so easy for me, but it is not difficult either. Then one morning I am in a jeep again, and away off, at the edge of the sky, I can see the round top of the church—San Pietro, St. Peter's. I have never been so excited—and before dark, I am in Rome. . . . I am no longer with the soldiers. I work in a restaurant near the river, the Tiber, for a while but I do not like the owner, even when he fixes papers for me to stay there—and when the war is over I go home to see my mother and father, my brothers, and my grandfather." She paused. "He is not alive now."

"No, not alive."

"You hoped to see him."

"Yes—of course."

"Many things have happened, Mike."

"Yes, many things."

"My grandfather was as surprised as me, when he saw the ring. He teased me. He said, 'Why do you go all the time, Angelina?—go here, go there, no one will have a chance to

catch you,' but I told him I do not want to be caught—and
then I have come to Naples, because it is smaller than Rome and
because I know it better, and no one has caught me yet—for
long."

"Not even Gerald Newell."

"No, not even he—but maybe he came the closest. It was a
very nice apartment. It had beautiful furniture—and a patio
with a couch where I could rest and dream. . . . Maybe I am
crazy to give it up—you think?"

"That's the last thought I would have on the subject."

"Then it is finished," she said smiling. "We will not talk of
Gerald Newell any more."

"No, it's agreed. It's definitely agreed."

"You would like some wine perhaps, Mike?"

"Yes, if you would—"

"I will get it from the others," she said. He watched her walk
away from him and lean over the man with the bow tie. He
thought how graceful she was. They would be chiding her about
the American. He watched the small tug-of-war for the wine
carafe. Then she turned and approached, and when she sat down
her eyes shone. He could feel the privacy in them reflected inside himself—almost like the privacy of love.

"The first time I saw you, you brought a bottle of wine—
remember?"

"Yes. I have thought of it."

"We drank it very quickly."

"Yes—and the whisky, you were also drinking whisky. I can't
remember if the wine was white or red—"

"It was white, I think."

"Yes, I think so. White would be more special."

"I went up past the house where we were that afternoon," he
said, "and up through the lane, until I reached the terrace. It was
so dark I could hardly see anything, but I wanted to find it. I
went through kind of a little alley. Someone was in the house,
but I sat out on the terrace wall for a few minutes, and smoked
a cigarette, I guess. I hadn't seen your family. I had no idea
where you were—"

"But you didn't think I would be out in the rain—"

He smiled. "No, I didn't think you'd be out in the rain."

"And then what did you do?"

"Then I walked around for a little longer and went back to the inn, the albergo in the square."

"I am surprised that you would remember so much, that you would do all this—"

"You remember what your mind goes back to often, don't you think?"

"Yes—"

There was a silence. "Well—that's all there is to the story. That part of it . . . The next morning I saw your mother and father."

"You do not think I remember—so well?"

"I've wondered about it. . . . I've wondered what you thought of me. Maybe you thought I was a fool—"

"A shy person—not a foolish one. It is not bad to be shy. A brave man can be shy, can he not? Would it be so surprising if I remember as well as you?"

"It would astonish me—"

"Not quite as well then," she said, her eyes smiling toward him. "But nearly." Her brows lifted a trifle, the eyes becoming more meditative. "Nearly as well. Perhaps because of the ring— and because of my grandfather—and when you were walking with me, I told you that I would be rich one day—and I asked you if I was acting like an American girl." The smile returned. "Anyway, I remembered your name."

"That astonished me most of all."

"Did it?" She laughed. "You have written it on a piece of paper for me once, inside the box for the ring. You said, 'I hope you will like this, Angelina'—and your name. I didn't know the whole name before, but right over there it came to me—when I saw your face. My heart was like this—not here, but in my throat."

"Mine too, Angelina. We'll drink to that, shall we?"

"Yes, that is nice."

They raised their glasses rather solemnly and touched them, drank, and put them down.

"I have sometimes wondered what became of you," she said. "I used to wonder, looking at the ring. I used to imagine that you made a great success."

"Did you ever imagine me coming to Italy again?"

"No, I didn't believe I would see you afterward, but sometimes I used to wonder what you were doing—in America. I do not think you told me."

"I'm in business, Angelina—not publishing, but the business of arranging insurance."

"Ah, the insurance!—so that if someone dies, he will leave money behind."

"Yes, that kind of thing, money for different kinds of emergencies—"

"You like this business?"

"I like it well enough."

"It is complicated—no?"

"It can be very complicated."

"And you have made a great success?"

"Not a great success, Angelina. Here and there, a little. Enough to keep on going—and to have a trip to Italy."

"And a house?"

"Yes, a house."

"A nice house?"

"Quite a nice house, not in the country—not in the city. In between them."

"You would like to be more in the country—"

"How did you know?"

"From your voice, from how you say the word."

"I would like to have a little more land. Not a farm, exactly— I wouldn't be much of a farmer—but some old trees, you know, and a lawn with fine grass."

"That is for later perhaps."

"Yes, maybe it's for later—"

"And your children, Mike? I think you told me you have children. I forget. One or two, maybe more—"

"No more than two—a boy and a girl."

"Yes, that is right, a boy and a girl. I remember now, but I forget who is older."

"The girl is older. Priscilla. She's fourteen, nearly fifteen, nearly all grown up. She is blond."

"*Una bionda!* Like her mother?"

"Yes, like Ruth."

"And the boy is like you?"

"Somewhat like me. He is thirteen—with brown hair and brown eyes."

"He has the same name as you?"

"Yes—the same."

"Some day maybe I will have children. I would like to have a little girl, I think. I do not know why, but I think it would be nice to have a little girl. Do you think it is impossible?"

"No—"

"It is not impossible. Only—only I never allow it to happen. . . . But—do you see this man over there with the others—the man with the long black tie, like so?"

"Yes, I see him."

"His name is Luigi Bertoli. He has asked me to marry him."

"When did he ask you, Angelina?"

"Oh, I have known him for a long time. It is not—not sudden. He is an artist. You should see the pictures he paints. They are nothing! At least they are nothing to me, or to anyone else. But to him they are from a genius. He says, look, here is a bowl of fruit—he is always painting things to eat—and I say, it is not a bowl of fruit, it looks like—how do you say?— it looks like garbage; and he is mad, oh very mad, and will not speak to me. But always he comes back."

"With another bowl of fruit?"

"Yes," she said, laughing, "with some more fruit, or with a painting of some meat on a dish, and I tell him the meat is already rotten and for him to throw it away, and he is in a rage. But sometimes we laugh, and sometimes I pose for him in the room where he lives, and he says put this on or put that on, or put nothing on; and he is very serious at first. I say to him—you are improving, Luigi, you have painted me for ten minutes without moving away from the canvas. He says no one understands his painting, and that is certainly true—but who knows? One day he may be famous, if he is not first in a hospital for his brain."

"He doesn't look quite so crazy—"

"No, I am joking, really. Only his painting is crazy—and his black tie. But he will put it around his neck if I marry him or not—and—" She looked down at the wine, "and we would live in his room, I suppose. He says he will buy a new bed and new curtains, and he makes a little money from decorating things— things on glass and china for the tourists, you know, and not crazy." She looked up. "Do you think I should marry him, Mike?"

"Do you think I should advise you?"

She smiled. "No, you should not. But he is not bad-looking—"

"No, he is handsome."

"And tall. I do not like anyone who is short. He is tall and thin, maybe a little too thin, but his face is not bad."

"No, it is nicely shaped, and it is sensitive."

"You only look at him once. Now you look at me."

"Yes, I know I do—"

"And maybe I don't marry him," she said. "Maybe I will go on looking. And you, Mike—what will you do? You will go home to America—"

"Yes—to America."

"Very soon?"

"Yes, in a few days."

"You will be in Naples after tonight?"

"No, not after tonight—not to stay."

"Then it is even more strange that you find me now."

"Even more strange."

"Where do you go from Naples?"

"To Capri, Sorrento—Amalfi—"

"Yes, they are beautiful . . . Take me with you—in your suitcase."

"Suppose I could, Angelina. Would you go with me?"

"Of course I would go—like before . . . But it is not before, is it?"

"No—I don't suppose it is."

"Of course it is not. And you will go back to the hotel to your wife, and you will say you do not wish to quarrel, and tomorrow you will go to Capri. Do you know I have never been to Capri, and it is no distance at all. . . . Do you think we will ever see each other again, Mike?"

"It happened once, Angelina. It could happen again—"

"America is not so close as Capri. Imagine going to America! Do you go on a boat?"

"No—in an airplane, Angelina. It is very fast. It takes only about a day."

"Imagine it—imagine how fast. Imagine! . . . But there must be other questions I should ask you. About my family. I should ask about them. They were angry about the letter?"

"No, not angry—but they thought you might be in trouble. Gino thought you might be."

"Gino did? Yes, it is always like that. Always Gino thinks I am in trouble. But I will write them, and I will send them a little money, and my father will say he does not wish to spend it. It is bad money, he will say." She smiled. "But he will spend it—after a while."

"Perhaps you'll go to see them. They would like that, I know."

"Yes, I will go to see them. I saw them when my grandfather had his funeral, but even then it was difficult. Even then there were arguments and the talk of marriage. Even my uncles said this to me. I think they would all die with surprise, if I bring them a husband—and Luigi Bartoli, he would die also . . ."

Then she was saying, "Do not look so sad, Mike—"

"I can't help being sad."

"Because of the time. It is time for you to leave—"

"Not really time. There couldn't be time enough—"

"I never think of time. Today, tomorrow—but it is not the same for you."

"No—not quite the same."

"Come," she said. "We will not say goodbye to each other here. We will go out through the door . . ."

They were standing near the plate-glass window.

"I should not go any further," she said. "You cannot tell who is running through the streets—"

"No, you can't tell. . . . Please thank Maria for bringing me here—"

"Yes, I will thank her."

"And explain about me to the others—"

"Yes, they will understand."

He reached for her hand and drew it to him, his arm that was free encircling her waist, his fingers against the soft, slightly bending darkness of the dress. Her lips were cool and suddenly pliant. Then they were smiling at him.

"How shy you are," she said, "and very kind."

"No, you are the one who is kind . . . It's hard to speak," he said, "very hard to say goodbye."

"*Non è necessario*, Michael."

She was staring at him, her eyes wistful, and as if they were appraising him, or as if she wanted to remember. There was a faint color in her cheeks. The smile hovered and became a little more full.

"I'll always think of you, Angelina." He waited a moment. "Take care of yourself."

"You also," she said. "I am so very pleased that you look for me."

Her hand withdrew. He was watching her go through the doorway. He stayed for a few seconds longer, looking diagonally in through the dusty glass. The man with the bow tie was rising. Angelina had joined him. Michael saw her arm gesture and push lightly against him, but the voices were indistinct and as muffled as the laughter from the others, when it came out to the street.

He re-entered the avenue; and once he glanced toward the café, at the lights under the awning, but if anyone else were searching for Angelina, it was not evident. Among the stone-scented shadows and under the hot, lush foliage of the trees, there was nothing out of place.

Michael watched the nose of the taxicab swerve into the Via Roma. It seemed an implausible conveyance—and implausible that he should be returning in it to Ruth. Disjointed phrases clung to him, words he had spoken, words he had not uttered— Angelina discussing with genuine amusement a possible husband. Abruptly he wished he knew what she had said about him to her friends. Was it important, though? She was safe with them. She belonged with them. . . .

He remembered her leading him away from the others, and the extraordinary sense of privacy he had felt with her; and with his knees jackknifed and his head bent forward anxiously as if to verify the progress of the taxi, he could see himself going to the village with her, or standing on some rocky promontory on Capri, but the thoughts swirled away from him, loneliness replacing them and a growing anxiety: an impression of momentous events, as if anything could happen on this night, as if anything could be found or lost—as if nothing in it had been quite real, and as if it had been more real almost than all he had known before.

The taxi halted.

"*Ecco l'albergo*, signore."

"*Sì—sì, grazie tanto.*"

He went into the hotel. At the desk he said to the clerk. "*La* Signora Allen—you have seen her?"

"No, signore—"

"She has not left any word for me?"

"No, signore. She has not left a message."

He entered the elevator. It climbed deliberately from floor to floor. He was in the subdued light of the corridor. He had reached the door of the room. His lips felt very dry. He rapped lightly on the door.

"Yes?" He heard Ruth's voice. "Who is it?"

"It's me, Ruth."

"Wait a minute," she said after a brief pause. "I'll be there in a minute."

He heard her crossing the room, a key moving in the latch. The door opened. She was in a white dressing gown. Her eyes seemed haggard and swollen.

"All right," she said. "Come in."

He walked a little past her, and turned.

"I'm sorry about the quarrel, Ruth—"

"Are you?" she asked quietly.

"Yes—I'm sorry—"

"Where have you been?" she asked.

"Out walking around . . . No tremendous distance."

"To the Vomero, for example?"

"Yes, I went up to the Vomero."

"And found your Angelina, I suppose."

"Yes, I found her. She wasn't with Gerald Newell. She was in a small restaurant, among her friends. She was quite safe. I talked with her for a little while."

"And that's all?"

"Yes, that's all."

"How tragic," Ruth said.

"No, it's not tragic. . . . It's much more tragic what we said to each other. Don't you agree?"

"I might agree with you—"

"I thought you might not be here—in the room, I mean."

"Where did you imagine I'd go?"

"I don't know exactly where, Ruth. You said you might go out—"

"Out to a small café by myself? How surprising if we'd met! . . . But actually—actually I am surprised you're back so soon. I thought of course you'd be gone a good deal longer—of course! Wouldn't it be natural for you to stay away the whole night?"

"No—hardly natural."

"It would be. It would have been." She brushed quickly at the corner of her eye. "Natural for you to be gone the whole night—and tomorrow. . . . Do you know what I did when you left? You'll be amused. I ordered something to eat from the dining room, but when it came I wasn't hungry for it, not a bit hungry—so I got undressed like this, and then I stood over by the window, looking down and looking down . . . and down . . . and then I felt rather trapped, you know?—and sick inside, sick at heart, and I was tired of standing there—and I never saw you come in." Her voice broke. "Never saw you walking along the street, never saw . . . Oh, Mike, I'm so sorry—"

"Darling—it's all right—"

"No, it isn't all right. It's only a little all right."

"I was afraid you wouldn't be here," he said. "I was very much afraid of that—"

Her body was shaking against him. His arm was around her. He tilted her chin upward. Her brow was all furrowed, the eyes streaming with tears. "I thought of going out, trying to find you, I wanted to find you—but I had no idea how to begin. . . . Oh, darling, I'm so sorry," she repeated. "I'm so terribly—terribly sorry."

GERALD Newell walked along the Champs Ely-
sées under the chestnut trees. The weather was perfect, he
reflected. The air had the gentle French touch, and a soft breeze
blew to lessen the heat. He had on his most expensive suit, one
he had left behind before his departure for Italy—a gray flannel
made in London. The suit and the new black Homburg and
the new necktie of blue silk made him feel almost jaunty. A
few luxuries could be afforded, now that he was for the moment unattached. He carried a pair of light gray gloves and a
thin bamboo cane. One might suspect he was a diplomat, or a
*boulevardier* in the old tradition, or a white Russian leisurely
strolling toward some lunch-time rendezvous with nobility.

He had relocated himself in Paris. It had taken him many
exhausting hours, but the apartment he had leased for a year
was more modern than the other had been, equally small but
cleaner. Paris was a city of innumerable facets. It was easy to
find an area not seen previously. The first days, even the first
weeks, in such a place could always be exciting.

He was near the Place de la Concorde when he saw the two
women walking in front of him. They wore nearly identical
black silk suits and twin sable neckpieces looped just above
the shoulder blades and slightly incongruous for so warm a day:
the furs a trifle dowdy and not worn flamboyantly or with
smartness, but with the assurance of wealth and irreproachable
position and middle age. Yet the two walked close together,
as if for protection, as if unwilling to leave the assurance open
to question. They were not Europeans, he decided. Most likely
they were from Philadelphia—or Boston, from a less cosmopolitan center than New York.

He followed them across the Place de la Concorde and

watched them pause and then enter a shop where lingerie was
on display. They came out purchaseless, smiling at each other,
exclaiming at the French prices. He was delighted with their
voices. They were cultivated—the broad New England "a"
clearly pronounced.

The women turned toward the Place Vendome. Gerald, a
few steps behind, saw them enter the Ritz. He followed them
into the bar, into the ornate room with its delicate gilt-backed
chairs and small round tables supported on columns. It was
coincidental, he thought. The bar at the Ritz had been his own
destination.

He chose a table discreetly nearby and watched the women
remove their sables and order martinis in condescending but
appalling French. The thought of the martinis evidently made
them laugh together after the waiter had left.

"*Oui*, monsieur?"

"*Un martini*," Gerald said impeccably.

"*Oui*, monsieur."

"One moment," Gerald said, crooking his finger ever so little,
speaking confidentially in French. The waiter bent down.
"Those two ladies behind you—do you know them?"

"No—but they were here yesterday, sir. In the evening."

"They were alone, as they are now?"

"Yes, all alone."

"They are staying at the hotel?"

"I think so, sir. They signed their bill yesterday evening for
the cocktails."

"I see," Gerald said. "I ask because I believe they may be
friends of mine, whom I have not seen for many years—so
many in fact that I have forgotten names. They are on the tip
of my tongue, but I cannot recall them. I am almost certain
they are the same people, but naturally if they are not, I would
not want to intrude." He produced a crisp note for five hundred fancs, folded it across and inserted it into the waiter's
hand. "Would you have a means of ascertaining the names for
me?"

The waiter smiled. "I will try, sir."

"You can do this without causing embarrassment?"

"Certainly, sir."

Gerald relinquished the note. "Not the slightest embarrassment," he whispered. "Perhaps you can write down the names for me. I would not wish them overheard, or to give the impression that my memory required refreshing. You understand?"

"Yes, sir, I understand."

The waiter disappeared. Gerald took his Homburg from the table and set it on an empty chair and put his gloves gently on top of the hat. He placed a gold-tipped cigarette in his amber holder. The ladies, he observed, had brought out a map of Paris. Their fingers, rather short but elegantly manicured, pointed across it. The jewelry was unobtrusive but costly. Gerald surveyed the rest of the room, his eyes moving swiftly from face to face, recognizing a few; but there was no one he needed to speak to, no one who would call out a sudden greeting.

He glanced at a copy of the *London Times* he had brought with him. The ladies were ideal. They could be marvelously exploited: lunch in the Bois, a trip to Versailles, tea at the Ritz; a late dinner at the Tour d'Argent, or at some similarly extravagant restaurant—and tomorrow perhaps a shopping spree to stores where the prices could be maneuvered with artistry to his advantage. "I am bringing my two friends to you, monsieur," or "madame . . . They wish to see only the very best—and for a reasonable sum." The humor in the remark would be lost on these two; the commission, to be collected later on, would be implied without even winking an eye. He might pay for the tea—a tiny investment compared with all the rest.

He was out of practice, however. In the old days names would not have been important; he would not have sought the services of a waiter. In the old days that mere suggestion would have affronted his sense of pride. I am less confident— but it will pass, he told himself. These are not schoolteachers. In the old days these two would have presented the most delightful challenge, as if they had been dropped from heaven.

The waiter set down the two martinis beside the map. He approached Gerald. Under the cocktail glass there was a piece of paper.

"It is unfortunate, sir—only one name is there, but I have

written it down as you directed. The name of the lady who signed the check last evening. The barman has helped me recall."

"Which one is she?"

"The one nearest the door, sir."

"Ah yes," Gerald said, without turning. "Perhaps I shall be able to remember the other myself. You have done very well."

"You are not going to examine the paper?"

"In a minute," Gerald said. "In a minute I shall examine it."

The waiter straightened and moved a few steps away. Then his attention was diverted and Gerald glanced at the paper and pushed it into his pocket. He had to smile at the waiter's tact and curiosity—and at the name. It was well known to him— not personally known, of course, but known through its association with other names—the names of people brushed against during years of traveling, names read in newspapers or listed in the paragraphs devoted to ship arrivals, names meticulously studied and catalogued. This woman's husband had died last year—or was it the year before? He had come to Paris occasionally on business. Invariably he stayed at the Ritz; but his wife had not been with him then. Gerald had not read her name in the newspapers. He had seen the husband, however, once or twice in this same bar. He could describe him perfectly.

The ladies were ordering a second round of martinis. They might order a third with the proper persuasion. When they had finished the second, he would join them. One had to time one's entrance—the exact moment. He could pretend having met the wife in Boston, at some large party where a casual encounter would have been most probable. "You see, I knew your husband better, though, dear lady . . . We had business dealings here in Paris—and in Switzerland. I helped him resolve a few problems in international law . . . Isn't it amazing how everyone meets in the Ritz bar? . . . No, I am absolutely free for the afternoon, I assure you. I couldn't possibly permit two attractive women to wander around Paris by themselves . . ." The other one might be a sister; but the relationship did not matter. She would be introduced.

Gerald avoided the waiter's scrutiny. The bar was filling

rapidly, the waiter was in constant demand. Gerald lit another cigarette. The gold tips would amuse the ladies . . .

It was time now, he thought—almost time. The words would come fluently as soon as he stood up. He sat with his fingers drumming softly against the round edge of the table . . . It was time—*le moment juste!* There was a slight trembling in his fingers. It became more noticeable. How absurd to be fearful! In the old days he had never been afraid . . . The trembling was in his shoulders now, almost imperceptibly, but as if his fingers had touched his shoulders. He continued to stare at the newspaper, at the stem of his martini glass. His fingers were cold. The edge of the table was cold.

The ladies were picking up their furs. They were beckoning to the waiter. Gerald watched them furtively. They were folding the map—rising to leave. They were discussing the amount of the tip, as if the waiter could not understand them. "How much did we leave last night, Maud—do you remember? I wish I could get these francs straight in my mind once and for all."

Gerald watched the purse open and close. The waiter was bowing obsequiously.

"Au revoir, mesdames."

"Yes—au revoir."

They went through the door, adjusting their sables. Immediately a young French couple took their place. Gerald's eyes returned slowly to his newspaper. He was conscious of the waiter.

"They were not the same people, sir—the same person?"

"No. I was in error. Not the same."

"It is too bad—"

Gerald looked up at him. "I would like . . . I would like another martini," he said.

Angelina climbed the flight of steps, their treads curved in the middle with wear. She carried a basket under her arm. The door at the top of the steps was open. She went into the room beyond.

"Ah, it's you," Luigi Bertoli said. "Finally!"

"You expected me sooner?"

"I thought it was arranged."

"I had a letter to write," Angelina said. "I told you—a letter to my mother. It takes me a long time to write a letter."

"I could have written it for you in half the time."

"Perhaps. But maybe you wouldn't have liked what I said. I wrote a little about you."

"And about the American soldier."

"Shouldn't I have mentioned him?"

"I'm very flattered to be mentioned with an American soldier," Luigi said.

"You only shook hands with him."

"He is like all American soldiers. They are all athletes who grow fat."

"His is not fat—but perhaps he doesn't enjoy starving."

"I'm flattered more and more—"

Angelina laughed. "Anyway, you won't starve today. See, I have some food. Some bread, some cold meat—"

"A banquet—to satisfy even American tastes."

"I will put it down," she said. "You're much too grouchy to eat it now. It would disagree with you."

"First you flatter me and then you think benevolently about my health," Luigi said. "I'm overcome with joy. . . . What did you say about me to your mother?"

"Simply that you have proposed marriage to me—and that I am considering the proposal."

"That is not news."

"It will be news to my family."

"You said I am an artist?"

"Yes, a famous one. They will not know the difference."

"You will destroy me with your kindness," Luigi said. "Did you say how long you might consider this proposal?"

"No, I didn't limit myself."

"You wished to arouse suspense?"

"One must make such an important announcement gradually, don't you agree?"

"Oh yes, gradually—over a period of years perhaps. I can always take back my proposal, you know—"

"Then I will write and say that you have. I will have the subject for another letter. . . . Do you wish me to pose for you, Luigi—or do you want to spend the rest of the day talking?"

"It was agreed that you should pose."

"But not how," she said, smiling at him. "Here in front of you, or up on the stand—or sitting on the edge of the bed?"

"On the stand, I think. The light is better on the stand."

"All right I will go to the stand—to your nice wooden platform . . . and face you like this. Do you want me to look sad, or happy—or as morose as the artist himself?"

"I'm not morose," he said. "I'm merely concentrating. . . . Here, we'll use the basket, I think—if the meat isn't too heavy. We will remove the meat and leave the bread. . . . There. That's better—hold it with your arm a little bent . . . Yes, like that."

"I don't know why you always make these arrangements," she said. "When it is finished, no one will be able to tell if I am holding a basket, or a piece of stone. You will have to write an explanation—"

"I will know, Angelina. I will know perfectly." He backed away from her. "And please don't smile. Compose your features, if you can."

"I will smile for a few minutes," she said. "Because I know you will paint the bread first. . . ."

She stood under the slanted window and watched him go behind the easel, his head raised to scrutinize her, his eyes suddenly intent. She thought of Gerald Newell with his typewriter; but this man was not like Gerald Newell. You could make fun of this man, and ruffle his pride, but you did not touch it underneath; you did not reach to its roots.

Then she was thinking of the letter she had written—and of the village and the terrace and the farm . . . A good deal of advice would come to her from the farm, advice and questions . . .

Luigi stepped to the side of the easel. "What did you write to your mother about the American, Angelina?"

"Why do you ask?"

"You were thinking of him. Your eyes were sad—or solemn."

"No, you're a poor mind reader." She hesitated. "It may astonish you, but I was thinking—I had just begun to think of children."

"Of children!" He put down his brush.

"You see, you are astonished. It hasn't been discussed, has it? How many children would you like, Luigi—eight or nine—or a dozen?"

"You shouldn't joke about such things! It's bad luck."

"It's not bad luck only to discuss something," she said. "You like children, don't you?"

"Yes—certainly. Certainly I do."

"Then perhaps I will marry you one day. . . . Maybe I'll marry you on the day—when you sell a painting."

"Ah! Then you'll have to wait until the end of the world—"

"No," Angelina said. "I'm not so sure." She was smiling toward him. "Maybe to see what you've painted, Luigi, the rest of the world will only have to turn itself—upside down. . . ."

Michael sat next to Ruth on the plane. It had cleared the runway minutes earlier, and objects on the ground had already grown tiny and fused with each other; but he continued to stare past her, his body shifted toward the window. The dome of St. Peter's was no longer visible. In a few minutes more the beach at Anzio would pass under them, and they would be out over the Mediterranean.

Michael waited until he could see the serrated blue of the water before he settled into his seat.

"Be sort of nice to be down there on a boat, wouldn't it?" he said.

"Yes, it would be lovely."

"But I guess maybe this is best after all. . . . We'll be home tomorrow."

"I can hardly believe it—can you?"

"No," he said. "It's hard to believe."

"Hard to believe we've only been gone a month. Do you think they'll have changed any? . . . The children, I mean—not us."

He returned her smile. "I guess we'll still be able to recognize them."

"It'll seem funny to be taking the train out from town again, won't it?" she said. "I hope we won't be too late. I'd like to see the house before it gets dark—"

"Don't worry about being late," he told her. "The flight's only begun."

"I wonder when they'll get the cable."

"They'll have it in plenty of time, darling. Probably this evening—"

"Yes, this evening. But I'm glad we sent it—even though it wasn't exactly necessary. They'd be expecting us anyway."

"Yes," he said. "They'll all be waiting."

He leaned back a little more. Then he was listening to the giant hum of the plane; and Ruth, sun-tanned beside him, had opened a magazine, and the passengers were moving about or settling themselves against the hours ahead.

Michael glanced at the ceiling. He was thinking of the dress for Priscilla and the ship model for Mikey. He could hear the exclamations of pleasure. The presents would be unpacked right away . . . It would be hot at home. There would be the hot smell of cinders and tar when they got off the train. He imagined how the road led from the station to his house, the heaviness of late spring already along it. On Monday morning he would be at the offices of Dilks and Stanley; but the secret of the extra week of holiday had been preserved, he was sure, and slowly his mind dropped away from all this, from other thoughts, from the final peaceful days of the trip; and the road he saw was more narrow, and it climbed through the hills—and at the crest of one of them it stopped—or he stopped, and was looking forward . . . It was the old image; yet it seemed altered He would need more time to fashion it completely.

He had turned affectionately toward Ruth. She was pointing to something in the magazine. Momentarily he wondered when, just when—at what time in the future—he might see his village, once more rising abruptly in the air like a castle—the safe castle, the one that was safe.